SAVAGE BONDS

BOOK TWO | SHADOWMIST PACK

E.V. MITCHELL

USA TODAY BESTSELLING AUTHOR

NEVER CAGE A WOLF YOU CAN'T CONTROL...

Every captive breaks.
Every secret is revealed.
There are no rescues.
No escape. No exceptions.

Lithia is no stranger to pain.
She's fought for her place, bled for her pack, and carved out respect as Shadowmist's first female beta. But when betrayal lands her in an underground prison, silver-bound and isolated, it's not pain that threatens to undo her.

It's the silence.

Until *he* speaks.

In a place built to shatter her, the broken, sarcastic nomad in the next cell becomes her anchor.

To escape their prison and expose the war brewing in the shadows, Lithia must face the ghosts of her past and decide if she can trust the one wolf with the power to save her soul... or destroy it completely.

REVENGE IS BEST SERVED BLOODY

ACKNOWLEDGEMENT OF COUNTRY

I acknowledge the Traditional Custodians of the lands on which I write, the Ngunnawal people, and pay my respect to elders both past and present.

I acknowledge the continued and deep spiritual relationship of the Australian Aboriginal and Torres Strait Islander peoples' to this land, and their unique cultural and spiritual relationships to the land, waters and seas, and their rich contribution to society.

Always was, always will be.

To the readers who saw a hole in a prison wall
and immediately thought,
"…yeah, I'd fist that."

You brave, horny disasters.
You trauma-bonded, violence-inclined little gremlins.
This book is for you.

And for Rooks —
Thanks for inspiring an emotional support glory hole.
No further context required.

CONTENT INFORMATION

Please note the following content information include SPOILERS for this book.

This book contains mature themes and may not be suitable for all readers. Please proceed with care.

- **Sexual content** – explicit scenes including primal mating, knotting, power imbalances, and possessive behavior. All are consensual.
- **Violence and gore** – including graphic interrogations, battle scenes, maulings, executions, and murder.
- **Torture / captivity** – imprisonment, chaining, and use of physical restraint.
- **Eugenics / cult** – discussions of creation of power through a eugenics-style movement by a cult.
- **Sexual assault threat** – references to sexual assault threat. No assault occurs.
- **Social rejection themes** – themes of societal rejection, loneliness, isolation due to trauma or forced due to imprisonment.

- **Psychological trauma** – including gaslighting, isolation, emotional abuse, internalized shame, forced fear/terror, and neglect.
- **Mental illness** – demonstrated Post-Traumatic Syndrome, hallucinations, and the risk of being driven to a mental break through magical or social means.
- **Death of humans and animals** – multiple characters die, sometimes brutally and without much warning. Animals (i.e. fish, birds etc) are killed to feed the characters. None of these animals are pets or main characters.
- **Power imbalances and toxic pack structures** – including commentary on patriarchal dominance and control.
- **Blood and bodily fluids** – descriptive and frequent, both from violence and consensual sex scenes.
- **General themes of war, survival, and rebellion** – including societal oppression and insurgency.

More information

If you have any concerns with the depictions in this story or would like further information before reading, please email Evie@EvieMitchell.com

END SPOILERS

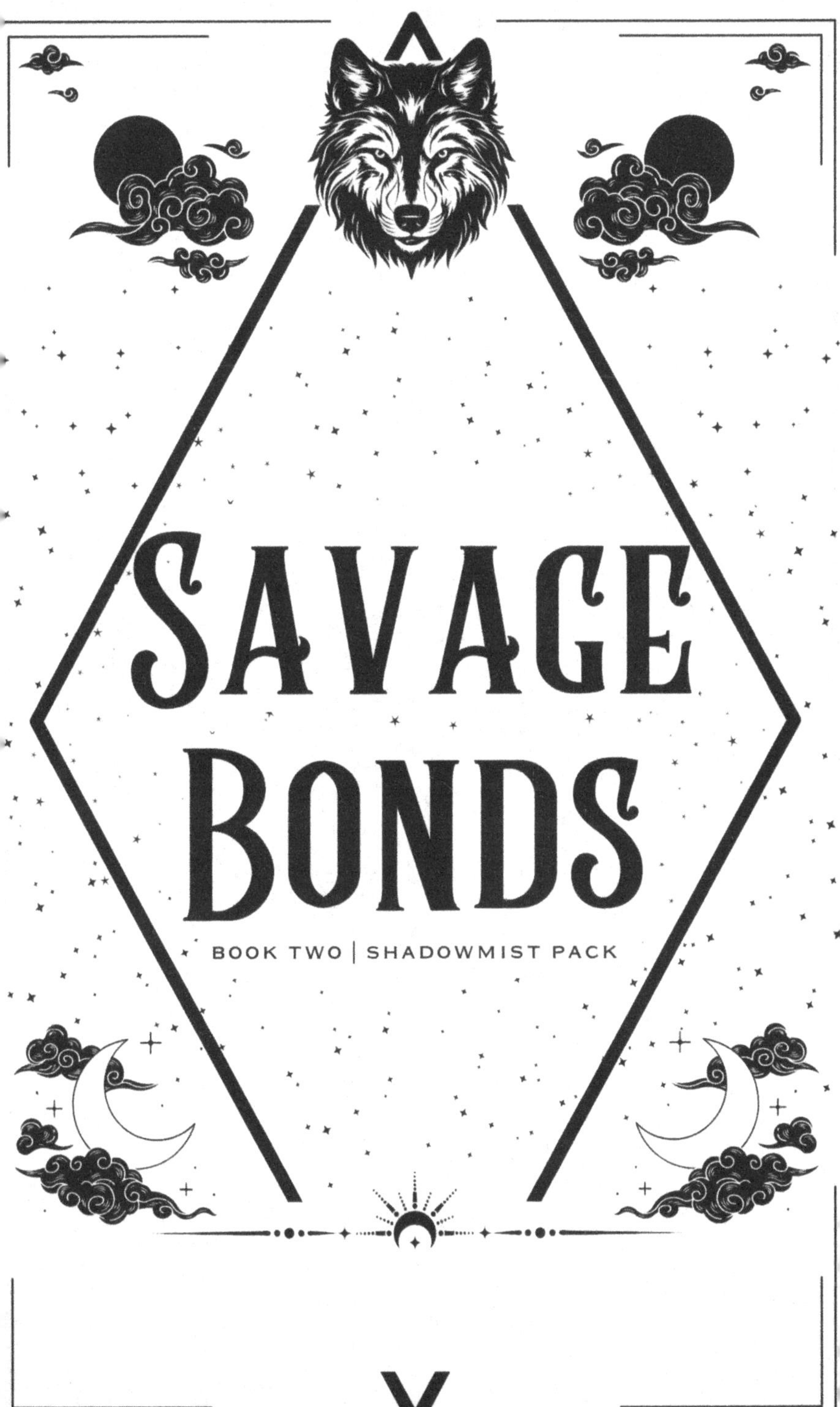

SAVAGE
BONDS
BOOK TWO | SHADOWMIST PACK

CHAPTER
ONE

I wake to darkness.

My head throbs, my limbs heavy, and everything smells like rot and silver. I've been unconscious for… hours? Days? Time has fractured into fragments of pain and silence. The only markers are the heavy footsteps of guards and sound of someone screaming their throat raw.

Rage crashes through me, white-hot and vicious. I'm the Beta of Shadowmist Pack, the first female beta ever. I don't cower in the dark like a beaten dog.

I'm going to paint these walls with their blood.

My wolf snarls her agreement from somewhere deep inside, though I can feel her weakness beneath the silver's poisonous burn. Let her conserve strength. When I break free —and I will break free—these bastards will learn exactly why you don't cage a Shadowmist wolf.

I roll into a seat, groaning at my body's protest. Silver cuffs burn around my wrists and ankles, the metal searing into already raw flesh. A matching collar sits heavy around my throat—thick, unforgiving, designed to keep me from shifting. My clothes are torn and filthy, what's left of my tactical gear hanging in shreds. Blood has dried in my hair, crusted along a gash above my left temple.

I don't know how long I've been here. Long enough for my skin to blister under silver. Long enough to feel the absence of my Alpha's presence.

Zella betrayed us.

The memory slices through me with savage clarity.

Five years. Five years of sparring side by side in the combat hall. Of shared meals and long watches and late-night laughter under moonlight.

Five years of the bitch lying through her teeth.

She waited until we trusted her. Until Kitara trusted her. And then she fucked us.

Traitor, my wolf snarls from somewhere deep, her voice strained under silver's grip.

I know, I answer softly. *We'll get our revenge.*

She took the Alpha Female.

Ryker will find Kitara, I assure her. *We need to concentrate on staying alive until we can get free.*

That wound of failing to protect Kitara is raw. I feel it more than the silver around my wrists, more than the ache in my head. Kitara is more than my Alpha Female—she's Shadowmist Pack's future. And Zella took her. Delivered her straight into the hands of a man who'd carve the gift from her bones if it meant power.

Thaddeus, the Grand Alpha.

I let my head rest against the cold stone wall, forcing my breathing to slow.

Control. Always control. That's how I lead. That's how I survive.

The silver burns like an eternal fire against my skin, and my wolf curls tighter inside me. She's trapped but not broken. Never broken.

Because my pack doesn't break.

We endure. We adapt.

And we avenge.

Some beta I am, failing to see the threat that walked among us.

I can't blame myself entirely though. After all, neither Ryker, my Alpha, nor Dane, my brother, saw Zella as a threat.

My brother. The thought of Dane sends a fresh wave of panic through my chest. Is he safe? Did he survive the ambush? The last thing I remember is the overwhelming force of Thaddeus's men descending on us during what was supposed to be a peace summit. The ambush was perfectly coordinated. They knew exactly where we'd be, and exactly how to hurt us.

Frustrated at my helplessness, I pull against the silver restraints only to regret it as the metal sears deeper into my already raw flesh. The silver poisoning has weakened my wolf and me. If this lasts much longer, I'm worried our connection will sever.

The cell is maybe eight feet by ten feet, carved from rough stone that looks like it belonged to a mine shaft. Which, I realize with growing dread, it probably had been. The walls are crude, chisel marks still visible in the rock face. No windows, just a single heavy door with a slot at eye level. A rusted bucket sits in one corner—my toilet, apparently. The floor is uneven stone, worn smooth in places by countless feet.

The silver cuffs around my wrists, ankles, and throat have no visible hinges or clasps. They were welded on while I was unconscious—a permanent fixture until someone decides to cut them off. A chain runs from my left ankle to a heavy ring bolted into the stone floor, giving me maybe six feet of movement in any direction. Enough to pace, to reach the bucket, to sit against any wall I choose. But not enough to reach the door.

The only light in the cell comes from under the door, slipping from the hallway outside in a thin, sickly yellow line that barely illuminates more than a few inches of floor. The rest is shadow and darkness.

The air is stale and damp, carrying the metallic tang of silver and something else—fear. How many prisoners have been held in this exact spot? The walls seem to whisper with their desperation.

This seems to be an abandoned mining operation repurposed for darker activities. If I'm where I think I am, I'm hundreds of miles from Shadowmist territory.

Hundreds of miles from any hope of rescue.

A metal door clangs somewhere in the distance, followed by the sharp echo of boot heels on stone. There are three sets of footsteps, plus the dragging scrape of someone being hauled between them. One of them is the unmistakable footsteps of the guard they send to torture me.

I force myself into a seat, determined to show no weakness even though every muscle in my body screams in protest. The silver cuffing my wrists, neck and ankles is not the only silver they've used to restrain me. During our interrogations they inject it directly into my bloodstream, waiting for me to break.

I'll never give the bastards the pleasure.

The sounds grow louder until they stop outside the cell next to mine. "Back again so soon, wolf?" one guard taunts. "Miss your old accommodations?"

A dull thud and grunt of pain answer—they've struck whoever they're dragging.

"Get him inside," another orders. "And check the hinges on the door again. Last time he nearly got out."

Keys jangle, a lock turns, and I hear the neighboring cell door swing open. There's a moment of struggle—flesh hitting stone, chains rattling—followed by a heavy impact as they throw someone inside.

The door slams shut, locks again. The guards leave and silence follows. I begin to doze, focusing on conserving my strength when a low, broken mutter pulls me back to consciousness.

The voice is male—rough and low, like gravel dragged over bone. "...told you I'd find her... you didn't listen... should've called for backup..."

It's not the kind of voice you easily forget. Despite being hoarse and frayed at the edges, it's deep and richly pleasant.

"I'm sorry... so fucking sorry..." The words rasp through the stone—a sound half-snarl, half-plea. "I'm sorry."

He repeats this six or more times before moving into a different repetition.

"Not real... can't be real... they're all dead because of me..."

Hours pass, his voice threading through them like a wire pulled tight. Sometimes his voice crackles with fury, sometimes it splinters into grief. Other times he sounds like he's sinking into hollow, wordless sounds that scrape at the dark.

It's a voice that fills the cell, the cracks, the empty air. It latches on, digs in.

I try to sleep, but his voice keeps pulling me back to wakefulness. There's something haunting about the way he speaks.

"...tried to save you... wasn't fast enough... never fast enough..."

By the time the guards next come for him, I've lost track of hours, days, time. I'm unsure how long I've been here between my fitful dozing and his conversations.

The man falls silent as the sounds of a brutal interrogation drift through the walls—questions are shouted, flesh hits flesh, his voice rises in defiance before falling into silence. When they leave him, the muttering has changed.

"Told you they'd be back."

There's a pause. Then another response, as if he's having a conversation with someone.

"I'm not telling them shit. You can tell them if you're so keen. Yeah, okay, bear. Sounds like you need to butt out and leave me be. Can't a wolf get a little peace around here?"

It's not long before I hear the scrape of a door and the even footsteps of guards returning.

This time, they don't go to him.

They come for me.

CHAPTER

TWO

My door swings open with a high-pitched whine. It bounces against the stone, echoing ominously.

A guard fills the doorway, his silhouette lit by the bright lights in the hall.

I wonder if they rehearse this nonsense.

"Ready to talk?" he asks. He's younger than I expected an interrogator to be, but the scent of anticipation that lays upon his skin is all the indication I need to know that he derives pleasure from watching another suffer. I assume that's why he was chosen—or volunteered—for this particular role.

Go fuck yourself, I think fiercely. But I keep my gaze fixed on the floor, saying nothing. I've learned quickly that any response only encourages him to become more creative with his interrogation techniques.

"The silent treatment again? That's fine. We've got all the time in the world." The slot slams shut, and his footsteps retreat.

I close my eyes, allowing myself to slump back onto the floor.

Thank the gods.

It seems I've been spared more torture—for today, at least.

A soft sound from the adjoining cell makes me freeze. It's barely audible, just a faint whisper that seems to be coming from near the floor. But in the oppressive silence of the facility, it might as well have been a shout.

I'm not alone.

"Silence doesn't work, you know." The voice comes again, barely more than a breath. Male, rough with exhaustion and resignation. "Trust me, I've tried."

I drop to my hands and knees, searching the base of the wall between our cells. There, near the corner where shadows are deepest, I find it. A hole no bigger than my fist, carved carefully through the stone. The edges are jagged, as if they've fortuitously crumbled rather than been carved out purposefully.

I press my face close to the opening but don't respond. Is this a trap? Or is my new neighbor as innocent in this mess as I am?

"Come on, I know you're there." His tone is mocking, but there's a desperate edge to his words. "What's the worst that could happen? They torture you? Beat the shit out of you? Pretty sure that's already on today's schedule."

Still, I remain silent, letting this wolf fill the silence.

"Let me guess," the voice continues. "You're weighing your options. You're wondering if I'm friend or foe, and trying to decide if talking to me is worth the risk." A pause, and when he speaks again, there's something raw in his voice. "News flash, I'm neither. I'm a fucking dead man walking. So might as well talk to me before I die."

That last admission catches me off guard. I can smell his pain through the hole, the blood and infection bitter in my nostrils.

This is either the most sophisticated trap I've ever encountered, or this man is genuinely a prisoner.

Despite myself, I find myself responding. "You talk a lot for a dead man walking."

A laugh, harsh and bitter. "A she-wolf then? Well, isn't this a treat."

"Want to die faster? Keep it up."

He chuckles. "Death starts to lose its sting when it keeps standing you up."

I shuffle closer. "How long have you been here?"

"Long enough to know that they don't kill you quickly. And apparently, I'm very hard to kill. What about you? Fresh meat, by the sound of it."

I bristle at the casual way he assesses me. "I'm not telling you shit."

"Smart. Trust no one, suspect everyone. That's survival 101 in this place." He sighs. "So what shall we talk about then? The weather? How are you finding the food down here? I myself had a three-course meal made by a private chef last night."

Despite myself I smile. "You're a dick, you know that?"

"Ouch. That stings." I hear him shuffle before he speaks again. "Let me guess. You're the strong, silent type. Probably think talking to strangers is beneath you."

"I think talking to potential spies is stupid."

"You think I'm a spy?" He laughs again, and this time it's genuinely amused. "Right, because these sheep are definitely smart enough to think of planting someone in the cell next to yours to trick you. That's some next-level psychological warfare right there, and I can assure you, they aren't that smart."

"Stranger things have happened."

"Fair point. Though if I were a spy, I'd probably be better at this whole 'gaining your trust' thing. I'd be all sympathetic and wounded, asking about your feelings and shit."

Despite the situation, I almost smile. "Instead of being an ass?"

"Exactly. I'm way too honest to be undercover. Three years

of having nothing but my own thoughts for company tends to strip away the social niceties."

"Three years?"

"Give or take. Hard to keep track when you never see the sun." His voice softens slightly. "Sorry if that's not what you wanted to hear. Hope's a dangerous thing down here."

We fall into silence after that. I find myself staring at the hole in the wall, trying to process what he's told me. Three years. If it's true, if people really are kept here that long, then my pack might never find me. I might die in this place, just another disappeared prisoner.

"So," he says after a few minutes, and his voice is gentler now, "what's your crime against the state? Besides having terrible conversational skills, I mean."

"None of your business."

"Fair enough. We're all entitled to our secrets." A pause. "But just so you know, whatever they want from you, it's better to make them work for it. The moment you give them everything, you become expendable."

"How do you know that?"

"I've seen a lot of people disappear over the years. The ones who cooperated went silent first. I can only guess what happened to them."

The casual way he says it makes my blood run cold. How many prisoners has he listened to? How many has he heard screaming, pleading, and then… nothing?

"Why?" I ask.

"Why what?"

"Why are you still here? If cooperation means death, why haven't they killed you?"

"Because I'm special." His voice is bitter now. "I have something they need, but I've never been cooperative enough to give it to them completely. It's a delicate balance."

"What kind of something?"

"The kind that keeps me breathing, even when I don't particularly want to be."

There's so much pain in those words that I feel something crack in my chest. This man—whoever he is—has been tortured for years, kept alive for some purpose he clearly despises, forced to endure isolation that would have broken most people.

"I'm sorry," I say, and mean it.

"Don't be. I made my choices. Now I live with the consequences." He's quiet for a moment. "What about you? Got anything they want badly enough to keep you alive?"

I consider how much to reveal. "Maybe."

"Then you might be here for a while. Best get comfortable."

Hours pass. We don't speak, but I find myself listening for the sound of his breathing, taking comfort in the proof that someone else is enduring this hell alongside me.

When the guards finally come, it isn't for me.

The metal door next to mine clangs open with a sound like a gunshot. I hear the scrape of boots on stone, then a familiar voice. It's the interrogator.

"Morning, smart-ass. Ready to tell us what we want to know?"

My neighbor seems to be ready for a fight. "Is this about my dress for the ball? Cause I really feel that taffeta and lace would be perfect."

"Still think you're funny." A meaty thwack is followed by a grunt of pain.

"Did you learn that technique at asshole school, or are you self-taught?" the wolf asks.

Another impact, harder this time. I find myself pressing against the wall that separates us.

"Keep running that mouth, dog. See where it gets you."

"Same place it's gotten me for three years. At least I'm entertaining myself."

The interrogation continues for what feels like hours. Every time they hit him, every time they demand answers, he has some smart remark ready. His voice gets rougher, more strained, but the attitude never wavers. His defiance never breaks.

By the time they finally leave, I'm equal parts impressed and horrified.

The guards shut the door to the corridor of cells and silence returns.

I wait, counting my heartbeats until I'm sure we're alone again. Then I crawl back to the hole.

"Still alive over there?"

A pained chuckle. "Unfortunately for them, yes. Though I think they're getting tired of my pretty face."

"How do you do it?"

"Do what?"

"Survive this. How are you not broken?"

There's a long pause. When he speaks again, his voice is quieter, more serious than before.

"Who says I'm not broken?" He shifts, and I hear the clink of chains. "You think surviving this makes me strong? I talk to myself for hours at a time. I have conversations with dead people." Another pause. "Hell, I'm not even sure you're real right now. Could just be another voice I've invented to keep myself company."

The raw admission catches me off guard. "I'm real," I say firmly.

"That's exactly what a hallucination would say."

"I can prove it," I challenge, though I'm not sure how.

He calls me on my offer. "How? By telling me something I couldn't possibly know?" A bitter laugh. "Problem is, my imagination's gotten pretty good over the years."

"But you're still here."

"Because the alternative is giving them what they want.

And what they want…" His voice hardens. "What they want would hurt a lot of innocent people."

"So you endure."

"So I endure," he agrees.

Damn. That hit somewhere deep. Respect, grudging but real, stirs in my chest.

"What about you? You planning to endure, or are you going to give up the first time they make you bleed?"

I glance down at my hands which I can barely make out in the dark. "They've already made me bleed."

"Hey, console yourself. You've got my company for a little while."

"Lucky me."

"I'm not that bad. I'm practically the prison's den mother at this point. Shall I give you the tour? It involves cookies—sorry, I mean torture. Definitely torture."

Despite everything, I find myself almost smiling. "What do you call this place?"

"Prison. Why, what would you call it?"

"Hell?"

"Also works."

We fall into a more comfortable silence after that.

"Are you still trying to escape?" I ask after a while.

His reply takes a long time to come. "Every day."

I close my eyes. "Me too."

CHAPTER
THREE
KIER

The voices had started sometime in the second year, when the isolation finally eroded my sanity.

At first, it had been my own voice echoing back at me, fragments of conversations with people who were long gone. My mind's desperate attempt to fill the crushing silence that had become my entire world. Then other voices joined in. The bear seer I'd failed to save, whispering accusations that grew louder each time she came to me. My long-dead pack members, reminding me why I'd chosen the nomad life in the first place. Conversations with wolves I'd known decades ago, arguments I'd had, words I wished I'd said.

And now there was a new one. Female, sharp-tongued, with a voice like broken glass that somehow still managed to sound beautiful. She's fast become my favorite.

"A redhead," I decide. "With big breasts and shapely hips."

"Are you talking to yourself again? Cause it's starting to get old."

I laugh, the sound echoing off the stone walls of the cell. "Hush. I'm just trying to imagine what you look like, imaginary friend."

"Imaginary friend?"

The voice sounds confused now, which is new. Usually my hallucinations are more predictable. They say what I expect them to say, accuse me of the things I already know I've fucked up. Rarely do they ask questions and prompt laughter.

It's clear to see why she's the favorite.

"Don't worry about it, sweetheart. You're just my brain trying to keep me from losing what's left of my mind." I shift on the stone floor, my body protesting. Another day, another beating

"I'm not a voice in your head," she growls.

"Sure you're not," I grin into the darkness. "You're my next fantasy. Fancy coming into this cell so I can imagine us—"

"Don't even *think* about finishing that sentence."

I chuckle. "So you're not a redhead and well endowed?"

"Sorry to disappoint."

I close my eyes, leaning against the stone. "Let's see. Are you a brunette, slim and sensual? Or perhaps you're a blonde with a wealth of curly hair. Or maybe—"

"I liked it better when I didn't have a sex fiend for a neighbor." She sighs heavily. "How can I shut you up?"

I tilt my head to one side. "What do you mean?"

"How can I prove I'm real?" The irritation in her voice is palpable. "What would convince you?"

"I don't know. Do something a voice in my head wouldn't do."

"Like what?"

"Surprise me."

There's a long silence. Then, "Go to hell."

The venom in her voice is... unexpected.

"Well," I say slowly. "That was definitely unsurprising. I've heard that from more visions than I can remember."

"I'm not a goddamned vision!"

I chuckle. "You're adorable."

I hear her mutter a curse then there's a weird scraping sound. "Alright, you dick. Get on the floor. There's a hole in the wall the size of a fist, can you see it?"

"I know. I made it the last time I was in this cell." I press my eye to the opening, but it's too dark to see anything.

"The last time?"

"I get moved around every few weeks. It's the guards' way of ensuring I don't escape."

For a beat I think she's left me, then finally she speaks. "Can you see me?"

"No. "

She curses in response, and there's another scrape, scrape, scrape sound.

I sit back, still not entirely convinced she's real. The voices have tricked me before.

"Tell me something about yourself," I say. "Anything."

There's a brief hesitation. "I'm from the Shadowmist Pack. Our Alpha is Ryker."

The name sounds familiar.

"I've heard of him," I admit.

"Most have." There's pride in her voice. "He'll come for me."

I don't voice my doubts.

"How'd they get you?" I ask instead.

"Ambush at what was supposed to be a peace summit." Her voice hardens. "Someone we trusted betrayed us."

"I'm sorry."

"Don't be. When I get out of here, I'll tear her apart myself."

The matter-of-fact certainty in her voice makes me smile despite the grim subject. "You sound pretty confident about getting out."

"My pack will come for me. Ryker doesn't abandon his people."

Her loyalty is fascinating. In my experience, pack bonds are rarely so strong.

"What about you?" she asks.

I hesitate. Names have power, especially in a place like this. I've kept mine close for years, offering the guards only silence or sarcasm.

"Not important," I say finally.

"Really? We're doing this? I tell you who I am, and you give me nothing?"

"Consider it a trust-building exercise." I lean against the wall, feeling more alert than I have in months. "I've been here long enough to know that caution keeps you alive."

"Fine," she huffs. "Keep your secrets, mystery man. But if we're going to be neighbors, I need to call you something."

"Call me whatever you want."

"How about 'Paranoid Asshole'?"

I laugh, genuinely amused. "Catchy, but a bit of a mouthful, don't you think?"

"I could shorten it to 'Ass.'"

"Now you're just being lazy."

I hear what might be a reluctant chuckle from her side of the wall, quickly stifled. "Fine. 'Nomad' it is, then."

"How'd you know I'm a nomad?"

"Call it a hunch.'"

I want to ask her name, but naming my hallucinations feels like crossing a line I'm not quite ready for.

We fall into silence, only the scraping sound filling the void. It's not uncomfortable. I'm still not entirely convinced she's real, but talking to her is better than sitting here in silence.

"So, Nomad," she says after a while, "since you've been here so long, what can you tell me about this place? Guards? Routines? Weaknesses?"

"Four guards on rotation in this section. Two per shift,

eight-hour shifts. The morning pair is the worst—the younger one likes to get creative. The night shift is older, more by-the-book."

"And the facility itself?"

"Old mining complex. Repurposed by Thaddeus. Three levels that I know of, possibly more. We're on the lowest."

"Exits?"

I smile at her hope—foolish she-wolf. "Planning your escape already?"

"Always," she says without a hint of humor.

Maybe this voice is my hope personified. Maybe it's the part of me that doesn't want to give up, the part that will always be looking for an exit.

Or maybe I'm full of shit.

"Main entrance is heavily guarded. Service tunnels might be viable, but I've never seen them. There's an old mining shaft somewhere on this level, sealed off decades ago."

She falls quiet. I hear her shifting, then another scraping sound.

"What are you doing?" I ask.

"Working on your delusion problem," she says, her voice strained with effort.

"What do you mean?"

"The hole. It's too small. I need you to help me make it bigger."

I hear her fingers scratching at the stone, trying to widen the opening between our cells.

"You won't make much progress without tools," I tell her. "It took me months to get it this size, and I had a metal fragment from a broken tray." Which was taken from me the last time they rotated me out of this cell.

"Then help me," she demands.

I hesitate, then move closer to the hole. "Let me see what I can do."

I work at the edges of the opening, my fingers already raw from years of similar attempts. The stone is old, crumbling in places, but still stubborn.

We work in silence for what feels like hours, taking turns chipping away at the edges of the hole. Every few minutes, I pause to brush away debris and check our progress.

"We need to be careful," I warn. "If the guards notice, they'll move us."

"Then we'd better not let them notice."

After what must be several hours of work, the hole is noticeably wider—still not large enough to see through clearly, but bigger than before.

"I think that's as far as we'll get today," I say, my fingers bloody and aching.

"One moment," she says, her voice is closer to the hole now. "I want to try something."

I hear her shifting.

"Can you see me now?" she asks.

I peer through the hole again then chuckle. "No. It's still too dark." I don't tell her it's really because she's not there. She may be imagined, but I don't want to hurt her feelings.

Can I get any more fucked up?

My wolf raises his head but doesn't answer.

Yeah. I know.

She makes a frustrated sound. "I have another idea. Stay there."

I hear more movement, then her voice again, directly at the hole. "Put your hand in."

"What?"

"Your hand. Put it in the opening."

Confused but curious, I slide my arm into the hole. It's still too small for my hand to fit far, but I can feel the cool air from the neighboring cell.

Then I feel something. Heat. At first it's a glancing brush, not even a proper touch. She makes a noise, there's a scraping then I feel it.

A fingertip pressing against mine.

The contact is electric. Real. Undeniable.

I jerk back instinctively, then immediately press forward again, desperate to confirm what I felt.

Her finger is still there, waiting. I touch it cautiously, my own trembling.

Warm. Solid. Real.

Fuck. She's real.

My wolf bolts to a stand, his fur rising as he begins to circle, pacing up and down, his tail slowly wagging from one side to the other.

"You're real," I whisper, grazing my finger over the pad of hers. "You're actually real."

"I told you."

I can't stop tracing her fingertip with my own, the simple human contact nearly overwhelming after years of isolation. I can feel calluses, and a small scar—she has the hand of a fighter.

"What's your name?" I demand. "Tell me."

Her finger retreats, and I make a sound—something between desperation and despair. Just as quickly she's back, the heat of her touch reassuring and welcome.

"Lithia."

"Lithia," I repeat, her name tasting sweet now I know she's truly real. "Lithia."

My wolf tips back his head, letting out a howl.

We've found another like us. We're no longer alone.

"I'm Kier," I murmur, desperately memorizing her feel.

I feel her finger twitch against mine, then press more firmly, as if sealing an introduction.

"Well, Kier," she says, and I can hear a smile in her voice for the first time, "looks like we're neighbors."

I laugh softly, the sound rusty but genuine. "Looks like it."

She withdraws slowly, and I feel her absence like a physical pain.

"We should rest," she says. "Conserve our strength."

"You're right." I sit back, leaning against the wall closest to her cell. Even if we can't touch, I need to be close to her. I run my thumb over the pad of my finger, touching where she touched. "They'll come for one of us tomorrow." It was the way of things in here.

"I can handle it."

"I know you can." I lift my hand to my nose and inhale deeply, imagining I can smell her scent against my skin. "I'm sorry I thought you were a hallucination."

"Apology accepted. I'm sorry you've been alone long enough to have hallucinations."

"Could be worse."

"How?"

"The voices could have been boring."

I hear what might have been a laugh, quickly stifled. "Were they good conversationalists?"

"Terrible. Until you."

She snorts. "Now we're bosom buddies, are you going to tell me what you know that could be important enough to land you in a place like this?"

I lean back against the stone. "Let's just say I have a habit of sticking my nose where it doesn't belong."

"And someone didn't appreciate it?"

"Several someones, actually. I'm very talented at making enemies."

"What kind of enemies?"

"The kind that run places like this."

She's quiet for a moment. "You were investigating them?"

"Something like that." I hesitate, then decide to give her a little more. "I was looking for someone. Someone who didn't deserve what happened to her."

"Her?"

"A kid. Well, not exactly a kid, but young. Innocent." The familiar weight of guilt settles on my chest. "I found her. Just not in time to help."

"I'm sorry."

"Yeah. Me too."

"Is that why you're here? Because you found her?"

"Because I found this place. And because I was too stupid to call for backup before trying to get her out." I close my eyes, remembering the moment everything had gone wrong. "Should have known it was a trap."

"You tried to save someone. That's not stupid."

"It is when you fail."

"At least you tried. Most people wouldn't have bothered."

I open my eyes, staring at the dark ceiling. "How do you know?"

"Know what?"

"That most people wouldn't have bothered. Maybe you just have shitty taste in people."

"Maybe. Or maybe I've learned not to expect much from people."

There's a carefully controlled pain simmering under her words that makes me want to ask more questions. But I've already pushed enough for one conversation.

"Well," I say instead, "for what it's worth, you're better company than the guards."

"That's a low bar."

"True. But you cleared it easily."

Another small sound that might have been laughter. "Thanks, I think."

"You're welcome, Lithia."

We fall into a comfortable silence after that. Not the crushing, suffocating quiet I've been living with, but a shared stillness that feels almost peaceful.

"Are you still there?" I ask after a while.

"Yes."

"Good. I was starting to wonder if I'd imagined the whole thing." I run my thumb over my finger once again, determined to hold on to the feel of her skin against mine.

"You didn't imagine me."

"You sure? Because this wouldn't be the weirdest conversation I've had with a hallucination."

"I'm sure."

"How can you tell?"

"Because I'm cold, hungry, and my wrists are rubbing raw from these restraints. I'd be pretty pissed if I'm a hallucination in this much discomfort."

"Good point." I move positions, trying to ease the ache in my back. "Was I lucid the entire time you've been here?"

She hesitates. "No. You seemed to be babbling to yourself for a while before finally speaking to me. But time's hard to track in here."

I hear her picking at the rocks around our hole, and I desperately wish she'd slip her hand through once again.

I curl my hands into fists, holding tight. *No. Don't become dependent on someone who's likely to be ripped away.*

"If you found this place and they still have the person you were looking for, why are they keeping you alive?"

I snort. "Good question. As far as I can tell, they keep me here because I know the location of someone they want."

"Ah."

I nod, knowing she can't see me. "I shared mine, is it time for you to share yours?"

"Share what exactly?"

I shrug. "I don't know. Anything. I've been alone for months. Any talk that doesn't involve torture is welcome."

She chuckles. "Fine. I'm useless at fishing."

I perk up. "Are you terrible at hunting too?"

"No, just fishing. I don't have the patience for waiting."

"Ah, so you're a live wire. You are a redhead, aren't you?"

"None of your business."

"Fair enough. But for the record, whatever color your hair is, I'm glad you're here."

"Glad I'm imprisoned and probably going to die?"

"Glad I'm not alone."

She's quiet for a long moment. Then, so softly I almost miss it. "Yeah. Me too."

I close my eyes, suddenly exhausted but more alive than I've felt in months. "Goodnight, Lithia of Shadowmist."

"Goodnight, Kier of this prison."

I smile, listening to her breathing gradually slow and deepen as she drifts into sleep. The sound is comforting in a way I can't fully articulate.

I press my palm against the wall that separates us, imagining I can feel her warmth through the stone.

Lithia.

You feel that? I ask my wolf, barely breathing.

Mate, is his answer.

His confirmation hits me like a physical blow. I lean my head back against the stone, my chest tight with an emotion so powerful it threatens to crush me.

Mate.

Three fucking years. Three years of talking to ghosts, of begging for death, of existing in a hell where hope is another form of torture. Three years of believing I was destined to die alone and forgotten in this concrete tomb. And now...

I lean my head back, exhaling slowly. "You're sure?"

Yes. My wolf presses against me from within, his intention clear. *She is ours. We will not die in this place.*

His affirmation changes everything. The walls of this cell are no longer my tomb—they're just an obstacle between me and my future.

Our future.

"No. We won't."

Not now. Not while she breathes. Not while she's close enough to touch.

My palm spreads wider against the stone, as if I could somehow reach through it to touch her. Everything has changed.

We've found her. Our mate.

Gods help anyone who tries to take her from me.

CHAPTER

FOUR

The slamming of a door jolts me from a restless sleep. I tense, listening to multiple sets of boots shuffle down the stone corridor. They stop outside my cell.

Damn.

This is it. My first real interrogation.

My mouth is cotton-dry, my tongue sticking to the roof of my mouth. When did I last have water? Yesterday? The day before? Time blurs in this windowless hell. My stomach clenches with a hunger so sharp it's become a constant companion, gnawing at my insides like a living thing.

"They're coming for you," Kier whisper-hisses through the hole. There's something different in his voice—an urgency with a hint of panic that makes my skin prickle with unease.

"I know," I mutter, dragging myself into a seat.

"Don't be a hero. Give them your name if they ask, maybe your rank."

Let them come, I think, settling my shoulders back. *Let them do their worst. They have no idea what they're dealing with.*

My heart hammers against my ribs, adrenaline flooding my system as footsteps approach my door. Fear tries to claw its way up my throat, but I swallow it down, transforming it into something sharper, more useful.

You want to play? Let's fucking play.

I force myself to sit up straighter, ignoring the way my vision wavers from the movement. My body trembles—not from fear, but from the effort of holding myself together when every muscle screams for rest, for food, for relief from the silver's constant burn.

Control, I remind myself, taking a slow, deliberate breath. *Always control.*

But beneath the surface, rage builds like a pressure cooker. White-hot fury at Zella's betrayal, at my own failure to see it coming, at these bastards who think they can break me. The anger is good—it's fuel, something to burn when the pain gets too much to bear.

I flex my fingers, testing the mobility in my hands despite the silver cuffs. My wolf stirs weakly, adding her snarl to mine. We might be trapped, poisoned, starving—but we're Shadowmist. We don't break.

"The important thing is to remember who you are," Kier tells me. "You are Shadowmist. You are Lithia. When they try to convince you otherwise, hold true to that."

"What do you—?"

The slot in my door scrapes open with a metallic shriek, cutting off my question. "Morning, sunshine."

The door swings open and three guards enter. The one in front is older, maybe late-fifties, with salt-and-pepper hair cropped military-short and a face mapped with lines—some scars, some deeply cut wrinkles. His eyes are cold, calculating, assessing me.

He's a threat, but it's the man to his right that worries me.

The second guard is the younger one from yesterday. He watches me with an eagerness that makes my skin crawl. His uniform is impeccable, his posture perfect, but there's something feral in his eyes.

Smells bad, my wolf tells me. *Rotten. Corrupt.*

I agree. He has the look of someone who enjoys causing pain, who gets a sick thrill from watching people break. The way his hands flex tells me he's itching to start, already imagining the sounds I'll make.

He's looking at me like I'm prey. Like he expects me to cower, to beg, to give him the satisfaction of seeing me crumble.

Wrong fucking wolf, asshole.

Despite the unease swirling in my gut—and the knowledge this man could do anything he wished to me—I meet his gaze head-on, letting him see the promise of violence burning in my eyes. Let him get his kicks elsewhere, I won't be feeding his sick appetite today.

But it's the third figure who catches me off guard. A small woman, barely five feet tall, with pale skin and eyes so light blue they're almost white. She hangs back in the shadows, trembling visibly, her gaze darting around the cell as if seeing things I can't. Her hands are wrapped in what appear to be silk gloves, and she flinches whenever the younger guard moves too close to her. For some reason, she reminds me of a little sparrow, fluttering its little tail nervously.

I inhale, catching her scent. Not a wolf. Some other type of were or fae or witch then. Impossible to tell without getting closer.

The older man crouches in front of me, his lips peeled into what could be called a grin if you were a satanist.

"You ready for a chat?"

"Fuck off." I turn away from him. "I'm in the middle of a facial, can't you tell?"

The punch catches my cheek. It's brutal, cracking against my cheek and tossing me to the ground. I taste blood.

From the cell next door comes a harsh, bitten-out curse, followed by the sharp rattle of chains. Like someone just lunged forward against their restraints.

Grunting, I force myself to sit up straight, glaring at the young guard who shakes out his hand with a smile.

Fucking sadist.

"I'm Jim," says the older one, staying just out of reach. "This is Bob"—he gestures to the young guard—"and that's Prudence."

I hide my confusion behind mockery. "Jim, Bob, and Prudence? What is this, a church social committee? Couldn't spring for some intimidating code names?"

Another punch comes from Bob, catching me in the gut. I let out a pained grunt, doubling over.

The sound of metal scraping stone echoes through the wall—like someone's pacing frantically in tight quarters, chains dragging across the floor with each agitated step.

He steps back, and I force myself to stare up at him, refusing to show pain.

"You sure you want to keep doing that? It might mess up your manicure." I nod at his hand. "Those cuticles look freshly polished."

Bob's face flushes crimson. "You won't find it so funny when I'm done with you, bitch."

"Easy, Bob," Jim cautions. "We need her coherent." He turns to me with a practiced smile. "Let's start simple. What's your position in the Shadowmist Pack?"

"I'm the one who gets to rip your throats out."

Jim sighs. "This'll go easier if you cooperate."

I spit blood onto his polished boots. "Bite me, bitch."

This time I'd ready for the sharp kick Bob delivers to my ribs. His boot slams into my side, and I hear the crack-pop of a rib giving way. Pain flares white-hot, stealing my breath. I fold over, choking on the scream I won't let them hear.

Fuck. That hurt.

A low growl filters through the stone—barely audible but unmistakably furious. The guards don't seem to notice, too focused on me.

"Ready to answer our questions?"

I drag my head up, blood on my lips and fire in my lungs.

"I'm going to count every mark you put on me," I rasp, voice low and steady. "Every single one. And when I get free, I'm going to return them tenfold."

Jim nods to Bob, who produces a small silver blade. The metal gleams with an unnatural light, clearly old silver.

This doesn't look good.

Bob presses the blade against my forearm. The metal burns, searing flesh.

I don't flinch. Don't blink. Just stare directly into Jim's eyes, letting him see the promise of death I'm making.

You're dead wolves walking.

"We know about the safe room beneath the main den," Jim says, watching my face closely. "But there are safe houses, aren't there? Locations only the alpha and his most inner circle know about. Tell us where they are."

The safe room's existence wasn't widely known even within the pack. The depth of Zella's betrayal hits me anew.

"Sorry to disappoint," I say through gritted teeth as Bob digs the blade deeper. "I'm just the muscle. They don't tell me the important stuff."

"We both know that's not true," Jim replies. "Ryker trusts you. You're his Beta. So I'll ask again—where are the safe houses?"

Bob twists the blade, and I can't stop the hiss of pain that escapes me.

"Look at Bobby go," I manage, forcing a smile. "Someone's eager to impress Daddy Jim. Got a performance review coming up?"

Bob's face contorts with rage. He moves the blade to my neck, just below my jaw.

"I'm going to enjoy breaking you," he whispers.

"Careful," Jim cautions. He turns toward the shadows. "Prudence. Come forward."

There's a howl from next door, but the guards ignore it as the small woman takes a hesitant step into the light. Her trembling is pronounced now, and up close I can see the hollows beneath her eyes, the unnatural thinness of her frame. She looks terrified.

"No," she whispers, her voice barely audible. "Please. Not yet. I need—I need to prepare."

"You've had enough time," Jim says coldly. "Do your job."

Bob grabs my hair, yanking my head back to expose my throat. "Look at her, Prudence. Do what you do best."

Prudence's strange, colorless eyes meet mine reluctantly. "I'm sorry," she says quietly.

Then her eyes begin to change. Her pupils expand until they swallow the irises entirely, turning her gaze into bottomless black pits. "She fears loss," Prudence says, her voice resonating oddly in the small cell. "She's lost before. Parents. Friends." A pause. "She fears it will happen again."

A chill races up my spine. *What magic is this?*

I force a laugh. "Nah, babe. My only fear is missing my hair appointment next week. Gotta keep the split ends at bay."

They all ignore me.

"Show her," Jim commands.

"Please don't make me," Prudence pleads, her black eyes never leaving mine. "It's too cruel."

"Show her," Jim repeats, his tone brooking no argument.

Prudence removes one silk glove, revealing a hand covered in strange, swirling patterns that seem to shift and move of their own accord. She reaches toward me, stopping inches from my face.

"I'm sorry," she says again. Then she touches my forehead.

The cell vanishes.

I'm nine years old again, hiding in a hollowed tree trunk with Dane. Above us, hunters move through the forest, silver weapons gleaming in moonlight. Below us, on the forest floor, our parents lie motionless, silver arrows protruding from their backs.

I clamp my hand over Dane's mouth to silence his sobs. "Be quiet," I whisper. "Or they'll find us too."

But the hunters turn toward our hiding place anyway. They've caught our scent. They're coming closer, silver blades drawn.

"Run!" I tell Dane, pushing him out the back of the hollow tree. "Run and don't look back!"

He does, disappearing into the underbrush. I turn to face the hunters, a child ready to die to give her brother time to escape.

Except this time, my wolf doesn't shift free, fierce and angry, killing them all despite her lack of training and experience.

Instead, they catch Dane. I hear his screams, his pleas for help.

"Lithia!" he cries. "Lithia, help me!"

I run toward his voice, but no matter how fast I move, I can't reach him. His screams grow weaker, then abruptly stop.

NO!

I break through the trees, and I find him. Not the child Dane, but the adult, my twin, my other half. Dead. Eyes open and unseeing, throat torn out.

Around him, other bodies. Ryker. Kitara. Elias. Levi. All the wolves I've sworn to protect, all dead because I failed them.

"No," I whisper, dropping to my knees beside them. "No, please."

"This is your future," Jim says, somehow part of this nightmare. "This is what happens when you resist us. Everyone you love dies."

The scene shifts. I'm in Shadowmist's main hall. Thaddeus sits in Ryker's chair, blood staining the stones beneath it. Zella stands at his right hand, smiling coldly.

"You could have prevented this," Zella tells me. "Could have saved them all by simply cooperating."

"Fuck off," I growl. "This isn't real."

The scene wavers, then resolidifies. Now I'm in my cell again, but there's someone else there too—a man I've never seen before but somehow know is Kier. He's on his knees before Jim, silver blade at his throat.

"Tell us what we want to know," Jim says, "or he dies too."

"Listen to them," Kier says, his golden eyes pleading. "Save me. Please."

The blade slices across his throat, blood spraying across the stone floor.

I scream, lunging forward. Grasping for Kier's falling body. A howl rips from my throat and I—

I crash into the wall of my cell, gasping and panting as reality snaps back into place. Prudence's hand hovers near my face, her eyes black and fathomless. Tears stream down her cheeks, mixing with the blood streaming from her nose.

Is this another vision?

I'm shaking, unable to control the tremors that rack my body. The visions felt so real—the blood, the screams, the death of everyone I've ever cared about.

"That's enough for today," Jim says, nodding to Bob. "We'll continue tomorrow."

Bob smiles cruelly, but Prudence just looks devastated. As they turn to leave, she whispers something only I can hear.

"I'm so sorry."

Then they're gone, the door slamming shut behind them, leaving me alone with the aftershocks of visions that still feel more real than the cell around me.

I curl into myself, trying to separate reality from the nightmare Prudence forced into my mind. Dane isn't dead. Ryker isn't dead. They're alive, somewhere far from here, probably searching for me.

And Kier. I saw his face in the vision, a face I've never seen before. Golden eyes in a lean, scarred face. How could I see someone I've never met?

"Lithia?" Kier's voice comes through the wall, urgent and concerned. "Lithia, talk to me."

I can't respond. Can't form words past the horror still gripping me.

"Dammit, woman, answer me!" His voice is sharp now, almost angry. "I know you're there. I can hear you breathing."

The edge in his tone cuts through my paralysis. "I'm here," I manage, my voice barely a whisper.

"I heard your screaming. What did the fear-seer show you?"

I close my eyes, the images still fresh and vivid. Fear-seer. The title is appropriate. "She… she showed me things… I…" I draw in a shuddering breath.

"Shit." There's real fear in his voice now. "What kind of things?"

"Everyone is dead. Everyone I care about." I swallow hard. "And you. She showed me you."

"Me? You don't know what I look like."

"I saw you anyway. Golden eyes. Lean face. Scars."

There's a long silence. "Ruggedly good- looking though, right?"

A choked sound escapes me—part sob, part laugh. I snort, the sound ragged in my throat. I wipe at my eyes, shame and grief still clinging to me like a second skin. "Gods," I whisper. "I get it now."

"Get what?"

"Why you didn't believe I was real when we first spoke." My fingers twitch against the stone. "Why you thought I was just another hallucination."

"Yeah," he says. "It's hard to tell what's real when good old Prudence can make anything seem possible. Though, to be fair to her, I was already fucked up before they dragged her in here a few months back."

I press my palm to the wall between us, desperate to cling to something solid. "I don't know if I'm awake, or dreaming, or somewhere in between. I can still see it—Dane bleeding out. Ryker broken. You…"

His voice cuts in, low and steady. "You're awake, Lithia. You're here. And so am I."

I hear him move.

"Slide your hand over here. Touch me. Let me show you how real this is."

I stick my hand in the opening, desperate for anything to anchor me. His touch is solid, the contact electric, a lifeline in the dark.

"I'm here," he says firmly. "You're not alone."

I press my finger against his, anchoring myself to the feeling. My breathing evens out slowly, the aftershocks of the vision beginning to settle.

"How is that possible?"

"I don't know. Prudence is some kind of fear-seer. I'd always heard rumors about supernaturals who can do this kind of thing." He shifts, and I hear chains rattle.

"She knows about you. What if she tells them we've been talking."

"They're not stupid." His finger grazes gently against mine. "If she tells them then they'll use it against you now. Threaten me to make you talk. Don't let them."

"I'm not going to be responsible for you being hurt."

His laugh is bitter. "They've been hurting me for three years, Lithia. What's a little more torture between friends?"

Despite everything, I feel the ghost of a smile touch my lips. "Are we friends?"

"We're whatever we need to be to survive this place." His finger presses more firmly against mine. "The important thing is that we don't break."

I focus on the warmth of his touch. Who would have thought the press of a fingertip would be the thing holding me together?

"That woman, Prudence," I say after a moment. "She's a prisoner too, isn't she?"

"Yes. Another captive they're using."

"She apologized. Before. And after."

"Don't mistake that for kindness." His voice turns hard. "She'll do exactly what they tell her to do to stay alive. No one is your friend here."

"Except you?"

He snorts. "I have ulterior motives."

"And those are?"

"I need you to keep me sane."

I'm quiet for a minute, fighting the pain that still rages through my body.

"She was terrified."

"We all are. If you're not, it means you're already dead." He shifts position but doesn't let his finger slip from mine. "Get some rest. Tomorrow will be worse."

"How could it possibly be worse?"

"Now they know your fears. And they'll use them against you in any way they can think of."

I close my eyes, the exhaustion of the day finally catching up to me. "Kier?"

"What?"

"Stay with me?" I twitch my finger against his, hating that I sound so vulnerable.

"Not going anywhere, Shadowmist." His voice is gruff but gentle. "Just try to sleep."

I sigh a silent breath of relief and close my eyes.

CHAPTER
FIVE
KIER

She's been out for six hours.

She's not sleeping. Not really. This is the kind of silence that follows pain sharp enough to knock you clean out. The kind of stillness that comes when your body can't fight the pull anymore.

And I can't do a goddamn thing about it. The rage burns through me like acid, eating away at what's left of my sanity. My mate—*my mate*—is lying unconscious on the other side of this fucking wall, and I'm chained here like a useless piece of shit, listening to her labored breathing and going out of my mind.

I should be holding her. Should be cleaning her wounds, checking her pulse, making sure she's warm and safe and breathing. Instead, I'm trapped in this concrete box, reduced to pressing my ear to stone just to catch the faint whisper of air from her lungs.

She needs me and I can't reach her.

The thought is a knife twisting in my chest. Three years of torture, three years of wanting to die, and none of it comes close to this agony. This helpless fury at being so close to her but unable to offer even the smallest comfort.

I press my palm flat against the wall, imagining I can somehow transfer strength through the stone. Willing her to feel that she's not alone, that someone is here, someone cares, someone would tear this entire place apart with his bare hands if it meant keeping her safe.

So I keep working. She deserves more than the press of a finger to comfort her after her beating.

And gods know, so do I.

The stone wall between us has stood for decades, maybe centuries. It wasn't meant to be broken by bare hands. But I've been working this same spot every time they rotate me back to this cell. This is my third time here, and each rotation I've managed to widen the hole just a little more.

Before, carving at the stone was just something to do—an act of defiance against the nothing. Something to focus on instead of losing my mind to silence and silver. I knew I'd never get out. Knew even if I broke through, it would just mean trading one cage for another. One cell for the next. Still trapped. Still alone.

But now?

My fingers are bloody, nails torn down to the quick, but I don't stop. If anything, I work faster. Because now she's here.

Now I want *in*.

I want to be in her cell. The hole isn't a mindless rebellion anymore. I carve because I need to reach her. She's my escape.

Lithia

Her breathing shifts—a sucked-in breath as if she's in pain.

She's waking.

The edges of the hole are jagged, slicing into my palms as I pry at the weakest points. I don't care. Pain is meaningless compared to the need to reach her.

"Lithia? Are you awake?"

No response. Just another pained intake of breath.

A piece of stone breaks away, cutting my wrist deeply as it

falls. I ignore it, reaching through the now-larger opening. It's still not big enough for more than my hand, but it's something.

I should have warned Lithia about the fear-seer and what would happen when those pale eyes looked into hers. But I didn't think they'd bring Prudence so soon. They usually start with physical pain, wait until the prisoner is weak before hitting them with the psychological torture.

Lithia's either very valuable or very dangerous. Or maybe she's both.

I curse under my breath, redoubling my efforts. The silver in my system makes my wolf weak, my strength a fraction of what it should be. But desperation fuels me now, fueling whatever strength I have remaining.

Lithia.

I break through, pulling stone from the hole and clearing the dusty rubble as best I can. I hide it as I've always done in the waste bucket. The woman who comes to swap them out twice a day never speaks of it, and I doubt the guards are clawing through our shit to check.

With the hole clear, I wiggle down, pressing close to the wall as I work my arm into the hole. I can fit my arm through past the elbow now, if I ignore the scratch and scrape of the sharp rock.

"Lithia?"

No response. Her breathing doesn't change.

I push my arm through the opening as far as it will go, feeling blindly for her in the darkness. My fingertips brush against fabric—her shirt—then find her shoulder.

At the contact, she jolts awake with a sharp intake of breath, pulling away from the wall.

"It's just me," I say quickly. "It's Kier. You're safe."

There's a pause, then I hear her shift closer to the wall. "Kier?"

"How are you feeling?"

She moves, and I hear a pained hiss. "Perfect. Like I could run five miles without breaking a sweat."

I smile. *There she is.*

"Bob's got steel-toed boots," I tell her. "Compensating for other inadequacies, I'm sure."

She snorts then groans. "How long was I out?"

"Six hours. Maybe seven." I flex my fingers, trying to ease the ache from hours of stone-breaking. "You had me worried."

"Don't be. I'm hard to break."

Of that I have no doubt.

Dawn approaches—or what passes for dawn in this windowless hellhole. I can tell by the subtle shift in the facility's sounds, the changing of guards, the distant clang of metal trays being prepared for morning meals, the soft shuffling of the cleaning crews beginning their rounds.

Three years of captivity have attuned me to the rhythms of this place, such as they are. They're the only way to mark time when darkness is constant. We won't have long before we're interrupted once more.

"I should have warned you about Prudence. I'm sorry."

"Even if you had time—and you didn't—would it have changed anything?" Lithia asks. "Maybe I'd have broken faster if I'd known what was coming."

"Maybe," I admit. "But I still should have told you."

She reaches out, her fingers finding mine through the hole. Her touch is electric, shimmering up my arm.

Mate.

"Tell me everything I need to know."

I thread our fingers together, wincing slightly as her fingertips brush over the raw wounds.

"Kier," she says sharply, her voice cutting through the darkness. "You're bleeding."

I can feel her fingers exploring gently, tracing the torn skin on my knuckles, the deeper gashes on my wrist. My hands are still wet and sticky with fresh blood from my work on the wall.

"How badly are you hurt?"

"It's nothing," I try to dismiss, but she's not having it.

"Bullshit. I can smell the blood, Kier. Your hands are torn apart." Her grip tightens on my fingers, careful of the wounds. "Tell me." The worry in her voice—for me, when she's the one who was just tortured—makes my chest tight.

"Just some scrapes from working on the wall," I admit. "I'm making the hole bigger."

"You've been clawing at stone with your bare hands?"

I don't answer.

She sighs heavily. "Fine. Tell me about Prudence."

"She's a fear-seer. Like all seers, it's a rare gift. Unlike others who might see the future or the past, she can see what terrifies someone and project it as visions that feel completely real."

Lithia's fingers flinched in mine. "Yeah. It definitely felt real to me."

I trace my thumb along her knuckles. "She's not evil. She's as much a prisoner as we are. They use her daughter as leverage."

Lithia's grip tightens. "They have her child?"

"Yes. They keep her deep in the mine somewhere. She's alive but sick. They tell Prudence that cooperation will earn her daughter better medical care. She does what she has to, to keep her daughter alive."

"Bastards." The venom in her voice could strip paint. "How do you know all this?"

"I've been in her mind."

"What?"

"Not intentionally." I shift position, uncomfortable with the admission. "One day they brought Prudence to my cell, and when she touched me to show me my fears, something… broke open. In both of us."

"What do you mean?"

"The barriers between our minds. I wasn't seeing my own nightmares—I was seeing hers. Her memories. Her pain." The memory still makes me sick. "I saw her daughter, Meg. Saw the moment they told Prudence that Meg was sick and needed treatment. Saw how they used that love to turn her into a weapon."

"Are you a seer as well?"

"Not that I know of." I turn her hand over, tracing the lines of her palm. "But the mind does strange things when it's pushed past its breaking point."

"Has it happened again?"

"A few times. Brief flashes when she's working on someone nearby. I feel her guilt, her self-hatred. That's how I know she means it when she apologizes. The pain in her mind when she hurts people—it's almost worse than what she shows them."

Lithia processes this. "Could I do it too?"

"Maybe. If you're desperate enough." I press my palm to hers, relishing the heat. "I don't recommend trying. It nearly shattered what was left of my sanity."

"How did you do it?"

I'm silent as I try to find the words to explain. "I guess the best description would be that I didn't fight the connection. It was my fifth session in three days and I just… gave up. When it started, I could see it all playing out before me, every sickened second. But instead of participating in the scene, it was like I was floating above it. As it continued, I noticed a weird pull from one side of the vision. When I followed it back to its source, that's when I found myself in Prudence's mind."

I swallow, remembering her thoughts. "To do what she does isn't just about unlocking our fears–it requires her to experience her own. There's a cost to everything."

Lithia's grip tightens on my hand. "Do you think I could break through?"

"If you don't, you'll be forced to endure whatever hell she shows you, just like everyone else."

I hear Lithia inhale sharply. "Does it get easier?"

"Never. Each time is worse than the last."

"How much worse?"

I search for the words to describe the horror. "They'll use what they learned from the first session. Your fears about losing people you care about—they'll build on that. Make it more specific, more personal. Lithia." I squeeze her hand. "I've been here three years. I know how this works. If you fight too hard, they'll continue to bring in Prudence or use other means to gather information until they can manipulate you. But if you give them small things—non-critical information, stuff that won't hurt your pack—they'll think they're making progress."

"It's not in my nature to roll over." She's quiet for a long moment. "What kind of small things?"

"Personal details. Your favorite color. What you like to eat. Names of wolves who aren't in positions of strategic importance." I squeeze her hand. "Things that sound valuable but aren't actually useful."

"And if they want more than that?"

"Then you give them a little more. But never the important stuff. Never anything that could genuinely harm your pack."

"You've done this?"

"Many times. The key is making them feel like they're winning while never giving them anything that actually matters."

"What have you given them?"

The question catches me off guard. "Nothing important," I say finally.

"That's not an answer."

"It's the only answer you're getting."

I can hear her frustrated sigh. "We're supposed to be in this together, aren't we? Partners in survival?"

"Partners don't always share everything."

"Bull. Partners trust each other."

The word "trust" hangs between us like a challenge. Trust. When was the last time I trusted anyone? When was the last time anyone trusted me enough to risk their life alongside mine?

"Trust has to be earned," I tell her.

She lets go of my hand, shifting back. "Good to know where I stand."

Fuck.

"I was looking for someone," I say finally. "A bear seer. A teenage girl named Adelaide. Her parents hired me to find her after she was kidnapped."

"Hired?"

"I track people. It's what I do." I shift position, my knees protesting against the stone floor. "Was what I did, I guess I should say. Finding Adelaide led me to a whole network of trafficking."

"Thaddeus?"

"And others like him. They collect anyone they think might be useful to their purposes. "

"Did you find her? Adelaide?"

My throat tightens. "Yeah. I found her."

"But?"

"Not in time." The familiar weight of failure settles on my chest. "They'd moved her an hour after I got captured."

Lithia's grip on my hand tightens. "I'm sorry."

"I should have acted quicker. Should have called for backup instead of trying to be a hero."

"You tried to save a child."

"Doesn't matter if you fail."

"Doing what's right always matters." Her voice is firm, certain. "Even when you fail. *Especially* when you fail."

I want to argue with her, but don't have it in me to protest actions that happened so long ago.

"What about you?" I ask. "You're a smart wolf. Why are you blaming yourself for being in here?" I can smell the bitter shame-scent of her guilt.

"That's different."

"Is it?"

"Yes."

"How?" I hear her move, shuffling away from the wall. "Talk to me, Lithia. What's eating at you?"

For a moment, I think she's going to shut down completely. Then she takes a shaky breath.

"I was supposed to protect my Alpha Female. She was taken because I failed to see the threat."

"Which was?"

"Zella. A fellow wolf."

I wince. "Pack or friend?"

"Both." Her voice hardens. "For five years she was in our pack. For five years I trusted her. I never saw what she really was."

"Sounds like she was good at hiding her true self."

"No, it's because I was arrogant. I thought I could read people. I assumed my instincts were foolproof." She lets out a bitter laugh. "Turns out I'm about as perceptive as a rock."

"So you're blaming yourself for not being psychic?"

"I'm blaming myself for failing in my duty. Kitara, the Alpha Female, trusted me to protect her. My Alpha, Ryker, trusted me. I couldn't protect her from the person sitting at our own dinner table."

The pain in her voice is raw, deep.

"Where is she now? Your Alpha Female?"

"I don't know." The admission seems to physically hurt

her. "They caught her. We were together for a little while then they separated us. For all I know, she's dead."

"But you don't think she is."

Her voice lifts slightly, surprised. "What makes you say that?"

"Because if you thought she was dead, you would have given up by now. You're fighting to get back to her, which means you believe she's still alive."

She's quiet for a long moment. "You're right. I can't feel her through our pack bonds—the silver disrupts that—but something inside me says she's still breathing."

"Why?"

Lithia's silent so long I assume she's not going to tell me. It's a surprise when she finally speaks.

"Kitara is a seer."

I close my eyes. "Which is why they want her here."

"Yeah."

I pull my arm out of the hole, shaking it out as I rotate to slip my other through. There's an ache in my shoulders and neck, but I'm so desperate for more of her touch that I'd rather die than not have my hand out and ready for when she next wants to touch me.

"Then hold on to what you know. They crave seers. Kitara is useful to them. Whatever instincts you think failed you before, they're telling you she's alive now."

"What if I'm wrong?"

"What if you're right?"

I jump when her thumb absently strokes along my knuckles.

"How do you do it?" she asks suddenly.

"Do what?"

"Stay sane. You've been here three years, Kier. Three years of this hell, and you're still fighting. How?"

The question cuts deeper than any torture they've put me through. Because the truth is, I haven't been sane. Not really.

The voices, the hallucinations, the conversations with dead people—I've been teetering between madness and sanity for longer than I know.

I assume I've been here three years. But for all I know it could be longer.

"I don't know," I tell her honestly. "Maybe this is just an elaborate shared delusion."

"That's a cheerful thought."

We fall into comfortable silence, her hand warm in mine.

The distant sound of the corridor door opening reaches us —the soft scrape of metal on stone that signals the beginning of morning rounds.

"Someone's coming," I murmur.

Lithia's fingers tighten around mine for a moment before reluctantly letting go. "Guards?"

"Yes, one with the bucket woman," I say, withdrawing my arm from the hole and adjusting my position. "She comes twice a day."

"The one who never speaks?"

"That's her."

The footsteps draw closer—light, hesitant steps that lack the confident stride of the guards. They pause outside my cell, followed by the familiar jingle of keys.

The lock turns, and the door swings open. She enters, small and hunched, moving with cautious efficiency. Today she carries not just the replacement bucket but also a small tray with what passes for breakfast in this hellhole—a bowl of thin gruel and a cup of water.

I remain still, pressed against the wall opposite the door, my head down in the non-threatening posture I've perfected over the years. Through lowered lashes, I watch her.

She sets the tray down near my sleeping pallet, then moves to exchange the waste bucket. As she lifts the old one, her eyes widen slightly at the stone fragments and bloody debris inside. Her gaze flicks to me, then to the wall I share with Lithia.

For one heart-stopping moment, I think she'll raise the alarm.

Instead, she makes a small adjustment to her movements, tilting the bucket slightly to shield its contents from the view of anyone who might be watching through the door's observation slot. With practiced motions, she transfers the bucket's contents to a larger container on her cart, making sure the stones are buried beneath other waste.

As she places the clean bucket in the corner, she pauses. Without looking directly at me, she reaches into her pocket and places something small beside the food tray. Then she's gone, the door closing and locking behind her.

I wait until I hear her enter Lithia's cell before moving. The object she left is a scrap of cloth, wrapped around something solid. I unfold it carefully to reveal a small piece of metal—part of a broken buckle or clasp, its edge sharpened to a crude point.

A tool. A weapon, even.

She's left me small gifts before. An extra piece of bread. A cloth to clean wounds. Never anything this obvious though.

The voices in my head begin to speak.

Could be a trap.

Could be a chance.

Could be escape.

Could be a test.

Could be...

Could be...

I carefully hide the metal shard in a crack in the wall near my sleeping area.

She might be our way out of here.

I can hear the scrape of Lithia's spoon as she eats her gruel.

"This is disgusting."

I huff out a laugh, picking up my own meal. "You get used to it. Mostly."

"I need to get out of here," she says after a moment. "My Alpha needs me. My pack needs me."

I need you.

I push my food around, watching the muck congeal into a weird grey lump. "If we're going to escape we need to do it together. Better odds than going solo."

She's quiet. "That makes sense. How do you think we should do it?"

"I'm not sure yet. But between the two of us, we'll work out something."

"We better." I hear her place her tray on the ground. "'Cause I think the meals might be what breaks me."

CHAPTER
SIX

"Time for another chat," Jim announces as the door swings open.

My wolf surges forward beneath my skin, hackles rising despite the silver's suppression. She may be weakened, but she's far from beaten. A low snarl rumbles through our bond as she recognizes the threat, her instincts screaming at me to fight, to run, to do anything but submit to these predators.

Danger, she warns, pressing against my consciousness with renewed strength.

I don't respond to Jim as Bob and Prudence shuffle in behind him. My wolf's agitation grows as she scents their intentions—violence, manipulation, pain. She paces restlessly beneath my skin, frustrated by the silver that keeps her caged.

I ignore the men and look at Prudence, watching as she moves to cower in the corner of my cell. She's pale and trembling, her eyes darting between me and the guards.

My wolf's snarl shifts to something almost protective as she senses the smaller woman's terror.

Scared, my wolf observes, her fury momentarily tempered by recognition of another victim. *Terror.*

I should hate her and what she does, but I can't. She's a mouse of a woman, small and petite. She barely looks old enough to be dating, let alone have her own pup.

I inhale, catching her scent. This time, I pay attention to it– or rather, what it's missing.

She carries the myrrh-like scent of a seer, dry and sharp at the edges. But there's no animal under it. No wolf, no lynx, no bear. Nothing.

She's human.

My gaze sharpens, raking over her again. Small. Fragile-looking. Skin so pale it seems like she'd bruise if you breathed on her wrong. Humans and weres didn't mix. Not really. Not in blood, not in magic, not in anything that mattered.

Sure, there were always whispers—witches and warlocks claiming seer blood, little hedge magics bubbling at the edges of the real world. But a true seer? One who could survive the weight of Sight without breaking?

They were rare in the were world, and even rarer still in humans.

I don't hate her—how could I? She's as much a victim as I am, trapped in this nightmare through no choice of her own. But I absolutely fucking loathe what she's being forced to do, the agony she's capable of inflicting. The world she's been dragged into is destroying her, piece by piece, and I can see it in every trembling line of her body. The guards haul me to a chair they place in the center of the room and chain my existing restraints to it. The additional silver burns fresh welts over yesterday's wounds.

I could fight. Should fight. But the silver already around my wrists, ankles, and throat has sapped my strength. Fighting will only make what comes next worse.

"Same questions as yesterday," Jim says, settling into his chair across from me. "Shadowmist's safe houses. Where are they?"

"And I'll give you the same answer," I reply. "Go fuck yourself."

Bob's fist catches my ribs before I finish speaking. The air rushes out of my lungs in a pained wheeze, but I don't cry out.

I'll never give them the satisfaction.

"Prudence," Jim says coldly. "You know what to do."

She pulls her gloves off and reaches toward me, her eyes locked on mine.

"Make it a good one," I growl. "I love horror movies."

Her fingertips brush my temple, and the world dissolves.

I'm standing in a cell much like my own, but the prisoner isn't me. A girl is chained to the wall, arms wrenched above her head, wrists raw where silver cuffs bite into her skin.

She's young. Sixteen? Maybe younger. Honey-colored hair clings to her damp cheeks, eyes wide and brown and terrified.

"I don't know anything," she's whispering. "Please—I don't know anything about the other packs. I can't just see things—"

Bob's voice cuts through, rough and impatient. "Adelaide, you'll see when we tell you to see or your family pays the price."

Adelaide.

Her name hits me like a rock to the gut. Kier's missing were.

The vision lurches, and I'm somewhere else. A cabin. Blood pools in sticky glistening puddles on the floor and streaked across the walls. Two people lay crumbled on the floor, their throats torn out.

The smell hits me even though I know it's not real—copper and grief and ruin.

Adelaide's parents.

My stomach twists. Even in the unreality of this vision, I can feel the despair bleeding off the scene.

Jim's voice slithers through the dark, wrapping around the edges of my mind. "This is what happens to those who resist. Tell us what we want to know, Lithia."

"Never."

The vision intensifies, the bears on the floor rising from their death, mouths wide and gaping, eyes glassy and flat.

I turn to run and find Adelaide behind me.

As the bears approach snarling and growling, she holds out a hand.

"You aren't alone," she whispers.

My breath catches, heart slamming into my ribs.

"Tell Kier it wasn't his fault. This had to happen—he had to meet you."

The world convulses. Adelaide's form wavering.

"Prudence will show you."

The world spins and I'm in another room, this one small and bare but for a thin mattress and some blankets on the floor.

Prudence kneels the bed cradling a baby to her chest.

A baby.

It's no older than three, maybe four months. Soft pale fuzz on her head, fists curled tight against Prudence's shirt, little mouth open in a silent, wobbly cry.

"I'm sorry," Prudence is whispering, over and over, rocking back and forth. "Please, please, don't take her. I'll do whatever you want. I'll do anything, just—"

Footsteps echo outside the door. A shadow moves under the gap.

"I can't lose her too," Prudence chokes out, clutching the baby closer, as if she can fold her small body around her and make them both disappear. "Please. I'll do anything."

The vision explodes outward, showing me flash after flash of Prudence's torment. The guards threatening her baby. The sessions where she's forced to rip apart other prisoners' minds. The nights she cries herself to sleep, hating what she's become.

And underneath it all, a desperate message meant only for me.

"If you escape—if anyone escapes—please. Please find her."

I slam back into reality with such force that the chair tips backward, my restraints cutting deeper into my wrists as I crash to the floor.

"Lithia!" Prudence cries out, her mask slipping for just a moment before she catches herself.

"Get her up," Jim orders Bob, who hauls me back into position with rough hands.

I'm shaking uncontrollably, the visions still burning through my mind. Adelaide's message. Prudence's plea. The knowledge that there are others here, other innocents being used against their will.

Prudence showed me weres, witches, warlocks, and fae. This is bigger than Thaddeus. This goes far beyond any one pack. This is an evil that has spread unchecked.

Until now.

"Well?" Jim demands. "Ready to cooperate?"

I look up at Prudence, meeting her terrified gaze. She did more than show me my fears—she shared her own. Told me about her daughter. Begged for help.

"I need water," I gasp, buying time while my mind reels.

Jim nods to Bob, who produces a cup. The water is warm and tastes of rust, but it helps clear some of the fog from my head.

"The safe houses," Jim prompts.

I lick the rust-tasting water off my lips, feeling the sting where they're split. My body is shaking, every nerve screaming, but Prudence has lit a cold fuse within me.

I need to stop this. And to stop this, I need to survive.

"Old mine shaft," I say finally. "Fifteen miles north of the main den. There's a hidden entrance behind a waterfall."

It's not a lie, exactly. There is an old mine shaft there. We just don't use it as a safe house—it's been flooded for decades.

Jim makes a note. "How many can it hold?"

"Fifty wolves, last I checked. More if needed." Again, not a lie. It's what it held before the floods came and filled it with muck.

"Supplies?"

"I don't know. That's not my department."

All truths that wouldn't harm anyone. Let them waste time searching for something that doesn't exist.

"Good," Jim says, clearly satisfied. "See how easy that was? Tomorrow we'll discuss the emergency evacuation routes."

They unchain me from the chair, leaving my permanent silver restraints in place. Bob shoves me toward the back of my cell, and I collapse onto the thin mattress, every muscle in my body screaming. The silver burns are getting worse, and my head pounds from the vision-induced trauma.

But I have information now. Adelaide's message. Prudence's plea. The knowledge that there are others here who need help.

Gods, what a mess.

They haul the chair out and slam the door shut, leaving me to the darkness.

I listen as they move down the hall then stop.

"Morning, sunshine," a guard's voice calls through the wall. "Miss us?"

"Like a rash," comes Kier's reply. "Did you bring flowers? I feel like this relationship is getting serious."

I hear the squeal of the old door swinging open followed by a fleshy thud and a grunt of pain.

"Still got that smart mouth, I see," Bob says.

"It's one of my best features," Kier growls. "That and my sparkling personality."

Another hit. Harder this time. I hear the crunch of bone, wincing in sympathy.

"Tell us who you were working with," a different voice demands.

"Not sure how many times I need to tell you dumbasses this but no one," Kier says firmly, though his voice has dropped to barely above a whisper. Each word sounds like it costs him effort. "I'm nomad. We lone wolves don't exactly play well with others."

The beating that follows is methodical, brutal. But through it all, Kier keeps talking smack.

"I have some feedback about your torture technique. Should I file that with you or your supervisor?"

Crack.

"It's mostly constructive criticism. Well, some constructive. Some just criticism." I can hear the exhaustion bleeding through now, the way his sentences are getting shorter, his words beginning to slur.

Thud.

"Has anyone ever told you"—he pauses, gasping for breath—"that you hit like my grandmother? And she's been dead for twenty years."

I press my hand over my mouth to muffle any sound. Kier is being tortured, and he's still making jokes. I'm impressed.

The interrogation continues for what feels like hours. Every time they demand information about his accomplices, Kier deflects with sarcasm. Every blow they land, he answers with mockery.

"You know," he says after a particularly vicious hit, "I'm starting to think you boys have anger management issues. There are therapists for that."

"Shut up," Jim snarls.

"Shut up? I thought you wanted me to talk."

I jump at a loud crash, followed by vicious sounds. It goes on and on until finally they stop, pulling away to allow Prudence to move in.

"Deal with this one," Bob orders. "And make it bad."

There's silence, the kind that makes my skin crawl. It's unnatural and oppressive, a pause of fear rather than peace.

I strain to listen, hearing only the soft shuffle of movement. Then a sharp intake of breath. Followed by another.

"No," Kier whispers, his voice barely audible. "That's not… you're not real."

The silence stretches again. I can picture Prudence's pale hands on his temples, her dark eyes boring into his mind, forcing him to see whatever nightmare she's crafting.

A whimper escapes him. Low and broken, the sound of someone trying desperately not to break.

"No," he gasps. "Stop."

But it doesn't stop. The whimpers become more frequent, punctuated by sharp breathing and whispered denials.

"They're not real," he keeps saying. "You're not real. None of this is real."

Then the first scream tears from his throat.

It's raw and agonized, the sound of a soul being flayed alive. Every muscle in my body tenses as if I could somehow absorb his pain through the stone wall.

Another scream. Longer this time, dissolving into broken sobs.

"I'm sorry," he cries out. "No. Don't!"

My chest tightens, and I bite my fist to keep from screaming at them to stop.

Think of all the ways they'll pay, my wolf says. *Think of all the ways they'll die.*

The screaming goes on for hours. Sometimes words emerge through Kier's anguish—names I don't recognize, pleas for forgiveness, desperate apologies to people who might be dead or imaginary.

By the time Prudence finally stops, Kier has gone silent again. But it's a different silence now. Broken. Hollow.

I hear the guards leave, laughing and joking as they walk down the long echoing corridor. The door to our area slams shut with finality.

Minutes pass. I wait, listening for any sound from his cell.

"Kier?" I whisper through the hole.

Nothing.

"Kier, are you there?"

A rustling sound, then his voice, distant and confused. "Adelaide? Is that you?"

My blood runs cold.

"I'm here," he continues, but he's not talking to me. "I know you're angry. You have every right to be."

"Kier, it's Lithia. I'm in the cell next to you. Remember?"

"Lithia? The bear seer wants to know why I failed her parents," he says sweetly. His saccharine tone chills me to the bone. "I'm sorry, Adelaide. Your parents died because of me."

Gods, he's talking to hallucinations.

"Kier, listen to my voice. You're in a prison cell alone. There's only you and me."

"Lithia of the sexy voice," He laughs, but it's empty, brittle. "My imagination is getting creative."

I frantically squirm my arm into the hole between our cells. "Kier, come here. Come to the hole in the wall."

"The wolves are here," Kier continues, his voice growing more distant. "They want to know why I left. Why I chose to leave instead of staying to protect them."

"Kier!" I wiggle my fingers. "You need to touch my hand. Feel that I'm real."

"More hallucinations. They always feel real at first."

I stretch further, ignoring the sharp edges that slice into my shoulder. "Kier, come here. Please."

My fingertips brush fabric. He jerks away with a sharp gasp.

"It's me," I say firmly. "It's Lithia."

Silence stretches between us. Then slowly, tentatively, I feel him move closer.

"Lithia."

"Yep, I'm here. Touch my hand."

His fingers find mine, trembling violently as they make contact. I grasp them firmly, anchoring him to reality.

"You're real," he whispers.

"I'm real. You're real. We're both here, and we're going to survive this." I squeeze his hand tight, desperately trying to draw him back.

"How long was I out?"

I swallow, closing my eyes. "They held you for hours. I don't know how you survived."

We sit in silence, my hand clasping his through the wall. I feel him slowly returning to himself, the trembling gradually subsiding.

"Thank you," he finally says, running a thumb over my knuckles.

"For what?"

His grip tightens on my hand, and I feel that electric current between us, stronger now after witnessing his vulnerability.

"For being real when everything else is madness."

I don't have a response to that. There's nothing I can say to make this better. Nothing I can do that will wash away the horror of this place.

How long before I break? How long before I'm the one Kier needs to pull back from the brink? How long before they move him or me?

"You know," he drawls dryly. "It's nice having an emotional support glory hole."

I splutter out a laugh. "Geezus, Kier. Way to ruin a moment."

"I live to surprise." He squeezes my hand. "In all seriousness, you can let go now. I'm okay."

Despite the pain in my shoulder, I keep holding on.

"Well I'm not. So don't let go."

And he doesn't.

CHAPTER
SEVEN

Time loses meaning, bleeding together into a strange, sick mix of waiting and torture. There's pain and boredom, and the brief spikes of adrenaline when my cell door opens.

I mark the passage of minutes not by meals—if you can call the gray gruel food—or by the rhythm of guard rotations, but by the scrape of stone and Kier's murmurs on the other side of the wall.

It's become my only escape.

When the pain wraps too tight around my ribs to breathe, when the silver sears deep enough I swear I can feel it in my bones, I press my fingers through that small, jagged opening and wait for Kier to touch back.

Sometimes we talk.

Sometimes we don't.

Sometimes it's just the quiet rasp of his breathing, or the warmth of his fingertips against mine, or the low rumble of his voice murmuring nonsense just to keep the silence from swallowing us both whole.

It's strange how quickly I've come to rely on him—this smart-mouthed nomad with too many scars and not enough self-preservation.

And it terrifies me.

I know what trusting someone can cost you. I know better than to let someone in. It's why I've forced myself away from the wall, curling on my mattress as I stare in the dark at the door to my cell.

I need to prove to myself I don't need him. I begin to name all those who've wronged me.

Jim, Bob, Zella, Thaddeus…

I shift, trying to alleviate the weight of the silver around my wrists, my ankles, my throat. My skin is blistered and bleeding. My head throbs. My wolf stirs sluggishly inside me, too weak to do more.

I'm beginning to doze when the psychic shockwave hits like a physical blow, tossing me across my cell.

"What the fuck!?"

I push to my knees, shaking my head against the ringing in my ears. Every supernatural creature within a thousand miles will have felt whatever the fuck that was.

My wolf stirs for the first time in days, lifting her head with hope.

Free, she whispers. *The Grand Alpha is dead.*

The knowledge arrives with absolute certainty, hitting me with the same devastating clarity as the power shift itself. That kind of psychic disruption only happens when an alpha of immense power dies violently.

Did Ryker kill him? Or someone else?

"You feel that?" Kier asks.

"The whole supernatural world felt that." I push to my feet, shuffling over to the wall.

"You okay?"

I rub my head. "Yeah. You?"

"Ready for my five o'clock massage but otherwise fine."

From the corridor outside, I hear shouting. Multiple voices, all talking at once, their words overlapping into chaos.

I press my ear to the door, straining to catch fragments of conversation.

"—can't be right—"

"—felt it too, that had to be—"

"—get out of here before—"

The guards hurry past my cell, leaving behind the sour tang of panic. In the days since my capture, I've never heard the guards sound anything but coldly professional. Now they're falling apart.

This can't be good.

"You hearing this?"

"Yeah. Guards are spooked, and it sounds like it's about more than the death of the Grand Alpha." Kier resumes his scratching at the wall. "Think your pack tracked you down?"

I want to believe that, but doubt gnaws at me. If Ryker had found this place, there would be violence. Alarms. The sound of battle echoing through stone corridors.

Instead, there's just nervous conversation and the pacing of unsettled guards.

Hours pass. The arguing grows more frequent, more heated. I catch fragments as different groups move through the corridor.

"—should evacuate while we still can—"

"Our orders were to maintain position—"

"What orders? From who? Dead men don't give commands—"

I lean down to the hole and begin to scratch, searching for a piece of rock big enough to use as a weapon. "This might be our chance to escape."

"I know." Something clatters through our hole.

"What this?" I reach into the crack, pulling out a metal shard. In the dim light from under the door, I can see it's part of a broken buckle sharpened to a crude point.

"The woman who empties our waste buckets left this for me," he explains.

"Kier, you should keep this. You might need—"

"No," he cuts me off. "You take it. When they come for you, you'll know what to do."

I finger the sharp tip, testing its strength. "Thank you."

"Don't mention it. Seriously. If anyone asks, tell them I gave you flowers and chocolates instead."

I almost smile. He's given me his only weapon, his one advantage in this hellhole, without hesitation. That he cares enough about my safety to leave himself defenseless catches me off guard. Something warm and unexpected unfurls in my chest. When was the last time someone put my wellbeing before their own? I can't remember.

The chaos in the corridor continues for hours. Guards rushing back and forth, radios crackling with contradictory orders. Some guards seem to be abandoning their posts entirely, while others argue about duties and chains of command.

Through it all, Kier and I wait, looking for our opportunity to strike. But luck isn't with us. The facility may be in disarray, but our cells remain locked, our silver restraints still burning against our skin.

As the hours pass, the chaos gradually subsides. It seems someone has taken control.

"Have they left us?" I ask Kier, who's still working on the stone next to my head. He stops scratching.

"No. It sounds like someone's taken control again."

"Damn."

Whatever routine may have existed is now gone, and mealtime passes without any sign of the woman who usually comes to feed us.

I manage to doze fitfully, exhaustion finally overcoming adrenaline. When I wake, there's a shadow under my door.

Fuck.

I slip the metal piece into my pocket, settling back against the wall.

Keys jingle, the lock turns and my door swings open to reveal three figures silhouetted against the dim corridor lighting.

I stiffen as a familiar scent touches my nostrils.

Zella.

She steps into my cell, her blonde hair catching the light from the corridor. I glare up at her, hating the way her blue eyes gleam with cold satisfaction. She's dressed in combat gear—black tactical pants, a fitted jacket, silver weapons gleaming at her hip and thigh. She looks every inch the warrior she'd pretended to be in Shadowmist, except now that facade has been stripped away to reveal the predator underneath.

Bitch.

Behind her stand two guards I don't recognize. Larger than the usual facility staff, with the controlled movements of elite soldiers rather than prison workers. They carry themselves differently, and there's a sweet sickness to their scent that wrinkles my nose.

They're no normal wolves. There's something not right with them.

"Lithia," Zella greets, smiling pleasantly. "Enjoying the accommodations?"

I want to rip her throat out. The silver restraints prevent me from even standing, but the wolf in me snarls and paces, desperate to tear into the woman who betrayed everything we'd offered her.

"Like a fucking plague." I force myself to meet her gaze, refusing to show the rage that threatens to overwhelm me. "Come to finish what you started?"

She chuckles, walking around my cell. "Not quite. I came because Thaddeus is dead, and someone needs to continue our important work."

I bite my tongue to keep from asking what that work is. I know it'll niggle her more if I give her nothing.

She glances over, and sure enough, her smile drops. "You're not curious?"

I lift one shoulder in a half-shrug. "Not particularly."

Her expression hardens. "You stupid little wolf. You have no idea what we're working on here. How great our purpose is."

I glance away, pretending to study the stone. "Doesn't seem so great since you're still making me shit in a bucket."

She strikes, digging her claws into my scalp and hauling my head back. Our gazes meet, and I see a fervor in her eyes that I've never seen before. It sends a chill down my spine.

"Evolution," she barks. "The supernatural world has been stagnant for centuries. Packs squabbling over territory. Councils debating endlessly while problems go unsolved. Our work is for the greater good."

"Your work involves murdering and enslaving people."

"We're building a better world. A world where abilities are created rather than left to the whims of nature."

"Who are you to play god?"

She lets me go, stepping back, and I nearly crumple forward, biting back a grunt of pain.

"I'm part of the solution, Lithia," she says softly, almost reverently. "It's the only way."

I lift my head slowly, meeting her eyes.

"Why?" I rasp. "Why the seers? The weres? The witches, warlocks, the fae? Why collect us?"

Her smile sharpens. Something *glints* there, something jagged and fanatical.

"You still don't see it, do you?" she murmurs. "This world —our world—wasn't meant to stay as it is. Nature left us scattered. Incomplete. One gift here, another there, hoarded by bloodlines, limited by birthright."

She paces slowly, hands clasped behind her back.

"But when you gather enough pieces..." Her gaze flicks to

me, alight with something fever-bright. "You can start rewriting the rules."

My stomach twists. My wolf snarls low inside, too weak to rise but strong enough to sense the danger coiling tighter.

"You're insane."

"No, I'm realistic." She straightens, her fervor fading back into cold professionalism. "But I didn't come here to debate philosophy with you, Lithia. I came to offer you a choice."

"And that is?"

"Join us. Use your position and knowledge to help build a better world than the fractured mess Ryker and his allies will create." She pauses, letting the words sink in. "Or be disposed of."

The casual way she says it, *disposed of,* sends ice through my veins. Not killed. Not executed. *Disposed of.* Like I'm a piece of equipment that's outlived its usefulness.

"Some choice."

"It's more than most get." She turns toward the door, then pauses. "You have until tomorrow to decide."

Tomorrow. My heart hammers against my ribs.

"Wait." The word comes out harsher than I intended, desperation bleeding through.

Zella turns back with raised eyebrows. "Changed your mind already?"

"I want to know about Kitara. Where is she? Is she alive?"

For a beat I don't think she'll answer me.

"Your precious Alpha Female was dead."

The casual cruelty of her words ignites rage in my chest. If I could shift, if I could break these restraints, I would tear her apart with my bare hands.

"I'll kill you for this. For all of it. The betrayal, the lies, for Kitara. I will kill you."

Zella laughs, the sound bright and genuine. "You know, I actually believe you would try. Your determination and loyalty are what make you such a valuable packmate. We could use you, Lithia. But if you're not interested, then you're a threat that needs to be put down."

She moves toward the door again, her guards falling into step behind her.

"Tomorrow, Lithia. Think carefully. The world is changing whether you help or not. The only question is whether you'll be part of the solution or part of the cleanup."

They leave, the door slamming shut with a finality that echoes through the stone chamber. The lock turns with a sharp click, sealing me in with the weight of what she's revealed.

Tomorrow.

"Kier?"

"I heard." His voice is tight with anger. "Every fucking word."

I close my eyes, breathing deep.

"What do you want to do?" he asks, resuming chipping at the stone.

It's a good question and a necessary one.

"I'm going to burn her goddamned utopia to the ground and piss on the ashes."

He chuckles. "Then I better get to work on getting us out of here."

The world Zella wants to construct—ordered, controlled, built on the bones of the unwilling—can die with its architect.

But first, I have to survive long enough to make it happen.

CHAPTER
EIGHT

KIER

The prison is quiet, the guards having settled into their night routine. We still haven't been fed, but the hunger in my belly can wait. I need to keep breaking down this godforsaken wall.

Lithia has until tomorrow morning, which means our opportunity of getting out of here is narrowing. Getting to her is the first priority. We can figure everything out from there.

There's a scuff of a shoe on concrete, and Lithia and I freeze.

"Was that—" she starts, falling silent.

I strain to hear.

There's a quiet jingle of keys then the faint scrape of the lock turning on my door.

I shift fast, throwing my body against the hole we've been working on, shielding it with my bulk.

The door creaks open, light spilling in—and I'm shocked.

I expected guards coming to execute me. Instead, it's the bucket woman. And she's alone.

Small, hunched, hair tied back under a stained scarf. Tonight, there's no waste bucket in her hands.

She reaches into her pocket and pulls out a single key, the

worn metal glinting dully in the dim light. It's not the rusted key she uses for the waste cart.

"You need to leave," she whispers, her voice barely audible as she glances nervously over her shoulder. "Tonight."

I stare at her, my mind racing. Is this a trap? Some cruel test the guards have concocted to see if I'll try to escape?

"Why?" I ask, my voice hoarse.

"They're planning to kill you tomorrow." Her eyes dart to the door again. "Any of you without a gift."

Lithia.

My wolf rises with a snarl. *No. Not happening.*

"Why help me?" I press, still not moving from my position against the wall.

She looks down, her fingers twisting nervously around the key. "Consider it my one good deed to atone for all the others." A bitter smile crosses her face. "Not that it makes up for anything I've allowed to happen here."

I study her face, searching for deception. All I find is exhaustion and regret.

"What about the guards?" I ask.

"Skeleton crew tonight. Most left after what happened with Thaddeus." She swallows hard. "Three guards on this level. One at the main door, two patrolling."

"And my silver restraints?"

"The key only opens the doors and removes the chains, not the cuffs. Those are welded on. You'll have to find another way to remove them." She presses the key into my palm. "There's a service tunnel at the end of the east corridor. It leads to the old mining shafts. Follow them up and out."

The silver around my wrists, ankles, and neck continues to burn, but the promise of freedom makes the pain secondary. "What about you?"

She shakes her head. "My fate was written a long time ago."

I hesitate, studying her. "You should come with us."

"No, I've been complicit for too long. There's no redemption for me." She glances nervously over her shoulder. "You need to hurry."

"Thank you," I say, though the words feel inadequate.

She nods once, then slips out the door, leaving it ajar. I hear her quick footsteps fading down the corridor.

The moment she's gone, I unlock my chains and move to the door and peer out. The corridor is empty, dimly lit by emergency lights spaced along the ceiling.

My wolf stretches, baring his teeth. *Freedom.*

"Lithia?"

"I'm here." Her voice is immediate, tense. "What's happening?"

"I don't really get it, but Bucket Woman just gave me a key to the doors." I palm the key. "We're getting out of here."

"It's not a trap?"

I glance back down the hall. "Apparently not."

"Thank the gods."

I slip into the corridor, moving quickly despite the weakness from the silver poisoning. My wolf strains against the metal, giving me just enough strength to function. I reach Lithia's door and try the key in the lock.

It doesn't fit.

I try again, angling it differently, but the key won't even enter the mechanism. "Fuck," I mutter, examining the lock more closely. It's a different model than mine—newer, with a different keyhole entirely.

"What's wrong?" Lithia asks from inside.

"The key doesn't fit your door," I reply, frustration building in my chest. "It's a different lock."

There's a moment of silence. "You need to go," she says finally, her voice flat. "Get out while you can."

"No." The word comes out as a growl. "I'm not leaving you."

"Don't be stupid, Kier. This might be your only chance."

I rest my forehead against her door, mind racing. I could try to find another key, but that would mean confronting guards—dangerous with the silver still weakening me. I could search for tools to break the lock, but that would take time we don't have.

Or I could leave—which would mean sentencing her to death.

The thought makes my wolf snarl in rejection. *Never.*

"Kier," Lithia says again, her voice gentler now. "Go. Find my pack. Tell them what Zella is doing. That's how you help me."

"No."

"What?"

"I said no." I turn back toward my cell. "I'm not leaving you."

I hear her frustrated growl through the door. "Dammit, Kier! This is no time for heroics."

"It's not heroics," I reply, already moving back to my cell. "We both go, or neither of us does."

"That's ridiculous! You need to leave!"

I slip back into my cell, closing the door until it's just slightly ajar—enough that it won't lock, but not enough to be noticeable to a passing guard.

I return to the hole in our wall, finding Lithia's arm reaching through. She's giving me the bird.

I chuckle.

"You had a chance to escape!"

"And I'll have another one," I say calmly, settling back against the wall. "A better one, when we can both take it."

I hear the slap of her palm against stone. "This is the stupidest thing I've ever heard. You've been here for three years, and you're throwing away your freedom for what? Some wolf you've known for a few days?"

"For you," I say simply.

She's silent for a beat. "You're a fool," she says quietly, but there's no heat in the words.

"So I've been told." I reach through the hole, extending my hand. After a moment, she takes it, her fingers warm against mine.

"We'll find another way," I tell her. "When they come for us tomorrow, we'll be ready."

"Ready to die, you mean." But she doesn't let go of my hand.

"Ready to fight. Together." I squeeze her fingers gently. "Get some rest. We'll need our strength."

She sighs, a sound of exasperation and resignation. "If we get out of this alive, I'm never letting you forget how stupid this decision is."

"I'd expect nothing less." I smile, settling more comfortably against the wall, her hand still in mine. "You can tell me all about it on our first date."

She makes a sound. "You're impossible."

"You didn't say no to that date," I murmur, my grin stretching slow and wicked in the dark. "I'm taking that as a yes."

"Kier—"

"I can picture it already," I go on, thumb lazily tracing her knuckles. "You, me, and a bed somewhere that doesn't have chains, silver, or sadists lurking outside the door."

"Seriously, Kier? All you want is sex?"

I chuckle, low and amused. "Sweetheart… I meant to *sleep*. Gods, your mind went there fast, huh? Filthy girl."

She makes a strangled noise but doesn't withdraw her hand.

I grin wider, settling back against the wall. "Good night, sweet Lithia. Tomorrow we're getting out of here."

CHAPTER

NINE

I've barely slept, too keyed up from Kier's ridiculous decision to stay rather than escape.

Every time I close my eyes, I hear him slipping back into his cell, closing the door behind him, choosing captivity over freedom.

Choosing me.

I would never have done that, I tell myself. *Especially not with a wolf I barely know.*

When my door didn't open, heartbreak hit, a sharp and vicious blade between my ribs. He had freedom while I was still trapped, still chained, still helpless. For one devastating moment, I thought I'd never see daylight again.

Then came the relief, so powerful I don't know how to process it. He didn't leave. This stranger, this broken nomad who owes me nothing, chose to stay in hell rather than abandon me to it.

I shuffle, guilt riding me hard. What right do I have to feel relieved? Kier should have run. He should have saved himself. I want him to save himself.

Don't I?

I don't know how to process all these emotions—or the

85

others brimming under the surface. The last time someone put me first, my parents died. They loved me, wanted me, knew me. This irrational, selfless choice to suffer beside someone he barely knows rather than escape makes no sense.

I don't feel worthy of a sacrifice this profound.

And I don't know what to do with the way it makes me feel. It's as if I'm coming apart and being remade all at once. Like something fundamental has shifted in my understanding of what I'm worth to another person.

The worst part? We barely know each other. We're bonded by trauma and desperation, by shared walls and whispered conversations in the dark. That's all.

But apparently that's more than enough.

"You awake?" Kier asks.

"No, I'm sleepwalking," I mutter, shifting closer to the opening. "Of course I'm awake."

He chuckles. "Still mad at me, I see." I hear him move, stone scraping as he settles into position. "Listen, I've been thinking about our options."

"We don't have options. You had one, and you threw it away," I point out.

"No, I postponed it." He sounds calm and confident—a terrifying mix. "When the guards come, that's when we move."

"Even if we overpower them, we're still wearing silver. We're weakened. And they'll have backup."

"Not necessarily. The bucket woman said the place is running on a skeleton crew. Most of Thaddeus's people scattered after his death."

"Zella's still here," I point out. "And her special guards."

"True. But they can't be everywhere." I hear the scrape of rock—he's still working on the wall between us. "We just need to create enough chaos to slip away."

I lean my head against the cool stone. "What's your plan?"

"If they come to my cell first, I'll play dead."

"What?"

"When they come, I'll be on the floor, not moving. When they check me, I'll attack."

"And if they come to me first?"

"Be ready to move. The moment your door opens, I'll create a distraction. You wait for your opportunity."

I nod, though he can't see me. "Okay. But Kier—" I hesitate, not sure how to say this. "If something goes wrong, if we get separated…"

"We won't," he says firmly.

"But if we do," I insist, "I need you to find my pack. Find Ryker. Tell him what's happening here."

There's a long pause. "I will," he finally says. "But it won't come to that."

The confidence in his voice almost makes me believe him.

Hours pass, tension building with each minute. We talk in low murmurs, planning contingencies, discussing the escape route. It helps keep the fear at bay.

When the door at the end of the corridor finally slams open, it's almost a blessing. Heavy footsteps approach—multiple guards, moving with purpose.

Kier's voice comes through the hole, barely a whisper. "Remember. Wait for your moment."

I move away from the wall, positioning myself near the back of my cell, palming the metal shard in my hand.

The keys rattle at my door first.

My door.

The lock turns. The hinges creak.

I hold my breath as two guards enter, flashlights cutting through the dark.

"There you are," one grunts. "You got an answer for Zella?"

"I'll do what she wants," I lie.

"Told ya," one says to the other. "Grab her. Zella wants her prepped for travel within the hour."

I force my body to remain still, head lowered, letting them think the silver's done its work.

One kneels beside me, fingers on the cuffs, muttering curses when the silver burns his fingers. He pulls a key from his pocket, releasing the chains.

The other guard steps closer, stun baton hanging loose.

Then—

A thud.

A choked grunt from the hallway.

"Hey—" the standing guard turns—

Too late.

A blur slams into him from behind.

Kier.

My first look at him is the impression of wild eyes, bared teeth, and hands wrapped around a man's throat as he drives him backward into the stone.

He's magnificent.

The second guard lunges for Kier, but I'm already moving. I land a blow with the shard to his temple, drilling it through his skull. He goes down like a sack of bricks.

I don't stop to check if he's dead.

Kier's guard is down, and the door to my cell is open. I sprint out, skidding to a stop as I find Kier locked in a brutal tangle with Bob. They tumble through the corridor, both of them snarling like the wolves they are despite the silver suppressing their shifts. Another guard lies motionless on the floor nearby.

Bob has a knife—silver, from the way it glints—and he's trying to drive it into Kier's chest. Kier holds his wrist, muscles straining against the poison in his system.

I grab the fallen guard's stun baton and lunge forward, driving it into Bob's side. Electricity crackles, and he convulses, his grip on the knife faltering. Kier wrenches it away and plunges it into Bob's throat without hesitation.

Blood sprays across the corridor as Bob drops, eyes wide

with shock. Kier stands over him, breathing heavily, silver restraints still in place but eyes burning with wild triumph.

For the first time, I truly see him.

What remains of his shirt hangs in tatters, revealing an expanse of scarred chest and lean muscle beneath layers of grime and dried blood. He wears worn jeans, bloodstained and filthy, his feet bare.

Three years of captivity have left their mark—old silver burns snake across his ribs, knife wounds crisscross his shoulders, and newer bruises bloom purple against pale skin. His face is all sharp angles and high cheekbones. He has a strong jaw covered in dark stubble, and a strong nose that looks like it's been broken at least a few times. His hair falls past his shoulders in tangled waves, once black but now streaked with strands of premature silver that catch the dim light. But it's his eyes that hold me—amber gold, almost luminous, with a fierce intelligence behind them.

This is the man who's been my lifeline for days, whose voice and touch kept me sane in the darkness. Seeing him now feels surreal, like a hallucination made flesh.

He studies me too, his intense gaze taking in every detail. Something shifts in his expression—surprise, recognition, something deeper I can't name. For a heartbeat, we simply stare at each other, the chaos around us momentarily forgotten.

"You're real," he whispers, so quietly I almost miss it. His hand starts to rise toward my face, fingers trembling slightly, as if he needs that physical proof to believe what his eyes are telling him. But at the last moment, he hesitates, pulling back.

I catch his wrist before he can retreat completely, guiding his palm to my cheek. His skin is rough, calloused, warm against mine.

"I told you," I murmur, leaning into his touch.

The contact sends a shock through me—not painful, but electric, like every nerve ending has suddenly come alive. My breath catches in my throat, and something low in my belly tightens with unexpected heat. His thumb traces the line of my cheekbone, and I have to fight the urge to close my eyes and sink into the sensation. It's been so long since anyone touched me with gentleness instead of violence.

His breath catches, and for a moment the world narrows to just this—his hand on my face, the wonder in his amber eyes, the electric current that seems to arc between us. My pulse begins to race and my skin flushes.

What is happening?

Kier's gaze sparks with amusement, burning with wild triumph. He pulls back, wiping blood from his face with the back of his hand.

"Nice timing," he says.

"Nice moves," I reply, my voice slightly rougher than intended as I turn down the corridor. "Now, let's get out of here."

CHAPTER

TEN

KIER

She's not at all how I imagined.

In my mind, I'd crafted a thousand different versions of her—tall and commanding, petite and fierce, redhead, brunette, scarred, tattooed. But the reality of her surpasses any image I could have conjured.

Her white-blonde hair falls past her shoulders in waves, tangled now from our ordeal but still framing her face beautifully. She has strong features—high cheekbones, a determined jaw, full lips. But it's her eyes that captivate me most—a blue so pale they appear silver.

Her body is a canvas of bloody history. An old scar runs down her face from her right temple to her cheek, mingling with the fresh bruises and cuts. It's a good thing I killed Bob, 'cause I'd have turned around and done it again after seeing her.

Battle-scarred and fierce, Lithia has the kind of presence that commands attention without demanding it. Others might look at her and see her current weaknesses.

They'd be fools.

What I see is the most magnificent creature I've ever laid eyes on. Every scar tells a story of survival. Every line of tension

93

in her body speaks of strength earned through adversity. The way she carries herself—head high, shoulders back—reveals an intelligence sharp enough to cut and a will that refuses to bend.

Beautiful doesn't begin to cover it. She's devastating.

I want her to be mine.

We move through the service tunnels, side by side. Even weakened by silver and injury, there's a natural grace to her movements. I've seen her fight now—precise, efficient, lethal. There's no wasted energy, no panicked flailing. She knows how to use every ounce of strength her body can give.

And gods help me, I can't stop watching her.

"East corridor?" she asks, her voice rough from the fight, eyes flicking to mine as I drop the last of the silver cuffs.

I nod once. "The woman said there's a service tunnel which leads to mining shafts. She said there's an exit that way."

We move fast. I take point, my senses sharp. The facility is unnervingly quiet, most cells empty. Whatever shitstorm Thaddeus's death kicked up, it's cleared out half the prisoners and nearly all of the guards.

Good for us. Bad for whoever's left.

At a junction, I pause, scenting the air. "Two guards ahead. Armed."

She holds the stun baton, extending it with an expert flick. "I'll go high, you go low."

I nod. We don't need more words. We move like we've done this a hundred times—she swings wide, I slide low. The guards barely register us before it's over—a gunshot, a flash of steel, a body hitting the wall, the thud of meat on stone.

I glance at her as she kneels by the fallen guards, rifling their belts. "Impressive."

She shoots me a look, tossing me the guard's gun. "I wasn't made Beta for my charming personality."

I huff out something like a laugh, and we keep moving.

The east corridor stretches ahead, old stone and rusted pipes, the smell of damp and moss thick in the air. At the end sits the door we need, the "SERVICE ACCESS" stamp barely legible under years of grime.

I pull out my key, praying the woman didn't steer us wrong, and slide it into the lock.

Click.

The door creaks open, revealing a narrow tunnel lined with old rock and darkness thick as tar.

"After you," I murmur, glancing back down the corridor.

Lithia slips past me, a pale streak in the dark, and I pull the door shut behind us. For a breath, the blackness is total. Then I thumb on a flashlight stolen from the guards. The light throws wild shadows on the tunnel walls.

"How far does this go?" she asks, voice low.

"Not sure," I admit. "But it should lead to the surface."

We move deeper, boots scuffing on damp stone, the drip of water echoing somewhere ahead. The tunnel forks and twists, but we follow it, unwilling to return.

"Do you know where you're going?" she asks after a sharp turn.

I glance back, the flashlight's glow flickering over her bloodied face. "No clue." I thumb my nose. "But the air we're following is the sweetest I've smelled in three years."

"Three years is a long time to wait for escape."

I give a faint, grim smile. "It was worth it."

She nods then glances away, scanning the walls.

"Not far now," I murmur. "Can you smell it?"

She inhales. "Trees."

The rot and damp of the tunnels is thinning, replaced by the sharp clean scent of pine.

Freedom.

An alarm sounds—a distant, muffled wail, vibrating through the stone.

"They've discovered we're gone," she mutters, picking up speed.

"Or the bodies," I add, matching her pace. "Either way, we need to move."

We break into a jog, the flashlight bobbing wildly in my hand. The tunnel widens into an old mining chamber, wooden beams sagging, rusted equipment collapsed in the corners. I pause, nostrils flaring.

"This way," I whisper, pointing right. "I can smell water."

The shaft narrows, forces us low. In places we crawl, scraping knees and elbows raw. Her breath hitches behind me —pain—but she doesn't slow.

Then I see it.

Light. Thin, pale, but real.

We scramble forward, clawing through a tangle of collapsed stone and vines until I can push through. My shoulders barely make it. I hear her squirm, squeezing after me, gasping into open air.

The world is overwhelming and for a brief moment I'm struck with fear. Everything feels so vast—the sky, the forest, the breeze. There's light here, and wind, and the sharp green bite of pine.

We made it.

I look over to find Lithia staring at me. Her white-blonde hair is tangled around her face, her skin is smeared with dirt and blood, her eyes like molten silver. My chest gives a sharp, painful pull.

"We made it," I rasp.

"For now." Her gaze flicks to the trees, calculating. "They'll be looking for us."

I nod. "We need distance. Which way's Shadowmist territory?"

"South, I think." She points in the direction. "But it's gotta be at least five hundred miles, maybe more."

"Then we'd better start walking." I offer her my hand, a

flicker of challenge sparking in my veins. "Unless you're too tired?"

Her eyebrow lifts, sharp and perfect. "I could run circles around you, Nomad."

A laugh I didn't know I still had bursts free. "Prove it, Shadowmist."

We run. We stumble. We push.

Through forest, over rock, down slopes sharp enough to shred muscle. We don't talk, don't stop. Just move. Every step is survival. Every breath is defiance.

We pause only when we stumble across streams. But we're up and going soon after, the danger no doubt coming.

And unlike those who might pursue us, the silver cuffs around our ankles, throats, and wrists mean we can't shift.

We're still pushing, the moon bright enough to light our way when I decide we've both had enough.

"We should find water," I murmur, throat raw.

Lithia nods, too tired for words.

I lead us southeast, my nose tracking moisture, until we stumble across a trickling creek. We drop to our knees, shoving faces into freezing water.

"Fifteen miles, maybe," I say, wiping my mouth. "Not enough."

"We need to keep moving," she rasps, but her body's shaking, her eyes glassy.

I shoulder her weight when she stumbles. Pretend not to notice when she leans heavily against me. Pretend not to care when every part of me warms at her touch.

Mine, my wolf howls.

We push on, and it's as dawn breaks that her body gives out on a rocky slope. I catch her, easing her down into a hollow beneath an overhang.

She's shivering and pale, clutching at her side.

"Let me see," I murmur, my fingers gentle. She lifts her shirt, and my jaw tightens. Her side is one deep mottled bruise. Her skin is split at the bottom of her rib cage, and there's a smell of blood that's both sharp and wrong.

I gently run my fingers over her side, feeling the ridges. "Looks like some broken ribs."

"Probably," she mutters. "But we need to keep moving."

"Not like this," I say, voice low, firm. "You're exhausted. If you keep pressing, you'll only slow us down when you fully collapse."

She leans against the stone with a grudging nod. I settle beside her, shoulder to shoulder, feeling the faint tremble in her body.

I watch over her until her breathing evens out, then slip away to scavenge the surrounding area. There's enough berries and herbs around to make her a poultice—and feed us a little.

Dark clouds are gathering on the horizon, and I can smell rain in the air. Good. A storm will help wash away our scent trail.

I return, finding her sound asleep. While she rests, I crush herbs and gently smooth them over her wounds. She gasps, jolting upright with a cry.

"Easy," I murmur. "I've got you." I smooth the paste over her broken skin.

"Where did you learn this?"

I shrug. "You pick things up when you're on your own." I pull my shirt off, tearing it into shreds.

"Kier!"

Ignoring her protest, I wrap the shred around her middle, binding her ribs as best I can.

"Sorry," I wince in sympathy when she gasps. "But it has to be done."

After she's eaten some berries and we drink from the creek, we begin to move again.

The first fat raindrops splatter against us as we crest the ridge, cold needles prickling through the thin fabric of our clothing. By the time we're backtracking through the valley, it's coming down in earnest. We spend the day crossing rivers then backtracking, smothering ourselves in mud and sap to hide our scent. Our progress is painfully slow but necessary. In wolf form, a were could hunt us down easily.

Years of being a lone wolf has taught me a few tricks, and now we have weather on our side.

The icy rain continues to batter us, coming down hard, plastering hair to skin. I curse under my breath, pulling Lithia closer as we push through the undergrowth.

When I scent the cabin—ash, dust, and wood rot—I'm half-carrying her. It's small, decrepit, barely standing, but it's four walls and a roof.

The lock is rusted but no match for my shoulder. We stumble inside, the storm muffled instantly, the scent of damp wood and lavender oil wrapping around us. The space surprises me—it's rough, sure, but someone once cared for it. A sheet covers a basic mattress, mason jars line a makeshift kitchen shelf, and a cracked record player sits on a trunk stacked with dog-eared paperbacks.

Rain patters against the windows, the sound oddly comforting after our harrowing escape.

Lithia sways, eyes heavy-lidded, lips tinged bluish. "Sit," I order roughly, guiding her down onto the mattress. Her lack of protest makes my gut twist.

Her skin's icy under my hands. "You're half-frozen," I murmur, my thumb sweeping absently over her skin.

The cabin has running water, and a quick search uncovers some cups. I bring her water, holding the mug while she sips.

"Thank you," she whispers.

"We're not out yet."

"But we're free." She closes her eyes. "And soon we'll be home."

As much as I appreciate her optimism, I can't say the same.

I find a few moth-eaten blankets in an old chest and some threadbare rugs rolled up in a corner. They smell musty but they're dry. I shake them out and layer them over Lithia, tucking the edges around her shivering form.

She's still shivering, but until I can find wood to feed a fire, that will have to do.

I move to the window, watching as the storm settles over the forest. Rain streams down the glass, and I can barely make out the trees through the downpour. In the distance, a wolf howls—but the sound is muffled, distorted by the weather.

We're free... for now.

CHAPTER
ELEVEN

KIER

Lithia's health deteriorates, and we're forced to stay in the cabin far longer that I'd have liked. The cuffs are impossible to remove, and despite searching the cabin high and low, I can't find a goddamned tool to assist. Without the proper tools, the silver continues to burn against our skin, slowing our healing and weakening our wolves. It's a constant reminder of our captivity, even as we sit in this ramshackle cabin pretending to be free.

She runs a fever, stirring hot one minute and shaking with chills the next. It's agony to watch how this fierce, proud wolf has been reduced to trembling weakness. The other half of my soul is withering away before my eyes, and I'm powerless to stop it.

Panic claws at my chest every time her breathing grows shallow, every time she cries out in her sleep. The desperate need to protect her, to heal her, to somehow absorb her pain into myself, burns hotter than the silver around my wrists. Three years of captivity taught me to endure my own suffering, but watching hers? It's breaking me in ways torture never could.

The poison from her infection has spread, leaving a toxic

trail through her system that her weakened wolf struggles to purge. My wolf paces frantically beneath my skin, snarling his frustration at our helplessness.

Fix her. Protect her.

But I can't. I can't even tell her what she means to me—not when she doesn't feel the bond the way I do.

Some hours I sit beside her bed, pressing cool cloths to her forehead, listening to her murmur broken phrases in her delirium. Others, I hold her, covering her with my warmth, fighting to stop her shivering. Each touch is both torture and necessity—my wolf demands contact with our mate, but every moment reminds me how fragile she is, how easily I could lose her before we've even had a chance to begin.

During her rare moments of lucidity, I coax her to drink broth I've managed to make from items left in the cabin and the few edible plants I can forage around the small hut. I'd hunt small game, but I don't dare leave her side.

The rest of the time, I pace the confines of our shelter, checking and rechecking her temperature and our defenses, always alert for the sounds of change.

In the quiet hours between her fever spikes, I find myself studying her. Everything about her is a fascinating contradiction—soft curves and hard edges, fierce strength and surprising vulnerability. Three years of isolation has left me unprepared for the reality of her, for the way my wolf responds to her presence with a bone-deep certainty I can neither explain nor deny.

I shake my head, forcing my attention back to the task at hand. The cabin needs to be secured if we're going to stay here while she recovers. I've already reinforced the door as best I could with the limited materials available, but the windows remain vulnerable.

Outside, the forest is quiet except for the occasional call of birds and the whisper of wind through pines. No sign of pursuit yet, but that doesn't mean they aren't coming. The storm bought us time, but these bastards don't strike me as the type to give up easily.

I gather fallen branches and begin fashioning crude alarms to place around the perimeter—simple arrangements of sticks that will snap loudly if disturbed. It's not sophisticated, but it might give us enough warning if someone approaches.

As I work, my mind drifts to Prudence and her daughter. To Adelaide. To the prisoners we left behind.

Guilt gnaws at me. I escaped, but they remain trapped.

We'll return for them, my wolf assures me. *But first, Lithia.*

I nod. *Yes.*

The cabin comes into view as I complete my circuit of the perimeter. It's not much—weathered logs and a sagging roof—but it's shelter. Protection from the elements and prying eyes.

Inside, Lithia is sleeping, her breathing steadier than it was last night.

I check her wound carefully, lifting the makeshift bandage to examine the angry red gash. The edges are starting to knit together, a good sign. The bruising around it has spread but changed color—from the deep purple of fresh trauma to the yellowish-green of healing.

Her eyelids flutter, and she grimaces, shifting slightly on the narrow bed.

"How long was I out this time?" she asks, voice rough with sleep.

"Most of the day," I reply, replacing the bandage. "How's the pain?"

"Better." She attempts to sit up, wincing with the effort. "Less like being stabbed, more like being run over."

I can't help but smile at her description. "Progress, then."

"Of a sort." She glances toward the boarded window. "Any sign of trouble?"

"None yet. I've set up some basic perimeter warnings, just in case."

She nods, approving. "Smart."

An awkward silence falls between us. In the prison, conversation had flowed easily—desperation and shared circumstances breaking down our barriers. But here, I'm aware of how little we know about each other.

I clear my throat. "Are you hungry? I found some canned goods in a storage cabinet. Ancient, but edible."

"Starving," she admits. "Prison gruel doesn't exactly stick to the ribs."

I move to the small shelf where I've arranged our meager supplies. Two cans of beans, one of corn, some jerky that's questionably old but still sealed in its package. A feast compared to what we've been eating.

As I prepare a simple meal using the cabin's small woodstove, I feel Lithia's eyes on me.

"Should you be using that?" she asks. "I'd think the smoke will give us away."

"If they're close enough to smell the smoke, they've already found our scents."

She nods, adjusting her position on the bed.

I stir the pot, tossing in some herbs.

"You seem at home here," she comments. "Doing the survival thing."

I shrug. "I'm a lone wolf. It comes with the territory."

"How long have you been a nomad?"

The question touches on a topic I rarely discuss, but after what we've been through together, I owe her at least some truth.

"Since I was seventeen," I say, stirring the warming beans. "About twenty years now."

"Your pack?"

"Dead." The word comes out harsher than I intended. I soften my tone. "During the Blood Wars. The usual tragic werewolf origin story."

She's quiet for a moment. "I'm sorry."

"It was a long time ago."

"Some wounds never fully heal," she says softly, and I know she's not just talking about physical injuries.

I bring her a plate—beans and corn mixed together, with a small portion of jerky on the side. Not appetizing to look at, but nourishing.

"What about you?" I ask, settling on the floor beside her bed with my own plate. "You mentioned your pack, but not how you became Beta."

She picks at her food, considering her answer. "I was born into Shadowmist. My parents were pack members—not high-ranking, just... pack. They were killed when I was nine protecting me and my brother from fae hunters. Much like yours."

The parallel surprises me. "Were you there?"

"Yeah. My brother Dane, he's..." She hesitates, pain flashing across her features. "He's my twin. We hid while our parents were killed. The Beta took us in. We spent most of the war learning how to fight from her."

"And you rose through the ranks."

She nods. "I had something to prove. A debt to repay. And a need to make sure no one I cared about would ever be unprotected again."

The fierceness in her voice stirs something in me. Admiration, certainly. But also recognition—I see in her the same driving purpose that has kept me moving all these years, even if our paths have been different.

"And now you're the Beta," I say. "Second-in-command to the most powerful pack in the region."

"And captured by the first traitor I should have seen coming." Bitterness laces her words. "Some protector I turned out to be."

"You survived," I point out. "You escaped. And now you'll warn your pack about what's coming. I'd call that a win."

She meets my gaze, searching for sincerity or mockery. Finding the former, she relaxes slightly. "Maybe. If we make it back in time."

"We will." I sound more confident than I feel, but she needs that right now. Certainty. Purpose.

We eat in silence for a while, the simple food tasting like a feast after days of near-starvation. When she's finished, I take her plate, pleased to see she's eaten everything.

"Thank you," she says suddenly.

"For the five-star dining experience?" I gesture at the empty plates. "Thank the owner for never tossing anything out."

"For staying." Her voice is quiet but firm. "You could have escaped without me. I'm grateful you didn't."

Her raw honesty catches me off guard. I look away, uncomfortable with gratitude I don't feel I've earned.

"I told you," I say gruffly. "It was the logical choice. Better odds together than alone."

The lie tastes bitter on my tongue. Logic had nothing to do with it. The truth—that she's my mate, that leaving her would have been like tearing out my own heart, that I'd rather die in that cell than live free without her—is too much. Too soon. She doesn't know what she is to me, doesn't feel the bond that's been driving me since the moment I recognized her. How do I explain that abandoning her was never even a possibility? That every instinct I have screams to protect her, to stay close, to never let her out of my sight again?

I can't.

There's a small smile tugging at her lips. "Still. Thank you."

I nod. "Get some rest. Your body needs sleep to heal."

"And you?" she challenges. "When was the last time you slept more than an hour at a time?"

"I'm fine."

"Liar." She shifts on the bed, making room. "There's space

for two, and we both need rest. I promise not to ravish you in your weakened state."

The unexpected teasing startles a laugh from me. "Very generous of you."

She pats the space beside her. "Seriously, Kier. Sleep. We can take watches, but you're no good to either of us if you collapse from exhaustion."

She's throwing my words back at me, but she's right, of course. I've been running on fumes, catching minutes of rest here and there but never truly sleeping. Until the silver is gone, its effects will linger—weakness, slowed healing, dulled senses.

But it's not just the silver making me hesitate. It's been years since I've slept beside another person. Years since I've had to worry about morning arousal or the unconscious movements that come with sharing a bed. And this isn't just anyone—this is *Lithia*. My mate. The woman whose scent has been driving me half-mad with want despite our circumstances.

The thought of lying beside her, breathing in her scent with every inhalation, feeling the warmth of her body just inches away, listening to the soft sounds she makes in sleep— it's both torture and temptation. What if I reach for her in my dreams? What if she wakes to find me curled around her like the possessive bastard my wolf wants me to be?

But the exhaustion weighs heavier than my concerns, and the practical part of me knows she's right. We both need rest.

After a moment's hesitation, I settle beside her on the narrow mattress, careful to leave space between us. The bed creaks under our combined weight, but holds. "Wake me in four hours," I say. "I'll take second watch."

"Deal."

I close my eyes, expecting sleep to evade me as it usually does. But whether from exhaustion or the strange comfort of having her nearby, darkness claims me almost immediately.

I dream of running through endless forests, silver arrows raining from the sky, a silver-eyed wolf always just ahead of me. When I jerk awake, heart pounding, the cabin is dark and empty except for the dying embers in the fireplace.

Lithia!

I hear her moving in the bathroom, and relax. She let me sleep longer than we agreed.

I rise quietly and walk to the window. Outside, night has fallen completely, the forest a tapestry of silver-blue shadows in the moonlight. I slip outside and make my way around the cabin, checking our perimeter warnings—all undisturbed—then return to add wood to the fire.

Lithia's passed out on the bed, the blanket curled around her.

As the flames grow, casting warm light across the small space, I study her again. In sleep, the fierce Beta softens. She looks younger, less burdened by responsibility and pain.

My wolf stirs, pressing against my consciousness with uncharacteristic insistence.

I push back against the instinct. *Not now. Not yet. She needs to heal. We need to get her home.*

But my wolf is persistent. *Ours. Claim. Protect.*

I shake my head, moving away from the bed to clear my thoughts. Whatever this pull between us—and I'd be lying if I said I didn't feel it—now is not the time to explore it. We're fugitives, injured, hunted. Romance is the last thing either of us needs.

A soft sound from the bed draws my attention. Lithia's face has tensed, her breathing quickening. A nightmare, by the looks of it.

I debate whether to wake her, then decide against it. Better she gets what rest she can, even if troubled. Instead, I move closer, gently placing a hand on her arm in silent reassurance.

She settles almost immediately, her features smoothing out. I withdraw my hand, surprised by the effect.

Outside, an owl calls, breaking the silence of the night. I move to the window, peering through a small gap in the boards. The forest is still, peaceful under the moon's glow. No sign of pursuit, no hint of danger.

But I know better than to trust the calm. Zella will be hunting us, and she'll have resources at her disposal that we can only guess at. Our reprieve is temporary, our safety an illusion.

"Kier?" Lithia's voice is soft with sleep. "Everything okay?"

"All quiet," I reply, turning back to her. "You should still be resting."

"I've slept enough." She sits up carefully, testing her injured side.

"You've needed it."

"So do you." She studies me in the firelight. "You look better, though. Less like death warmed over."

I snort. "Such flattery."

A small smile touches her lips. "I'm known for my charm."

"How's the wound?" I ask, nodding toward her side.

"Healing, I think."

"Good." I move toward the bed where she's resting. "Let me check your wounds before I make dinner. Make sure the infection hasn't returned."

She nods, shifting to give me better access as I settle on the edge of the narrow mattress.

My wolf stirs beneath my skin, pleased by her nearness. Three years of isolation have left me starved for physical contact.

"This might be tender," I warn, gently lifting the edge of her makeshift bandage.

The wound has healed significantly—no longer the angry red of infection, but a healthy pink. It seems that we might make it out of this after all.

I reach for the small pot of healing salve I'd made from herbs, warming it between my palms. The ritual is familiar now—I've done this dozens of times over the past few days—but something feels different tonight. Maybe it's because she's fully conscious, fully present, instead of lost in fever dreams.

"How does that feel?" I ask, my voice rougher than intended as I smooth the balm over her skin.

"Better." I notice the way her muscles tense as I brush her skin.

I work methodically, my fingers tracing the edges of the healing wound, making sure the salve covers every inch. Her skin is impossibly soft beneath my touch, warm and alive in ways that make my chest tight. I've touched her before, but this is different. She's aware of every brush of my fingers, and I'm aware of her awareness.

The silence stretches between us, broken only by the sound of our breathing. Mine is steady but deliberate, controlled. Lithia's is shallower, with the faintest catch.

I should be clinical about this. Professional. But the way she's looking at me—those pale blue eyes following my every movement—makes it impossible to pretend this is just wound care.

When I move to check the bruising along her neck, I have to lean closer. The angle puts my face inches from hers, close enough to see the tiny scar that cuts through her left eyebrow, close enough to catch the subtle scent that's uniquely her beneath the herbs and healing salves.

My knuckles brush against the smooth expanse of her abdomen as I work, and she inhales sharply—a soft gasp that has nothing to do with discomfort. The sound goes straight through me, and I watch, fascinated, as goosebumps ripple across her skin in the wake of my touch.

Time seems to slow. I'm hyperaware of everything—the way her lips part slightly, the rapid flutter of her pulse at the base of her throat, the way her fingers curl into the rough blanket beneath her. The cabin feels smaller, the air thicker, charged with an emotion I don't dare name.

My gaze flies up to meet hers, and what I see there makes my breath catch. There's no mistaking the heat in her eyes or the way her pupils have dilated. She's as affected by this as I am, and the knowledge sends fire racing through my veins.

"Kier," she whispers, my name barely a breath.

The sound of it—soft, needy, uncertain—nearly undoes me. I can see the questions in her eyes, the same confusion I'm feeling.

I'm leaning closer without realizing it, drawn by something primal and undeniable. Her scent surrounds me, making my wolf pace restlessly beneath my skin. Just a few more inches and I could taste her, could finally discover if her lips are as soft as they look.

Her breathing hitches, and I can tell she's thinking the same thing. The space between us feels electric, crackling with tension. All I'd have to do is close the distance, and I could finally give in to the pull that's been driving me mad.

But then I catch sight of the silver cuffs still burning against her wrists, notice the slight pallor that speaks of recent illness, and remember how fragile she felt in my arms when the fever had her in its grip.

Reality crashes back like a bucket of ice water. She's injured. Recovering. Still weak from infection and silver poisoning. And here I am, taking advantage of her vulnerability, letting my own desperate loneliness cloud my judgment.

What kind of wolf does that make me? What kind of protector puts his own desires above her wellbeing?

The thought is enough to shatter the spell completely. I stand abruptly, putting distance between us before I do something we're both not ready for—something she might regret when she's thinking clearly again.

I clear my throat. "We should be able to move in a few days, if you keep improving at this rate."

I don't look back to see her reaction, don't trust myself to maintain this distance if I see disappointment or apathy in her eyes.

"I guess. If we're not found before then."

I nod, acknowledging the unspoken concern that hangs between us. "I'll scout further tomorrow, make sure we truly are alone out here."

"Be careful," she says. "We don't know who or what might be searching for us."

The worry in her voice catches me off guard. It's been so long since anyone cared about my safety that I'm not quite sure how to respond.

"Always am," I say finally, focusing on restocking the fire. "You should eat again. Keep your strength up."

She accepts the change of subject without comment, allowing me to prepare another simple meal from our limited stores. As she eats, we discuss the area, the mountains, the best route to Shadowmist territory once she's healed enough to travel.

In the light of the flashlight, we pour over rough maps I found in a drawer, trying to triangulate our position and work out the best possible paths and potential dangers. The planning feels good—concrete, practical, something to focus on besides the pain and uncertainty.

"You know this area well?"

I shrug. "Not overly, but I've tracked through most of the northern territories at some point or another. Goes with the job."

"And what exactly is that job?"

"I find stuff that's been lost. Items, information, people. Sometimes those things go missing by choice, sometimes not."

"Like Adelaide."

The girl's name sends a pang through my chest. "Like Adelaide."

She changes the subject, asking about my tracking methods, my life as a nomad, how I find clients.

I answer, grateful for the shift to less painful territory. As we talk, I find myself revealing more than I usually would—small details about my travels, the places I've seen, the strange jobs I've taken on over the years.

In return, she tells me about Shadowmist. About Ryker and his mate, Kitara. About her brother Dane and her friendship group. About the structure and strength of the pack, their territory, their allies.

There's something in her voice when she talks about Ryker and Kitara—a softness, but also a deep sadness that makes my chest ache.

"They sound like they had something special," I say carefully, noting her use of past tense.

"They did." Her voice catches slightly, and when she speaks again, there's a wistfulness mixed with grief that she probably doesn't realize she's revealing. "True mates. Their bond made them stronger, not weaker. When one hurt, the other felt it. When one fought, the other stood beside them. They were... complete together. Our pack could feel it."

The longing she's trying to hide bleeds through her careful words, mixed with the pain of loss. She wants what they had —that bone-deep connection, that certainty. But she also believes it's gone forever, destroyed by whatever happened to Kitara.

She wants it. She's just afraid to reach for it and convinced she's already lost her chance to see it again.

"That kind of bond..." I say quietly, "it must be devastating when it's broken."

Her jaw tightens, and I see her fighting back emotion. "Ryker will never be the same. When your true mate dies..."

She doesn't finish the sentence, but the implication hangs heavy between us.

That's why she's so afraid, I realize. *She knows what losing love can do.*

"And you?" I ask eventually, the words scraping my throat raw. "No mate? No partner waiting for you to return?"

Say no.

My wolf paces beneath my skin, ears flattened, ready to tear apart anyone who might have a claim on her. The thought of another man touching her, holding her, makes my vision edge with red. I grip my hands into fists, nails biting into my palms as I wait for her answer.

A shadow crosses her face. "No. I mean... there was someone who I thought might but..." She shakes her head. "No, it's better to not do that."

Someone.

The knowledge there was once another hits like a physical blow. My chest tightens, jealousy flooding my system with toxic heat.

What wolf thought they could touch her when she's mine?

"Do what?" I ask instead of reaching over to claim her with a bite.

"Form attachments." She looks away. "They're a liability in my position."

The pain in her voice cuts through my selfish jealousy like a blade. Someone hurt her. Made her believe that caring meant weakness, that love was a luxury she couldn't afford.

The protective instinct that roars to life surprises me with its intensity. I want to find whoever did this to her and rip their throat out. But more than that—and this terrifies me—I want to prove her wrong. I want to show her that the right person wouldn't be a liability. That the right person would make her stronger, not weaker.

Me.

As I watch her, I can see the walls going up behind her

eyes, the careful distance she maintains. Pushing now for her to tell me more would only drive her further away.

"Fair enough," I say, the lie bitter on my tongue. It's not fair at all. It's a fucking tragedy that someone as fierce and loyal as her thinks she has to be alone.

But what can you offer her? my rational mind demands. *A nomad with no pack, no home, no future? You're exactly the kind of liability she's trying to avoid.*

"Being a nomad doesn't exactly lend itself to long-term commitment either." I reach forward to stir the fire.

"It's simpler that way, isn't it? Fewer complications."

"Fewer people to lose," I agree quietly.

Our eyes meet in silent understanding. We've both lost too much, seen too many we care about taken by violence or circumstance.

But I also know those words are the biggest lie I've ever told. Because looking at her now, even damaged and guarded and convinced that caring is dangerous, I know I'd rather risk losing her than never have her at all. I'd rather have one day of her choosing me than a lifetime of wondering what if.

You're fucked, I realize. *Completely and utterly fucked.*

"I'm worried about them," she admits. "I should be there."

"Your pack is strong. They've survived this long without you. A few more days won't make the difference."

"You don't know Zella," she says darkly.

"Then tell me," I encourage. "The more I know, the better I can help when we reach Shadowmist."

She looks surprised. "You're coming with me? To my pack?"

The question catches me off guard. "Of course. You think I'd get you this far and then just wave goodbye?"

"Most would," she says. "Especially a nomad with no pack allegiance."

"I'm not most people." I meet her gaze steadily. "And

whether you want to admit it or not, you're still recovering. You'll need backup until you reach your territory."

She studies me for a long moment, as if seeing me for the first time. "Why are you doing this, Kier? Really? You've already gone above and beyond what anyone would expect."

I'm not ready to give her the honest truth, so I deflect. "You promised me a date."

She laughs, then winces, pressing a hand to her injured side. "Don't make me laugh. It hurts."

"Sorry," I say, not sorry at all. The sound of her laughter feels like a victory.

She rubs her side gently. "You sure you want a date? I'm difficult and stubborn and terrible at expressing gratitude," she teases.

"Apparently those are qualities I find appealing."

She snorts, slapping my arm. "Stop making me laugh."

Outside, the wind picks up, branches scratching against the cabin walls. The temperature is dropping—I can feel the chill seeping through the old logs despite the fire.

"You should get back in bed," I tell her. "It's going to be a cold night."

She doesn't argue, which tells me how much she's still hurting despite her improvements. As she settles back onto the mattress, she asks, "Will you stay this time? Or are you going to keep the noble vigil all night?"

"I'll stay," I say simply, joining her on the narrow bed. This time, I allow our shoulders to touch. The contact is innocent, practical—shared warmth on a cold night—but it feels significant nonetheless.

"Kier?" she says after a moment, her voice soft in the darkness.

"Hmm?"

"I'm glad it was you. In the cell next to mine."

"Yeah, me too."

CHAPTER

TWELVE

I'm going to lose my temper if I stay in this cabin one more hour.

The walls feel like they're closing in, the air thick with the scent of woodsmoke and confinement. I've been cooped up for days while my ribs healed, and now that I can move without wincing, restlessness sizzles under my skin.

Plus, I stink.

The bucket baths we've been managing with lukewarm water heated over the cabin's ancient wood stove aren't cutting it anymore. I need to feel clean for the first time since our escape.

The storm that rolled in during our mad escape lingered for a few days, turning the ground damp. The weather is another reason we've been able to stay here for so long, our scent washed away by the torrential rain.

But the rain is now long gone, and the longer we stay here, the greater the risk of discovery.

We'll need to move.

I press a hand to my side, testing the wound. It's hot and painful, stealing my breath when I move.

"Damn. Okay. Another day or two."

I stare at the window, chewing on my bottom lip. Kier went out an hour ago to check our perimeter, so I should have privacy.

Perfect time for a real wash.

I grab the bar of soap we found in the cabin's supplies and slip outside. The cool air hits my face, and I breathe deeply, pine and the green scent of growing things.

The stream near the cabin has swollen with the recent rainfall, running deeper and faster than before. I follow it downstream, looking for a pool deep enough to actually submerge in.

I find it around a bend—a natural basin where the water has carved out a deeper pocket, maybe chest-deep in the center. Steam rises from the surface where the warmer stream water meets the cool air.

And standing waist-deep in the middle of it, completely naked, is Kier.

I freeze behind a large pine, my breath catching. He's fishing with his bare hands, holding almost impossibly still as he waits for the right moment to strike. His back is to me, water lapping at his hips, and I can see every line of muscle.

I should leave. Should turn around and go back to the cabin and act like I never saw this. But I can't make myself move.

His shoulders are broad, tapering down to a lean waist. Scars map stories across the expanse of his back, some thin and silvered with age, others newer and still slightly raised. His muscles shift and flex as he adjusts his stance, and I can see the tension coiled in him, every fiber focused on the hunt. Water droplets cling to his skin, catching what little sunlight filters through the canopy above.

Then he moves, lightning-fast, and comes up with a writhing fish in his grip.

"Gotcha," he murmurs, and his voice carries clearly across

the water. He twists, wading toward the bank to deposit his catch, and that's when I see… everything.

His chest is broad and defined, with a light dusting of dark hair that trails down his flat stomach in a tantalizing line. More scars mark his torso—silver burns across his ribs, what looks like claw marks over his left pectoral, a thin blade scar that runs from his collarbone toward his shoulder.

But it's the evidence of his arousal that makes heat flood my cheeks and pool low in my belly. Despite the frigid water, he's hard—thick and heavy and absolutely impossible to ignore. The sight sends a bolt of pure want through me so intense it nearly buckles my knees.

Heat floods my cheeks as I try to look away and fail completely. My wolf stirs beneath my skin, recognizing something in him that calls to her on a level I don't fully understand.

Beautiful, she whispers, and I can't argue. He is beautiful—not in a pretty way, but in the way a blade is beautiful. Dangerous and purposeful and absolutely mesmerizing.

Heat curls low in my belly, and I press my thighs together, confused by the intensity of my reaction. This is Kier. When did he become… this? When did looking at him start making my pulse race and my skin feel too tight?

Want, my she-wolf growls.

"No, we don't," I mutter under my breath, but my body and my wolf don't seem to be getting the message.

Kier tosses the fish onto the bank. With knife in hand, he begins to prep his kill.

"You planning to hide behind that tree all day, or are you going to join me?"

I jump, my heart slamming into my throat. He hasn't once glanced my way and is still standing knee-deep at the water's edge, but somehow he knows I'm here.

"I wasn't hiding," I call back, stepping out from behind

the pine with as much dignity as I can muster. "I was... waiting my turn."

He turns then, completely unselfconscious about his nudity, eyebrow raised in that infuriating way of his. "Your turn for what? Voyeurism or fishing?"

"I need to wash," I say primly, trying to keep my eyes on his face and not... other areas.

"Well, don't let me stop you." He wades back into deeper water, settling into his fishing stance again. "Water's not too bad once you get used to it."

I hesitate at the water's edge. Getting undressed with him right there feels... significant somehow. Like crossing a line I can't uncross.

"Oh, and Lithia?" he calls without looking at me, voice infuriatingly casual. "I'd ask if you brought me a pole, but, well..." He gestures vaguely downward, a smirk curling his lips. "We can both see you did."

My brain stutters. My face flames.

He chuckles, the sound deeply wicked. "Ignore it. I'm just glad to see you up and about."

I let out an incredulous laugh, torn between shoving his head under the water and holding him there until the bubbles stop, or pretending this whole conversation never happened.

"You're terrible," I huff, trying for dignity as I unbutton my shirt.

"So you keep telling me." He chuckles, turning back to the water.

I strip efficiently, trying not to think about the fact that he could turn around at any moment. When I step into the water, it's shockingly cold, making me gasp.

"Liar," I accuse through chattering teeth. "This is freezing."

"You'll adjust."

I wade deeper, soap in hand, keeping my eyes firmly on

the rippling surface. "Easy for you to say. You're obviously part polar bear or something."

A soft snort. "I'll take the compliment."

The water laps around my waist, sending a shiver through me. "I'm regretting this. I'm not built to handle hypothermia just to get clean."

"Consider it character building."

I glance over my shoulder and catch him watching me out of the corner of his eye, just briefly—a flicker, gone before I can call him on it. My stomach does a stupid, traitorous little flip.

"Eyes forward, Kier," I say, but there's no bite to my words.

He laughs, low and rough. "Oh, I'm being a gentleman. You're the one making it difficult."

I roll my eyes, sinking down to wet my hair. As I rise, my foot slips on the slick rock below.

I let out a startled yelp, arms flailing, and suddenly he's there, catching me with a splash and a grunt. His hands are firm on my waist, holding me steady, and for one breathless second, our bodies are too close, the chill of the water forgotten entirely.

I suck in a sharp breath, bracing for the moment his gaze drops—but it never does. His eyes stay locked on mine, intense, steady.

My heart thunders against my ribs, heat blooming low in my belly. *Gods, why does he have to be like this?*

He lets out a quiet breath, something almost like a laugh, and then gently—carefully—sets me back on my feet.

"There," he murmurs, brushing a wet lock of hair from my face. "All good."

I swallow. "Thank you."

"Don't mention it." But his eyes are dark, intense in a way that makes my pulse skip. "I... you're beautiful, Lithia."

The simple honesty in his voice steals my breath. No one's

ever called me beautiful—not like that, like it's just a fact he can't help but state.

"Kier..." I don't know what I'm going to say, but he's already let me go and is turning away, giving me privacy I didn't ask for.

My skin prickles with a thousand confused feelings as I touch the place where his hand held me.

"Sorry," he mutters. "Didn't mean to make this weird."

But it is weird. And charged. And absolutely nothing like the practical, survival-focused dynamic we've maintained in the cabin.

"You didn't make anything weird," I find myself saying. "You made things... interesting."

He glances back over his shoulder, a slow smile spreading across his face. "Interesting good, or interesting bad?"

"Jury's still out."

He laughs, the sound rich and warm in the cool air. "Fair enough."

We fall into companionable silence—him fishing, me scrubbing days of grime from my skin. But I'm hyperaware of every movement he makes, every flex of muscle as he moves through the water.

And he's aware of me too. I can feel it in the way the air between us crackles with tension, in the way his breathing has gone just slightly uneven.

This is dangerous territory. I know it, he knows it, but neither of us seems inclined to retreat to safer ground.

When I finally climb out of the water, clean and shivering, he keeps his back turned until I'm dressed.

"Better?" he asks, finally facing me again.

"Much." And it's true—I feel renewed. "Thanks."

"Thank you for the distraction from the mind-numbing boredom of fish stalking."

We collect his catch, five fish in all, and head back to the cabin together. As we walk, I find myself glancing over at him, letting my eyes linger longer than they should.

Kier is… attractive. More than attractive. The realization hits me like a physical blow—I'm attracted to this man. Not just grateful, not just trauma-bonded, but genuinely, viscerally attracted.

Something tightens low in my belly, heat pooling once more.

I want him.

I nearly stumble.

Well, shit.

Back at the cabin, Kier sets about preparing the fish with practiced efficiency. I watch his hands work, steady, sure, competent, and try to ignore the way my pulse quickens every time he glances my way.

"You're staring," he observes without looking up from filleting.

"I'm supervising," I correct. I place a pot of water on the wood stove and light it, then settle into one of the mismatched chairs around the small table to wait.

When the fish is ready, he cooks two simply—one seasoned with herbs we found in the cabin's stores and cooked over the fire, the other boiled in the water until it turns into a thick fatty stew. The smell makes my stomach growl audibly.

The fish is perfect—flaky and tender, seasoned just right. I make an embarrassing sound of appreciation around the first bite.

"Good?" Kier asks, amused.

"Amazing," I manage around another mouthful. "Where did you learn to cook?"

"Twenty years of fending for yourself teaches you a few things." He takes a bite of his own fish. "Trial and error, mostly. I've had some truly terrible meals."

"I can't cook at all," I admit. "Pack life means there's always someone else handling meals. I never learned."

"I could teach you."

The offer hangs between us, casual but somehow weighted. Teaching implies time together, a future beyond just surviving the next few days.

"I'd like that," I say quietly.

We eat in comfortable silence, and I'm struck by how domestic this feels. Sharing a meal, talking about mundane things, the fire crackling softly in the background. It's been so long since I've felt... peaceful.

Being Beta of the Shadowmist is a full-time job. There's always someone needing my help, or some issue I need to solve. Rare are the days when I get to just be.

Which is why it's even stranger that I'm in the middle of a life and death situation and feel the most peaceful I've been in years.

When we finish eating, Kier rummages through the cabin's supplies and emerges with a deck of cards, worn but still intact.

"Go fish?" I ask, watching him pull the cards from their deck.

He snorts. "How about poker?"

"I don't really know how to play. Never had much call for it in pack life."

"I'll teach you." He shuffles the cards with practiced ease. "Fair warning though—I'm pretty good."

"I'll try to keep up."

He starts with the basics—the different hands, how betting works, reading other players.

"So a flush beats a straight?" I ask, furrowing my brow as I stare at my cards.

"Yes, but a straight flush beats both."

"This is complicated."

He deals our first hand, patiently explaining each step. I

play hesitantly, making obvious rookie mistakes—betting when I should fold, folding when I have decent hands. He wins easily, as expected.

"Not bad for a first try," he says encouragingly. "You'll get the hang of it."

We play several more hands. I continue to ask him for guidance. He wins consistently, taking our small pot of dried raisins we'd plucked from a can of trail mix.

"You're starting to catch on," he says after I win a hand. "Natural instincts."

"Really? I still feel like I'm just guessing."

After about an hour of play, he's won the vast majority of hands. I'm down to maybe a quarter of my original "chips", but he's looking pleased with his teaching skills.

"One more hand?" I suggest, looking at my dwindling stack. "Winner takes all?"

"Are you sure? I don't want to clean you out completely."

"Come on," I niggle. "What's the worst that could happen? Maybe I'll get lucky."

"All right." He deals the cards, his hands flying. "But don't say I didn't warn you."

I peek at my cards and have to hide a smile. Decent hand, but it doesn't matter—I'm going to win this regardless.

He bets moderately, clearly not wanting to be too aggressive against his struggling student.

I look at my cards again, then at him, then push all my remaining chips forward. "All in."

He blinks in surprise. "You sure?"

"Sometimes you have to take risks, right?"

He studies his cards. "All right, I'll call. But Lithia, don't feel bad if—"

"Let's see what you've got," I interrupt sweetly.

He flips his cards over with a slightly apologetic smile. "Sorry. Full house."

It's a very good hand. Any normal player would be devastated.

I look at his cards, then at mine, then let my expression shift from nervousness to something else entirely.

"That is a good hand," I say, my voice completely different now—confident, amused. "But not good enough."

I flip my cards over with a grin that's pure shark.

Royal flush.

His jaw drops. He stares at the cards, then at me, then back at the cards. "That's…"

"The best possible hand in poker," I say sweetly, dropping the innocent act entirely. "Also known as unbeatable."

"Wait…" His eyes narrow as understanding dawns. "You hustled me!"

"Yep," I admit, unable to suppress my grin. "Dane and I used to clean out half the pack during the winter months."

"You absolute—" He leans back in his chair. "You've been playing me this entire time."

"Have I?"

He throws a raisin at me, which I catch easily. "I was being nice to you!"

"I know. It was very sweet." I laugh, delighted by his outrage. "You have to admit—I had you completely fooled."

"For a while," he concedes grudgingly. "But I should have known. Nobody's shuffling is that bad naturally."

"That was a nice touch, wasn't it?"

We sit there grinning at each other across the table.

"Your brother sounds like trouble," Kier observes, shuffling the cards once more. "Teaching his sister to hustle the pack."

"He is. Was. Still is, actually." I laugh, watching those deft fingers work. "But he's my trouble."

"Family's complicated."

"Do you have siblings?" I realize I don't know much about his life before becoming a nomad.

His expression shifts, becoming more guarded. "A younger sister. She didn't make it out of the attack that killed my pack."

"I'm sorry."

"Long time ago." But there's old pain in his voice, carefully controlled. "She would have liked you, I think. She was fierce like you—never backed down from anything."

The comparison warms me. "What was her name?"

"Natalie." A small smile touches his lips. "She had this laugh—completely infectious. Could make anyone smile, even when everything was going to hell."

We're quiet for a moment, both sunk in memories of people we've lost. The fire pops, sending sparks up the chimney.

"She would have been a better poker player than both of us," he adds, breaking the somber mood. "Do you wanna go another round?"

We play for another hour, the conversation flowing as easily as the card games.

This time he doesn't hold back. He reads me like an open book, calling my bluffs and folding when I have good hands. Within twenty minutes, I'm down to my last few raisins.

"You have to be cheating," I mutter, glaring at my terrible cards.

"You're a sore loser," he corrects.

I throw my cards down in defeat. "I fold. You win. Again."

"Good game," he says solemnly, then grins. "Better luck next time."

"There won't be a next time."

He laughs. "You just need to stop giving away your cards. You have a very expressive face."

"No, it's not."

"You sure about that?" He leans forward slightly, studying my face with those impossibly golden eyes. "Right now, for instance, you're frustrated but trying to hide it. Your jaw is tight, and you're pressing your lips together to keep from saying something you think might be too harsh."

My breath catches. He's right—completely, perfectly right.

"How do you do that?"

"Do what?"

"See so much."

His expression grows serious. "I've been forced to learn how to read people quickly. Survival depends on knowing who you can trust and who you can't."

"And what do you see when you look at me?" The question slips out before I can stop it, more vulnerable than I intended. But I genuinely want to know. What does he see? The broken Beta who failed to protect her Alpha Female? The damaged wolf who can't let anyone close? Or something else entirely?

He's quiet for a long moment, his gaze moving over my face like he's memorizing every detail.

"I see someone who's been carrying the weight of the world on her shoulders for so long, she's forgotten how to set it down," he says finally. "Someone who thinks she has to be perfect, untouchable, because if she shows any weakness, the people she protects might get hurt."

His voice is gentle, but his eyes are knowing. "I see someone who cares so deeply it scares her. Someone who would rather suffer alone than risk letting anyone else carry even the smallest part of her burden."

"Stop." The word comes out rougher than I intended.

"I see someone beautiful," he continues, ignoring my protest. "Not just physically, though you are. But beautiful in the way you refuse to break, no matter what they do to you. Beautiful in your loyalty, your strength, your absolute refusal to give up."

I can't breathe. No one has ever seen me like this—not the role I play, but the person underneath. The broken, scared person I keep hidden from everyone, even myself sometimes.

"Kier..." I don't know what I'm going to say. Don't know how to respond to such raw honesty.

He leans back in his chair, completely relaxed, a small smile playing at his lips as he watches me process his words. There's nothing but warm affection in his expression—no recognition, no sudden awareness, just the same easy companionship we've been building over these past days.

"You're staring again," he observes, that familiar teasing note in his voice.

But I can barely hear him over the roaring in my ears. Something is happening—something fundamental shifting inside me as I look at his face in the firelight.

My wolf lifts her head, suddenly alert. She tastes the air, her attention sharpening with laser focus.

What is it? I ask her silently.

She doesn't answer in words. Instead, she sends me an image, a feeling, a bone-deep certainty that makes my blood sing.

Mine.

The thought doesn't come from me. It comes from her, from some primal part of myself that recognizes truth when it sees it.

Ours.

The realization hits me like a physical blow. I stare at Kier —really look at him—and everything suddenly makes sense. The way I felt safe with him from the very beginning. The electric current that runs between us whenever we touch. The way my wolf has been calling for him, trying to tell me something I was too stubborn to hear.

Mate.

The word echoes through my mind, not thought but known. Ancient, primal, undeniable.

Kier is my mate.

"Lithia?" His voice seems to come from very far away. "You okay? You look like you've seen a ghost."

I can't speak. Can't breathe. Can barely think past the overwhelming certainty flooding through me.

He's completely oblivious. Still leaning back in his chair, still wearing that easy smile, completely unaware that my entire world just tilted off its axis.

My wolf is singing, practically vibrating with joy and certainty. She's known, I realize. Maybe not from the beginning, but she's been trying to tell me.

"No," I breathe, the word barely audible.

"No what?" Kier asks, leaning forward with concern. "Lithia, what's wrong?"

He doesn't know. The thought is both relief and terror. *He doesn't feel it.*

But my wolf is insistent, pressing at me—Kier's scent, the way he's cared for me, the rightness of being near him. She's absolutely certain, and wolves don't make mistakes about these things.

The knowledge sits in my chest like a stone, heavy and undeniable. Kier is my mate. This complicated, infuriating, wonderful man is the other half of my soul.

And he has absolutely no idea.

"I need air," I say abruptly, standing so fast my chair topples backward.

I flee the cabin like something is chasing me, bursting out into the cool night air. But I can't outrun the truth burning in my chest.

Mate. Mine. Ours.

My wolf's certainty echoes through me, and for the first time since our parents died, she's completely, utterly, joyfully sure of something.

I just wish I could say the same.

THIRTEEN

I return to the cabin, shaken but resolved. There's no mates for me. No one I want enough to hold tight.

Once this adventure is over, I'll let Kier go. I have to.

"We'll leave the day after tomorrow," I announce, watching Kier's back as he stokes the fire.

He turns, studying me with that unnerving intensity I've come to know over our days in the cabin. "You sure? Your side—"

"Is healing," I say firmly, cutting him off. I lift my shirt to show him the wound. The angry red gash has faded to a thin pink line, the bruising around it more yellow than purple now. "I'm not saying it's perfect, but it's good enough."

Kier rises from his crouch by the hearth, wiping his hands on his makeshift pants. He'd found some of the outfits left by the cabin's owner and refashioned them into something cleaner than the filthy prison clothes we escaped in. The result is ridiculous—a patchwork of faded floral fabric that somehow still manages to look good on him.

Turns out our cabin's owner is less hunter and more hippy.

"It's not just about the wound," he says, approaching to examine my side. "The silver—"

"Is still a problem, yes." I gesture at the cuffs we still haven't managed to remove. "But it's a problem whether we're here or on the move."

The silver has been our constant companion, the cuffs impossible to break. Despite searching the cabin thoroughly and even venturing into the surrounding forest, Kier hasn't found anything strong enough to break them. They continue to burn against our skin, a constant reminder of our captivity, slowing our healing and keeping our wolves subdued.

"I'm as healed as I can get out here," I continue, pulling my shirt back down. "Zella will have search parties combing every inch of these mountains. We've been lucky so far, but luck always runs out."

Kier nods reluctantly. "What are you thinking?"

I move to the old map we've pinned to the cabin wall, dragging my finger southward. "Shadowmist territory is still at least another three hundred miles from here in a straight line." I tap the mountains marked on the map. "It's also rough terrain and we can't shift. Which means even if we push hard, that's at least a three to four weeks' journey on foot."

"And that's if we're fully healed and don't run into bad weather or trouble," he adds grimly.

"Exactly." I run a hand through my hair, now clean thanks to the cabin's rusty but functional pump. "We need to get moving. Find a town, maybe. Steal a vehicle if we have to."

Kier raises an eyebrow, amusement quirking his lips. "You're suggesting grand theft auto, Beta? What would your Alpha think?"

I snort. "Ryker would probably ask why we didn't steal something faster."

He laughs, a sound I've come to treasure for its rarity. In the days since our escape, Kier has slowly emerged from the shell that three years of imprisonment created. The hallucinations have faded, the moments of confusion grown less frequent. But there's still a guardedness to him, a careful distance he maintains even in our close quarters.

Except at night. At night, when the temperature drops and we huddle together on the narrow bed for warmth, that distance collapses. He curls around me protectively, his arm draped over my waist, his breath warm against my neck. I tell myself it's practical—survival, nothing more—but my wolf knows better.

Ours, she insists each time, and I push the thought away.

I can't afford attachments. Especially not now, when my failure still burns fresh.

Kitara.

I push down the grief that threatens to envelop me. If Kitara's gone, then Ryker won't be far behind. True mates are bound together. Where one goes, the other must follow, and if our Alpha Female is dead, then our Alpha will turn feral searching for her.

A feral that will see him stuck in wolf form for the rest of his days, his mind as fractured as his heart.

Just get home. Then you can deal with all the what ifs.

Kier moves to our small pile of supplies, interrupting my thoughts. "We'll need food, water containers, clothing, and better bedding than this." He holds up the threadbare blanket we've been sharing. "Not to mention weapons."

"I've been thinking about that." I join him, rifling through the supplies. "We should check the shed out back again. There must be something we missed."

"I've been through it three times, Lithia. Just some old fishing gear and rotted wood."

"Then we'll make do." I pick up the knife, testing its weight. "Do you want the gun or the knife?"

He gives me a look that's equal parts amusement and offense. "I'll make do with the knife. You take the gun."

I roll my eyes. "Okay, macho man."

He studies me, rubbing his chin. "You're really determined to do this."

"I need to get back to my pack." I meet his gaze. "And we can't stay here forever."

He sighs. "All right. Day after tomorrow. But if you're not ready—"

"I'll be ready," I say firmly. "We've waited long enough."

The truth is, the cabin has become a dangerous comfort. Away from the prison's horrors, it would be easy to forget the urgency of our situation. But every day we linger is a day Zella moves forward with her plans—plans that will destroy everything I've sworn to protect.

"I'll start preparations," Kier says, already moving toward the door. "See what I can hunt that we could take with us. You should rest."

"I've rested enough." I stand straighter, ignoring the twinge in my side. "I'll check the perimeter."

He hesitates, clearly wanting to argue, but nods instead. "Just don't push too hard. We need you at full strength."

After he leaves, I circle the cabin slowly, checking the crude alarms he's set up. The forest is quiet, birds calling to one another in the afternoon light. No sign of pursuit. No hint of danger.

But I know better than to trust the peace. Zella is ruthless and methodical. She wouldn't have given up just because we escaped. She'll be hunting us—if not for recapture, then for elimination. We represent a threat to whatever sick vision she's building.

Evolution, she had called it. As if slavery and torture could be justified by some twisted ideal of progress.

What kind of "greater good" requires the suffering of innocents? What kind of "evolution" builds its foundation on fear and pain?

I complete my circuit of the cabin, ending at the small

stream that runs nearby. Kneeling on the bank, I stare at my reflection in the clear water. My face is thinner than it was before my capture, my pale blue eyes shadowed with exhaustion and haunted by memories. The scar that runs from my temple down my cheek seems more pronounced.

But it's the silver collar around my throat that holds my attention. A symbol of captivity that I still can't shed.

With a growl of frustration, I splash the water, destroying the image. My wolf stirs restlessly inside me, weakened by the silver but growing stronger each day. She wants freedom as desperately as I do.

Soon, I promise her. *We'll be home soon.*

By the time Kier returns, the sun is setting. He carries two rabbits, already skinned and cleaned, and a handful of wild onions.

"Dinner," he announces, holding up his catch. "And breakfast for tomorrow."

"Nice work." I help him prepare the meal, working in comfortable silence as twilight deepens outside.

We've fallen into routines during our stay here—Kier handles most of the hunting and scavenging, having more experience with living off the land, while I take charge of cooking and security. It's an easy division of labor that plays to our strengths.

Sometimes I wonder if it would be this simple if he were to join my pack, if we could find this quiet rhythm with others around.

Silly. He's nomad. Why would he want to stay? Why do you want him to stay? You've said it yourself, you have no use for attachments.

My wolf whines, stating her objection to my decision.

Hush, I tell her.

"What's the plan once we reach Shadowmist?" he asks as we eat.

I consider the question carefully. "Warn the Alpha and the

pack about Zella's operation. Mount a rescue for the other prisoners if possible."

"And after that?"

I pause, fork halfway to my mouth. "After?"

"After you've delivered your warning. After the rescue, if it happens. What then?"

The question catches me off guard. I've been so focused on getting back, on completing my duty, that I haven't thought beyond it.

"I go back to being Beta," I say finally. "My job is to protect the pack. I need to make sure nothing like this happens again."

And atone for my failure.

Kier nods, returning his attention to his food.

"And you?" I ask.

He shrugs, a casual gesture that doesn't quite hide the tension in his frame. "Continue my nomad ways, I suppose. There's always someone looking for a tracker."

The thought of him simply walking away after everything we've been through sends an unexpected pang through my chest. My wolf whines, pressing against my consciousness.

Stay, she urges.

I push the feeling aside. "You'd be welcome in Shadowmist," I hear myself say. "After helping me escape, Ryker will grant you a place in the pack."

Kier's eyes flick up to meet mine, his usual smirk tugging at his mouth—but it's thinner this time, like a thread pulled too tight. Behind the sarcasm, I catch it, a flicker of something raw, aching, so quickly masked I almost doubt I saw it at all.

"You sure? Packs aren't usually keen on taking in strays."

He's bracing himself, pretending he doesn't care, pretending he's used to the door closing. But his eyes—gods, his eyes—betray him.

"You're not a stray," I say more sharply than intended.

"You're a…" I struggle for the right word. Friend seems inadequate. Partner too intimate. "An ally," I finish lamely.

A smile tugs at the corner of his mouth. "An ally. Is that what we are, Lithia?"

There's a challenge in his tone that makes my pulse quicken. "What would you call us, then?"

He studies me for a long moment, something unreadable in his gaze. "I'm not sure there's a name for what we are."

The air between us feels suddenly charged, heavy with things unsaid. I break eye contact first, returning to my food with forced casualness.

"Well, whatever we are," I say, "you'll always have a place with Shadowmist. Come, go, stay, leave, doesn't matter to us. We'll always welcome you."

He doesn't answer immediately, and when I glance up, he's watching me with an intensity that makes my skin warm.

"Thank you," he says finally.

We finish the meal in silence, the unspoken tension gradually easing into our usual comfortable companionship. As night deepens, the temperature drops, reminding us that winter's chill is approaching.

Kier adds wood to the fire, the flames casting his face in warm light and dancing shadows. The firelight catches in his dark copper hair, highlighting strands of premature silver threaded through the waves.

At thirty-eight, he's only a few years older than myself. But we've a world of experience between us. I've seen battle, I've lost loved ones—and so has he. But the last three years sit on his shoulders and burrow under his skin, marking him in ways I'll never understand.

I watch him, a now-familiar warmth spreading through my chest. It's a feeling I've been fighting since our escape. A pull that goes beyond gratitude or camaraderie.

My wolf has no doubts about what it means. She recognized him immediately, knew him for what he was to us even through the prison walls. But I've spent too many years guarding my heart to surrender to instinct so easily.

"We should sleep," Kier says, breaking into my thoughts. "Tomorrow will be busy."

I nod, moving to the bed we've shared these past days. The mattress is lumpy and smells faintly of mildew despite our best efforts to clean it, but it's still better than the stone floor of a prison cell.

Kier takes his time banking the fire, checking the doors and windows one last time before joining me. The bed creaks as he settles beside me, his warmth seeping through the thin barrier of our clothes.

"Lithia," he says softly, "if you're not ready—"

"I am," I interrupt. "I need to get back to my pack."

He sighs, a quiet sound in the darkness. "I know. I just... I don't want you pushing yourself too hard."

"You don't think I can do this?" The question slips out before I can stop it, blunter than I intended.

There's a long silence, long enough that I wonder if he'll answer at all. When he does, his voice is so quiet I have to strain to hear it.

"No. I know you can. But I don't want to break the only good thing I've found after three years of hell."

His simple honesty steals my breath. I don't know how to respond, don't have words equal to the weight of his confession.

Instead, I find his hand in the darkness, threading my fingers through his. It's a small gesture, inadequate to express what I feel, but it's all I can offer right now.

See? my she-wolf asks. *He's ours.*

Kier squeezes my hand gently, accepting what I can give without demanding more. We lie there in silence, hands clasped between us, until sleep finally claims us both.

CHAPTER

FOURTEEN

Morning brings a flurry of activity as we prepare for our departure. Kier heads out early to hunt and forage while I transform what rags and blankets I can find into a makeshift pack. We'll need to carry water, food, and what few weapons we've managed to cobble together.

By the time he returns with more rabbits and a handful of early spring greens, I've assembled a rough backpack torn from strips of cloth and hastily sewn together with a dull needle and some old thread.

"Impressive," he says, eyeing my work.

"Thanks," I say with a smile. "It'll make do in a pinch."

We spend the rest of the day in preparation—smoking meat over the fire, filling water containers, fashioning crude weapons from kitchen knives and broken furniture. By sunset, we're as ready as we'll ever be.

Our last night in the cabin is quiet, filled with anticipation and unspoken concerns. We go to bed early, resting before our big push.

Despite my tiredness, I drift between wakefulness and

sleep, Kier's arm draped over my waist. My mind is full of thoughts of what's to come, what's become of my pack, what we'll have to face.

And somewhere in those thoughts rests a question I can't quite silence. Where does Kier fit in?

My wolf has her answer, of course. But I've spent too many years building walls around my heart to allow someone to slip in so easily, even when the pull is this strong.

Everyone I love dies, a voice whispers in the back of my mind. It's the fear that's shaped my life since I watched my parents die. It's the reason I've kept all potential mates at arm's length.

Attachment is a luxury I've never allowed myself. A vulnerability I can't afford. Even now, with Kier's steady breathing beside me and his arm a comforting weight around me, I fight the pull.

Dawn breaks crisp and clear, the forest awakening around our small cabin. I rise before Kier, slipping from the warmth of his embrace to check our supplies one last time. Everything is ready—our crude pack filled with what food and water we can carry, our makeshift weapons secured.

When Kier joins me, his eyes still heavy with sleep, I'm already dressed in the cleanest clothes I could piece together from the cabin's meager offerings.

"Ready?" he asks.

I nod, offering him cold meat. "Let's go home."

He shoulders our pack, eating the meat from the spit as we leave the cabin. The forest is quiet around us, the morning mist clinging to the trees with like ghost-fingers. Despite the silver restraints still burning against our skin, there's a lightness to our steps.

We're moving toward safety.

As we walk, I find myself stealing glances at Kier. He moves with a silent, confident grace through the underbrush, his golden eyes constantly scanning our surroundings. Three years of captivity haven't diminished his instincts or his will.

I wonder what he was like before he entered that prison. Did he always seek to protect the people around him, or did the prison force him to make choices he otherwise would never have made?

As if sensing my thoughts, he glances back, catching me watching him. A smile tugs at his lips.

"See something you like, Beta?" he teases.

Heat rises to my cheeks, but I refuse to look away. "Just making sure you can keep up, Nomad."

His smile widens to a grin. "Race you to that ridge?" He points to a rocky outcrop about half a mile ahead.

Despite the ache in my side and the silver restraints, I find myself grinning back. "I have broken ribs."

"Excuses."

I eye the ridge. It's not that far, and my ribs are healing nicely. What the hell. I need the energy burst.

I break into a run, weaving through trees and leaping over fallen logs, leaving Kier in my dust. He barks out a laugh, and I hear him give chase.

For a few precious minutes, we're not escaped prisoners or wounded fighters. We're just wolves, reveling in the simple joy of movement.

I reach the ridge barely a step ahead of him, laughing as I turn to face him. "I win!"

He's laughing, his smile wide and easy and breathtaking. "So you did."

For a moment, we just stand there, grinning at each other like fools. Then his expression sobers, his gaze shifting to something over my shoulder.

"Lithia," he says quietly, "look."

I turn, following his gaze, and my breath catches for an entirely different reason.

From this vantage point, we can see for miles—the forest

stretching below us, the mountains towering behind. And in the distance, a plume of dark smoke rising into the clear morning sky.

"Wild fire?" I ask, though I already know the answer.

Kier shakes his head. "Too dark and controlled." He points to another plume, farther east. "There's another one. And there."

I count five distinct smoke columns, forming a rough circle to the north of the area we've just left.

"Search parties," I say grimly. "Burning as they go."

Kier nods. "They're systematically searching the area. Working inward and down toward the mountain."

"They're looking for us."

"And making sure we can't hide." He turns to me, his expression grave. "We need to move."

I nod, the brief moment of lightness gone. "We'll keep to the high ground as much as possible. Use the streams and rivers to hide our scent."

We set off again, pushing harder now, silent as we move through the forest. The journey we'd planned had been a slower one, accounting for our injuries. Now we're in a race against time.

The sun climbs higher, the air warming, but a shift rides the breeze—faint, acrid, unmistakable.

Smoke.

I pause, lifting my nose to the wind. Kier does the same beside me, his brow furrowing as he tastes the air.

"That's... close," I murmur.

He rumbles his agreement, scanning the tree line.

Another gust of wind, this time sharp enough to sting the back of my throat. My stomach knots.

"They're not behind us anymore," Kier says, voice tight.

A crow caws overhead, harsh and jarring in the unnatural hush.

"We're not outrunning this, are we?" I whisper.

His jaw tightens, eyes flicking golden as the wolf stirs just beneath his skin.

"No," he murmurs. "We have to go into it."

FIFTEEN

KIER

The smoke is everywhere now—thick, choking clouds that turn the morning sun into a sickly orange glow. We're moving through a nightmare landscape of burning trees and falling ash, the heat like an oven against our skin.

"This way!" I shout over the roaring flames. I pull Lithia toward what looks like a gap in the fire line. The silver around our throats makes breathing harder, each inhalation a struggle against metal and smoke.

Behind us, voices cut through the crackling inferno. Human voices, coordinated and closing fast.

"Hurry," Lithia gasps, stumbling over a fallen log. "They're driving us toward—"

A pine tree erupts, sparks shooting skyward as it topples across our path in a violent crash, flinging burning branches and flaming nettles. We skid to a halt, trapped between the fallen tree and the advancing flames.

"Fuck," I breathe, spinning in a circle. The fire has closed around us on three sides, leaving only one narrow corridor— straight toward the voices of our pursuers.

Lithia's face is streaked with soot and sweat, her pale eyes reflecting the orange glow of the flames. "We can't go back."

"And we can't go forward." I scan the burning forest, looking for any option, any way out. "Unless..."

I point to a steep rocky slope rising to our left, barely visible through the smoke. "Can you climb?"

She follows my gaze to the treacherous-looking cliff face. "In this smoke? With these restraints?"

"It's better than burning alive."

Another tree crashes down behind us, sending up a shower of sparks that spark and sizzle against our skin. The voices are getting closer—I can make out individual words now, orders being shouted between the searchers.

"There! I saw movement!"

"Circle around, cut off their escape!"

Lithia meets my eyes, and I see the same desperate determination I feel burning in my chest. "Let's go."

We scramble toward the cliff face, using our hands as much as our feet on the loose scree. The silver cuffs make every movement awkward, throwing off our balance. Behind us, the fire roars closer, and ahead, the rock face seems to stretch endlessly upward.

"Don't look down," I call to Lithia as we climb, my fingers finding precarious holds on the rough stone. "Just keep moving."

A gunshot echoes through the smoke below us. Then another.

"They see us," Lithia pants, hauling herself up another few feet. Blood seeps from her palms where the rock has torn them open, but she doesn't slow.

We climb in desperate silence, the heat from below making the rock face almost too hot to touch. My lungs burn with each breath, and my vision wavers from smoke and exhaustion. The silver poisoning isn't helping—my strength is maybe half of what it should be.

Fifty feet up. Sixty. The voices below grow fainter, but the fire is spreading faster than we can climb.

"Kier." Lithia's voice is tight with strain. "I can't—"

I look down to see her clinging to a narrow ledge, her injured side bleeding through her shirt. She's pale, shaking with exhaustion and pain.

"Yes, you can," I tell her, scrambling down to her position. "Just a little farther."

"No." She shakes her head, tears cutting clean tracks through the soot on her cheeks. "I'm slowing you down. You should—"

"Don't you fucking dare," I snarl, grabbing her chin and forcing her to meet my eyes. "We do this together or not at all. Remember?"

She stares at me for a moment, something fierce and desperate flickering in her gaze. Then she nods, taking my offered hand.

I force her ahead of me, following her climb. One handhold at a time, one foot after another, pushing through pain and smoke and the terrible heat rising from below. The world narrows to just this—rock under our hands, air in our lungs, the solid warmth of each other beside us.

I lose track of time, of distance, of everything except the need to keep moving up. The fire below sounds like a freight train now, consuming everything in its path. But ahead, through the smoke, I can see the edge of the cliff face.

"Almost there," I gasp, following Lithia's painful ascent. As she reaches the edge of the cliff, I reach up, boosting her onto the stone outcrop. I haul myself over, finding her flat on her back, gasping for air. She's climbed the fucking thing on pure stubborn will. I flop beside her, sucking in lungfuls of the slightly cleaner air.

Below us, the forest burns. The entire valley is engulfed in flames, smoke rising in towering pillars that block out the sun. And somewhere in that inferno, our pursuers are either dead or retreating.

"We made it," Lithia whispers, her voice raw from smoke.

I want to agree, but something's wrong. The smoke up here is different—not just wood smoke, but something chemical and sharp that makes my eyes water.

"Lithia." I grab her arm, pointing to the horizon. "Look."

She follows my gaze and her face goes white.

An aircraft circles in the distance—helicopters dropping something that makes the flames burn hotter and faster.

"They know we're here."

As if summoned by my words, the sound of rotors cuts through the air above us. A helicopter, emerging from the smoke like a predator, already swinging in our direction.

"Run!"

We scramble across the rocky plateau, looking for any cover, any escape. But there's nowhere to go—just bare rock and empty sky, and the helicopter closing fast.

The searchlight finds us, cutting through the smoke to pin us like insects in its glare. Over the rotor noise, I hear a voice amplified by a megaphone.

"Stop running. You're surrounded."

I grab Lithia's hand, pulling her toward the far edge of the plateau. Maybe we can find another way down, another route—

The rock explodes inches from my feet, shards of stone spraying across the plateau. Not a warning shot. They're trying to kill us.

"This way!" Lithia yanks me toward a narrow crevice in the rock face. It's barely wide enough for a person, but it's cover.

We squeeze into the narrow crevice in the rock face, gasping as the helicopter's searchlight sweeps past. There's another shot, but it lands about three feet to our left. The angle of this crevice is all that's keeping us from becoming Swiss cheese.

But our relief is short-lived.

The sound of rotors cuts through the air above us—another helicopter, different from the first. Through the gap in the rocks, I watch in horror as it drops a line of liquid fire across the plateau above us, the chemical accelerant igniting instantly.

"Fuck, they're boxing us in," Lithia breathes.

Fire below us, climbing the cliff face with terrifying speed. Fire above us now, spreading across our only escape route. And somewhere in the smoke, helicopters circling like vultures, making sure we have nowhere to run.

The smell of smoke grows thicker. The fire is climbing toward us from below while the new blaze spreads across the plateau above, following the wind currents down through the rock formations. Through the narrow opening, I can see orange light dancing closer from both directions, hear the roar of flames consuming everything in their path.

"Kier," Lithia's voice is tight. "The fire—it's coming up."

I can feel the heat building, see the glow intensifying from both directions. We're trapped, sandwiched between walls of flame, with nowhere left to run.

The heat is becoming unbearable. Sweat beads on our skin despite the fear, and each breath burns our lungs. Through the gap, I can see flames licking at the rock face not twenty feet away from below, while the fire above spreads closer with each passing second.

"We're going to burn," she whispers.

"I'm sorry," I say, my voice rough. "I should have gotten you out of here. Should have—"

"No." She grabs my face, forcing me to look at her. "Don't you dare apologize."

Her pale eyes reflect the orange glow, wide with terror and acceptance. My chest tightens watching her—this fierce, beautiful woman who's become everything to me in a matter of days. If we're going to die, if this is our last moment—

I crush her back against the rock, my mouth crashing to hers with a hunger that's been building since the second I saw her—hell, maybe since before that. She meets me with the same wild, reckless need, a moan vibrating from her throat as she fists her hands in my shirt, pulling me closer like she's trying to crawl inside me.

I pour three years of isolation, days of unspoken tension, the terror of impending death into a kiss that tastes of smoke and salvation.

I'm unprepared for the taste of her. The feel of her. Her mouth is soft and warm and perfect. I relish the sweet slide of her tongue against mine, the way she gasps when I bite her bottom lip, the shift of her hips under my hands.

I growl low in my chest, crowding her harder into the stone, fingers sliding into her hair, tugging just enough to hear the sharp intake of breath she gives me. Her nails drag down my back, a sting that shoots straight to my blood, and I swear the fire behind us is nothing compared to the heat sparking under my skin.

She arches against me, mouth parting wider, hungry, desperate, devouring. The smell of smoke wraps around us, sweat-slick skin, pounding hearts, adrenaline and the electric crackle of something too big to name. I slide a hand down, gripping her thigh, hiking it around my hip, needing her closer, needing her *more*.

We're going to die. We both know it.

So I kiss her like a man starved, like a man drowning, like a man who wants to leave his mark on her soul before the fire takes us both.

The fire roars closer, but I don't care. Nothing exists except the heat of her mouth, the way she rocks against me, the small sounds she makes against my lips.

I press harder against her, trying to shield her from the

approaching flames. Desperate to make these final seconds of life perfect. My hands tangle in her hair as I deepen the kiss, pouring everything I can't say into our desperate fucking kiss—

The rock behind her gives way.

SIXTEEN

We tumble into darkness, stone scraping my arms, my back—Kier's arms wrapping tight around me as we crash into something cold and hard.

Cold explodes over us—icy, rushing water that punches the air from my lungs. I gasp, hands flailing, water roaring past my ears.

Kier is already there, pulling me up, gripping my arms. "Are you hurt?"

I choke on a laugh, half hysterical. "We're alive."

We're alive.

Above us, the cracked wall glows—orange, flickering, alive with fire. The heat must've split the stone, dropped us into an underground water system.

I glance at him—soaked, bleeding, his wild dark hair clinging to his face, his golden eyes burning in the dim light.

"Fuck," Kier mutters, looking around. "We're actually alive."

My chest tightens, emotion catching hard in my throat.

I shouldn't. This isn't the time. We're injured. We're hunted. I should be focused on survival, on escape, on anything *but* the sharp pull in my chest when I look at him.

But gods help me, I can't stop.

I step into him, sliding my hands into his hair to pull his mouth to mine.

The kiss hits like a punch—hot, raw, desperate. There's no room for careful, no room for gentle. His hands are in my hair, mine drop to clutch at his shoulders, and we're both shaking, soaked, delirious.

His mouth claims mine, and I let him, opening under the press of his tongue, dragging him closer. I need him under my skin, I need the heat of his body. He's the only thing keeping me anchored right now, the only thing stopping me from losing all control.

His teeth scrape my bottom lip, and I gasp, holding him tighter, tilting my head, needing *more*.

Every inch of him is solid muscle and heat and tension wound tight, trembling against me as his hands slide down to my waist, hauling me flush. I can feel every sharp edge, every scar, every line carved by captivity and survival.

I shouldn't want this.

But I do. Gods, I *do*.

I pour it all into our kiss—fear, exhaustion, fury, relief. All the things I can't say, all the things I don't have time to unpack. Right now, it's just mouths and hands and heat in the dark.

When we finally break apart, I'm gasping, dizzy, my pulse a wild drumbeat in my throat.

Kier leans his forehead to mine, breathless, smiling. "You're something else, Shadowmist."

I laugh, shaky and real, and brush his hair back from his face. "Come on," I whisper, threading my fingers through his. "Before something else tries to kill us."

Kier flicks on the flashlight and we begin to wade through the thigh-deep icy stream, following the current which tugs at our clothes as we stumble through.

"Underground streams usually lead to some kind of exit,"

Kier says, his voice echoing against the wet cave walls. "Hopefully it'll be somewhere without people trying to burn us alive."

"Your optimism is inspiring," I mutter, but I keep my fingers laced through his as we trudge forward.

The tunnel narrows, forcing us to duck our heads. Water sloshes around our thighs, numbing my skin. At least the cold helps with the burns and cuts we've collected during our escape. My ribs are aching from the fall, but our days of rest seem to have done their work.

"So," Kier says after we've been walking for several minutes. "We gonna talk about that kiss?"

"Technically there were two," I mutter.

"True. We gonna talk about those *kisses*?"

I nearly stumble on a submerged rock. "You want to discuss our romantic prospects while we're half-drowned in a cave?"

"I'm a multitasker." I can hear the smile in his voice. "Besides, I figure it'll be a more interesting conversation than, 'what did you get up to today, love?'"

I snort. "Is that what you call it? An 'interesting conversation'?"

"Well, your tongue was doing most of the talking, so you tell me."

Despite everything, I laugh. "You're terrible."

"And yet, you kissed me." His fingers tighten around mine. "Care to explain that, Beta?"

I consider deflecting again, but what's the point? We've nearly died multiple times. Pride seems like a luxury I can no longer afford.

"I thought we were about to die," I say finally. "And if I was going to burn alive, I wanted to know what it felt like to kiss you first."

"That matches my thoughts." He stops to help me over a particularly tight crevice. "And now that we're not dying?"

I drop into the water on the other side, gasping at the cold. "Now I'm wondering if you've always been this annoying or if it's a new development."

He chuckles. "You gonna talk about those walls you've built? Or should I just pretend I don't notice them?"

"You gonna talk about your imaginary friends?" I counter.

"Touché." He goes quiet for a moment. "They weren't friends, for the record. More like… ghosts. Reminders of all the ways I'd failed."

I wince. "I didn't mean—"

"It's fine." He squeezes my hand. "Adelaide was the worst. I'd see her standing there constantly. I'm not sure if it's because she was the youngest, or because she was the reason."

We splash through a deeper section, the water rising to our waists.

"Why did you think I was another hallucination?" I ask, remembering our first conversations through the wall.

"Can you blame me? A beautiful voice appearing in the darkness after years of isolation? It seemed too good to be true."

"Beautiful, huh?"

"Don't let it go to your head."

I smile. "What would you have done if I had been just another voice in your head?"

"Enjoyed the company, I suppose. Your particular brand of sarcasm is a definite improvement over the guilt trips my other hallucinations specialize in."

"Glad to hear I rank higher than your guilt-induced delusions."

"Top tier hallucination, that's you."

We round a bend, and the tunnel widens slightly. The water level drops to our knees, making walking easier.

"Your turn," Kier says.

"For what?"

"To share. Fair exchange and all that. I told you about mine, now you tell me yours."

"What do you want to know?"

"You're the Beta of Shadowmist. Strong, fierce, gorgeous. How is it you're single?"

I nearly stumble. "Who says I'm single?"

"You did, back in the prison. Are you now telling me there's some poor bastard waiting for you back home?" His tone is teasing, but I notice the faint clench of his jaw in the glow of the flashlight.

Damn, I did too.

"No," I admit. "There's no one."

"That's what I thought. So what's the story there? No eligible wolves in Shadowmist?"

I roll my eyes, though he can't see it in the dark. "Plenty of eligible wolves. Just none I'm interested in."

"None?" His voice lifts, playful, but when I glance at him, I see his brow pinched. "Not one worthy suitor caught your eye?"

"I don't do relationships," I say flatly.

"Ever? Or just currently?"

"Ever."

"Any particular reason? Or just not a fan of companionship, cuddling, mind-blowing sex, breakfast in bed—"

"I have my reasons."

"Care to share with the class?"

I sigh. "No."

He's quiet for a while as we walk. "It was your parents right? Their death made it easier not to love at all."

I bristle at his question. "It's not about easy."

"Isn't it?" He stops walking, turning to face me in the semi-darkness. "You sure this isn't fear talking?"

"Excuse me for not wanting to watch everyone I care about die," I snap.

"So instead you're choosing to die alone? Brilliant strategy."

"Better than your approach. What exactly is your long-term plan, Nomad? Wander forever? Never belong anywhere?"

"At least I'm doing something with my life rather than staying in pack purgatory no doubt making everyone around me miserable."

We're both breathing hard now, anger crackling between us like static.

"You don't know the first thing about what I feel," I hiss.

"I know you kissed me like your life depended on it. I know your wolf recognizes mine. I know you're terrified of what that means."

"You think you've got me all figured out, don't you?"

"I think we're both fucked up in ways that fit together surprisingly well."

The statement is so unexpected, so perfectly ridiculous, that the anger drains out of me. A reluctant laugh bubbles up. "That's your romantic pitch? 'Our damage is compatible'?"

His teeth flash white in the darkness. "Is it working?"

"It's… not the worst I've heard."

He steps closer, his hand finding my waist. "I've spent twenty years alone, Lithia. By choice, mostly. I know what it means to keep people at a distance and convince yourself it's safer that way."

"Now you've seen the error of your ways?" I try to keep my tone light, but my voice wavers.

"Now I've met someone who makes me wonder if being alone is really a better choice."

I don't know what to say or how to respond to this man.

"I'm Beta of Shadowmist," I say finally. "My duty is to my pack."

"I'm not asking you to choose."

"Then what are you asking?"

He's quiet for a moment, his thumb tracing circles on my hip. "Just don't shut me out. Not yet. Not without giving this —whatever this is—some thought."

We follow the river for a while longer, quiet but for the occasional discussion about directions or hazards.

I mull over his words.

Don't shut me out.

Gods, I want to. He's already under my skin. But I've spent years building walls so high no one could climb them, walls even *I* couldn't see over. I buried my grief beneath duty, buried my hunger for touch beneath discipline, buried every soft, reckless part of myself beneath cold steel.

When we get back to Shadowmist and the dust settles, I'll shore up the walls, patch the cracks, and forget this momentary weakness.

But the truth is, I'm not sure I want to.

The tunnel curves sharply, and something changes in the air—a freshness, a hint of open space ahead.

"I think we're almost out," Kier says, pointing the flashlight in that direction.

"Let's hope it's somewhere without helicopters and psychopaths."

He reaches for me, helping me over a boulder. "Your standards are low. I like that about you."

I elbow him in the ribs as I drop down. "Keep it up and I'll leave you down here with your imaginary friends."

"They'd just tell me how I screwed up with you too."

"Smart hallucinations."

He laughs, and I grin, glad the tension between us is broken.

For now.

CHAPTER

SEVENTEEN

KIER

Three fucking weeks on the road, and I still can't get that kiss out of my mind.

We emerged from the tunnels miles from where we'd entered, the roar of helicopters nothing but a distant memory. Since then, we've kept to the wilderness, avoiding towns and roads, sticking to forest paths and animal trails. The silver restraints still burn against our skin, preventing us from shifting—a constant reminder of our captivity that we haven't been able to break despite our best efforts.

The journey to Shadowmist territory should have taken two weeks at most. Yet here we are, still trudging through forests and valleys, taking the long way around. Neither of us has pushed to speed up our journey.

We both know why.

The moment we reach Shadowmist, everything changes. Lithia goes back to being Beta, surrounded by pack responsibilities, and I go back to being… what? A nomad? A guest? A strange wolf with no place or purpose?

So we drag our feet. Take detours. Make camp early. Break camp late.

Our excuses range from weather to injuries to exhaustion. All of them are true. None of them are reasons to delay.

She's been gone from her pack for three months. It's time to return her to her people.

"We should reach the southern border of Shadowmist territory by tomorrow evening," Lithia says, dropping an armful of firewood beside our small campsite.

I nod, continuing to clean the rabbit I've caught for our dinner. "Good. Your pack will be relieved to see you."

She makes a noncommittal sound, busying herself with the fire. We've fallen into comfortable rhythms over these weeks—I hunt, she builds the fire. I cook, she cleans up. We work together without needing to speak, moving around each other with ease.

"Are you nervous?" I ask, skewering the rabbit on a makeshift spit.

She glances up, firelight dancing across her face. "About?"

"Going home. Facing everything. Telling them about Zella's plans."

Her expression darkens at the mention of the traitor's name. "I'm Beta. It's my job to report threats."

"That's not what I asked."

She sighs, running a hand through her hair—still pale as moonlight despite the days of travel and dirt. "Of course I'm nervous. I failed them. I failed Kitara."

Grief flickers across her face before she shuts it behind her trap door of emotions.

"You didn't fail anyone," I argue, settling the rabbit over the fire. "No one saw Zella coming. You need to stop blaming yourself."

She nods, her gaze returning to the fire. I watch her, wondering what she's thinking. Since that desperate kiss in the tunnels, we've maintained a careful distance during daylight hours. We talk about everything there is to share—

except the electric tension that crackles between us whenever we get too close.

But at night, when we lay our makeshift bed of pine boughs beneath the stars, all pretense falls away. She curls against me, her back to my chest, her body fitting perfectly against mine. I wrap my arm around her waist, bury my face in her hair, and we pretend not to notice how my body responds to her closeness, how her breath catches when I pull her tighter.

Every night I tell myself I'll keep my distance. Every night I fail.

The rabbit cooks slowly, filling the small clearing with its savory aroma. We eat in comfortable silence, watching the stars emerge above the trees.

"Will you stay?" Lithia asks suddenly, her voice quiet in the night.

My chest tightens, hope and fear warring inside me with brutal intensity. *Stay.* The word I've been desperate to hear, wrapped in careful politeness that makes my wolf snarl in frustration.

I look at her, surprised by the question. "At Shadowmist?"

She nods, not meeting my eyes. "For a while, at least. Ryker will want to thank you for helping me."

Ryker. Not her. Not because she wants me here, but because her Alpha will feel obligated. The disappointment cuts deeper than it should, slicing through the fragile hope I'd been nurturing.

She's asking me to stay, but only as a duty. It's not good enough.

I rise from my position by the fire, crossing to where she sits with deliberate slowness. Her breath catches as I settle beside her—close enough that our thighs brush, close enough that I can smell the scent that's been driving me slowly feral.

"Lithia." My voice comes out rougher than intended. I can

feel the heat radiating from her skin, can hear the slight hitch in her breathing as I lean closer.

She turns to look at me, and I see it—that flicker of want she tries so hard to hide, the way her pupils dilate despite the firelight. She shivers, a soft sound escaping her throat that goes straight to my cock.

"If you're asking me to stay," I murmur, "ask for yourself, not your alpha."

Her jaw tightens, and for a moment I think she'll retreat behind her walls again. But she surprises me.

"Then stay. I've gotten used to having you around."

My chest tightens.

"Geeze, Shadowmist. Way to beg," I tease. "I'll stay. For a while."

She nods, and there's a slight relaxation of her shoulders. We finish our meal in silence.

As night deepens, we prepare for sleep. The routine is familiar by now—lay out the pine boughs, bank the fire, check our surroundings one last time. But tonight, something's different. The knowledge that tomorrow brings an end to our solitude hangs heavy between us.

I settle onto our makeshift bed, leaving space for her to join me. She stands for a long moment, gazing at the stars, before slipping in beside me. As always, she fits herself against me, her back to my chest, my arm around her waist.

Her scent—gods, her scent—is everywhere, in my mouth, in my lungs, drowning me in heat and wolf and the sharp, addictive edge of her need.

Her fingers slip under mine, guiding my hand up, over her ribs, over the beat of her heart, until I'm palming the soft weight of her breast.

I suck in a breath sharp enough to cut.

"Lithia," I rasp—part warning, part plea.

"Kier, don't." She swallows. "Just… touch me. Please."

Fuck. *Fuck.*

My cock throbs so hard it's almost painful. My chest heaves, fighting to stay still, fighting to be a gentleman—but the moment she arches back, the curve of her ass grinding against me, I snap.

I slip my hand beneath her shirt, dragging my palm over bare skin, up to her nipple. It pebbles instantly, tight and eager, and I roll it between thumb and forefinger, relishing the strangled little sound she makes.

"More," she whispers, and it's like handing a starving man a feast.

I press my mouth to the curve of her neck, biting down just enough to hear her gasp, her fingers flying to the back of my head to hold me there. My other hand skims lower, dipping beneath the waistband of her pants, past the heat of her skin, across her damp curls into the wet, molten slick of her.

I graze two fingers over her slit, teasing but not really touching.

"Kier."

Biting her earlobe, I slip a finger into her wet heat, finding her clit and loving it with the barest of touches.

"Gods above," I choke. "You're soaked."

She writhes when I stroke over her clit—just once, a slow, filthy drag of my fingers. Her body arches like a bowstring pulled too tight.

I work her slowly at first, learning every gasp, every sigh, every broken little plea she tries to bite back. I circle her clit, slowly, testing pace then pressure. I alternate shapes and directions, discovering she's more sensitive on her left, she loves pressure but not pace. Not until she begins to beg for it.

"Fuck, you're gorgeous," I growl, grinding my cock into her ass. I'm hard as stone and desperate to be in her. But tonight's not about me.

I slip two fingers into her heat, and her walls clench

around me, greedy and hot and perfect. Her hips cant, and she begins fucking herself on my hand.

"Please, Kier," she whispers. "Don't stop—oh gods, please, don't stop."

"Never," I growl. "Never stopping, baby. I'm going to make you come so hard you forget your fucking name."

She jerks when I curl my fingers just right, hitting that spot inside that makes her entire body light up. I press my thumb to her clit, stroking hard, steady, relentless, her thighs trembling around my hand.

"Look at you," I murmur, voice ragged, lips dragging over her ear. "Falling apart for me, my little Beta. So good. Such a good fucking girl."

Her breath is breaking now, little sobbing sounds as she claws at the blankets, at me, at anything she can hold onto as I work her higher, until—

"Come on," I whisper. "Let me feel it. Come for me, Lithia. Come on my fingers. Let me hear it."

She shatters with a raw, guttural cry, her body locking around my hand. Heat floods over my skin as she comes, hard, helpless, wrecked.

I hold her through it, whispering filth and sweetness, kissing the salt from her skin, the tears she doesn't know she's crying.

When she turns to face me, her mouth finds mine instantly —no hesitation, no armor, nothing but raw, desperate hunger.

Her hand moves to my cock, palm stroking hard and sure through my pants. I groan into her mouth, throbbing under her touch, so fucking close it's embarrassing.

But when she fumbles at the button, I catch her wrist, panting against her lips.

"Not like this," I murmur, shaking with the effort it takes to stop. "Not in the dark. Not when I can't see every inch of you, taste every inch of you, make you come until you're too wrecked to stand."

She trembles, jaw tight, eyes wild. "Kier—"

I kiss her again, deep and slow.

"When you're ready, when you're mine for real, I'll give you everything. Every filthy, fucking thing you want."

She exhales shakily, resting her forehead to mine. "Your mistake. I'm only here for the taking tonight."

I smile against her lips, tasting her, feeling her heartbeat echoing through both of us.

"Whatever you want, baby. Just know, you're already mine."

She lets out a humorless laugh. "Don't get cocky, Nomad."

I roll us until she's under me and I'm on top. "Cocky? I'll show you cocky."

I kiss my way down her body, shifting aside clothing until we can feel skin against skin. Her breath catches as I reach her stomach, my hands gripping her hips, thumbs pressing into the hollows there.

"Weren't you going to wait?" she breathes, watching me through half-lidded eyes.

I look up at her, letting her see the hunger in my gaze. "No, *you'll* have to wait. I'm having my dessert."

Her laugh turns into a gasp as I yank her pants down her legs, spreading her thighs with firm hands. The scent of her arousal hits me like a physical blow—rich and heady and fucking perfect. I growl low in my throat, unable to help myself.

"Kier—"

I silence her with the first broad lick, and her words dissolve into a broken moan. Her hands fly to my hair, gripping tight enough to hurt, but the pain only sharpens my focus. I work her with my tongue, alternating between slow, deliberate strokes and quick, teasing flicks that make her hips buck.

"Fuck," she hisses, thighs trembling as I suck her clit between my lips. "Oh gods—"

I hum against her, the vibration making her jerk, her back arching off our makeshift bed. I slip two fingers inside her, curling them just right to hit that spot that made her come before, and she nearly shatters right then.

"So perfect," I murmur against her, not letting up for a second. "So fucking beautiful, Lithia."

She's close already, wound tight from our earlier play, and when I focus all my attention on her clit, sucking hard while my fingers work inside her, she comes with a sharp cry, her body convulsing under my hands.

I work her through it, gentling my touch but not stopping, riding the waves with her until she collapses back, gasping and boneless.

"Kier," she manages, her voice wrecked. "That was—"

A howl cuts through the night—close, too close, and unmistakably wolf.

Lithia bolts upright, instantly alert despite her post-orgasmic haze. I roll off her in one fluid motion, crouching ready for an attack, my wolf rising close to the surface despite the silver restraints.

The howl comes again, louder, and then the undergrowth at the edge of our campsite explodes.

A massive gray wolf bursts into the clearing—silver-streaked and battle-scarred, muscles rippling under thick fur. His lips are pulled back in a snarl, yellow eyes locked on me with murderous intent.

He lunges for my throat, moving faster than anything his size should be able to. I barely manage to throw myself sideways, hitting the ground and rolling to my feet in one desperate movement.

"LEVI! STOP!" Lithia's voice cracks like a whip.

The wolf freezes mid-leap, paws hitting the ground hard enough to send dirt flying. He skids across the clearing, his massive head swinging toward Lithia, yellow eyes widening in what can only be described as shock.

Lithia stands, half-dressed but utterly commanding, every inch the Beta of Shadowmist. "Stand down."

The wolf—Levi—snarls again, but it's halfhearted now, his gaze darting between us. Then, with a ripple of muscle and bone, he shifts. The transformation is fast, fluid, a testament to his power.

Where the wolf stood, a man now crouches—tall, broad-shouldered, with long dark hair and battle scars.

"Lithia," he says, his voice rough with emotion. "You're alive."

"I am," she confirms, quickly pulling her clothes back into place. "And you just attacked my friend."

Levi rises to his full height, easily six-foot-four of solid muscle. His yellow eyes—unchanged from his wolf form—narrow as they lock on me.

"*Friend*," he repeats, the word dripping with skepticism.

I straighten, fighting the urge to shift and meet his challenge. With the silver restraints, I'd be at a severe disadvantage, but the wolf in me doesn't care.

Back, he snarls at the newcomer. *She's mine.*

"Levi." Lithia steps between us. "This is Kier. He helped me escape. He saved my life."

Levi's gaze doesn't leave mine. "And now he's what? Claiming his reward?"

I snarl, my patience snapping. "Watch your fucking mouth."

A dangerous smile spreads across his face. "What are you gonna do about it, newcomer?"

I bare my teeth, a growl rumbling in my throat. "She's not yours."

"No? She's my pack's Beta. *My* Beta."

The emphasis on "my" isn't subtle, and I feel my wolf straining against the silver's suppression.

"Both of you, stop it," Lithia snaps. "Levi, where's Ryker?

Is he feral? What's happened since I've been gone? How did you find us?"

The questions seem to bring Levi back to himself. His shoulders relax slightly, though the hostile glare he gives me doesn't waver.

"Ryker sent search parties out the moment you were taken. We've been combing the mountains for months." His gaze softens as he looks at Lithia. "We never stopped looking for you."

The shift in his expression tells me everything I need to know. This isn't just pack loyalty.

This wolf—this massive, powerful wolf is in love with Lithia.

And I just had my face between her thighs.

Fuck.

EIGHTEEN

Much to my chagrin, Levi decides to stay the night, bedding down in our small camp.

"We'll reach the border by mid-morning tomorrow," he says, feeding another branch to our small fire. His eyes never leave me for long, tracking my movements with an intensity that's unsettling.

Relief wars with a sickly sinking feeling in my chest. Seeing Levi should feel like coming home. And part of it does. He's pack, he's safety, he's proof that Shadowmist survived my absence. But the way he watches me, the careful hunger in his yellow eyes as they catalog every detail of my appearance, makes my skin prickle with awareness.

He knows.

I can see it in the tightness around his eyes, the way his nostrils flare slightly when he catches our mingled scents. The knowledge sits between us like a blade, unspoken but razor-sharp.

I've always known about Levi's feelings, the way he looks at me when he thinks I'm not paying attention, the distance he maintains to keep from crossing lines I've never invited him to toe. Seeing him now is deeply uncomfortable.

Guilt. That's what this feeling is. Guilt that I can't return what he's offering, guilt that I'm grateful he interrupted us, guilt that part of me wishes he hadn't found us at all.

"How far to the main den from the border?" Kier asks, his voice neutral as he sharpens a stick with his knife.

Levi's jaw tightens. "Another half-day's journey. I'll have you there by sunset."

The way he says "you" makes it clear he sees Kier as separate from me—a temporary addition, not a permanent fixture.

I catch Kier's eye across the fire, but his expression reveals nothing. He's letting me handle this, respecting that these are my pack dynamics to navigate.

I rub at the raw skin beneath my restraints. "Will Elias be able to remove these?"

Levi nods. "He'll have something in his toolbox that'll work."

"And the pack?" I ask. "How have they fared with Kitara gone?"

Levi tilts his head to one side. "Kitara?"

I swallow, glancing away. "Has Ryker gone feral?"

Levi leans back. "No? Why would he?"

"Because Kitara's gone."

Levi scratches his head. "Lithia, what are you talking about?"

I frown. "Kitara. She's dead."

"Who told you that?"

"Zella." I straighten. "Are you saying—?"

He reaches across and places a hand on my knee. "Kitara is alive and well. Zella is a liar."

The relief that floods through me is so powerful it makes my chest ache. All this time, all these months thinking she was gone, that I'd failed her completely—and she's alive. The weight of that guilt suddenly lifts, leaving me dizzy with emotion.

I close my eyes, breathing deeply.

She's alive.

"I should check the perimeter," Kier announces, rising smoothly to his feet.

I recognize what he's doing—giving us space, though the slight tightening around his eyes betrays his discomfort at leaving me alone with Levi.

"I've already secured the area," Levi says, not bothering to hide his distaste with Kier.

I try not to roll my eyes.

"I guess I'll go for a stroll then," Kier replies with a casual shrug, before disappearing into the darkness beyond our camp.

The moment he's gone, Levi turns to me fully. "I don't like him."

His bluntness shouldn't surprise me—Levi has never been one for subtlety—but I find myself unprepared for it nonetheless.

"Kier saved my life," I say carefully. "We survived together. I owe him a debt."

His lips curl back. "So you're fucking him to repay that debt?"

"Levi!" I stand, turning from him. "If these cuffs were off, you'd be on the ground paying for that."

He huffs, running a hand over his face. "You're right. I shouldn't have said it. I'm sorry. I just... Lithia. It's been three months."

"Levi—"

"Three months," he cuts in, his voice tight. "Three months of not knowing if you were alive or dead. Of imagining what they might be doing to you. I searched every cave, every abandoned building, followed every whispered rumor."

His hand finds mine, gripping with an intensity that borders on painful. "I never stopped looking. Not for a single day."

The raw need in his voice resonates in my chest. Levi and I have a history—not romantic, but something deeper than simple friendship. We've trained together, fought together, protected the pack side by side for years. There had always been potential for more, an undercurrent of possibility we never fully acknowledged.

"I know," I say softly. "And I'm grateful."

"Grateful," he repeats, the word bitter on his tongue. "I didn't do it for your gratitude, Lithia."

Before I can respond, he releases my hand and stands. "Get some rest. We leave at dawn."

I watch him move to the opposite side of the camp, his broad shoulders tense beneath his shirt. The space he leaves behind feels colder somehow, heavy with unspoken words and expectations I'm not sure I can meet.

When Kier returns from his circuit, he says nothing about Levi's mood, simply settles beside me with a respectful distance between us—close enough for comfort, far enough for propriety.

"Try to sleep," he murmurs. "Tomorrow might be overwhelming."

I curl into my makeshift bed of pine boughs finding myself caught between two worlds—the one I left behind, and the one I found in darkness.

Without Kier's heat, sleep is elusive. My mind races with thoughts of what awaits us at Shadowmist. Will the pack accept Kier? Will Levi's possessiveness create problems? How will I explain what happened, what I learned about Zella's plans?

When dawn breaks, we break camp in silence. Levi takes point, setting a brisk pace through the forest. Kier and I follow, the silver restraints slowing our movements but not our determination.

As we cross into Shadowmist territory just before noon, I feel it immediately—a shift in the air, in the scent of the forest, in the very energy around us. My wolf surges against the silver's suppression, recognizing home.

But my attention isn't on the familiar pine and granite that marks our borders. Instead, I find myself watching Kier, cataloging every micro-expression as he experiences Shadowmist for the first time. The way his gaze sweeps the towering pines, how his nostrils flare as he scents the rich earth and clean mountain air, the subtle shift in his posture as he takes in the sheer vastness of our territory.

Do you see what I see? I wonder. *Do you see the beauty and possibility of this place? Does it feel like home, or another cage?*

There's a tightness in my chest I don't want to examine too closely—a desperate need for him to understand why it's worth protecting, why I've chosen to settle here.

You want him to stay. The admission whispers through my mind before I can stop it. *You want him to choose this. Choose us. Choose you.*

My wolf whines softly, pressing images at me of Kier running these trails, learning our territory, finding his place among our people. It's a fantasy I have no right to entertain, but seeing the careful way he studies everything around us, I can't help a small part of me from hoping.

"Welcome back, Beta Lithia," Levi says formally, his role as Gamma, third in command, momentarily overtaking his personal feelings.

The journey through Shadowmist territory is both familiar and strange. Trees I've known since childhood seem taller, streams deeper, the mountain paths wilder after my absence.

By mid-afternoon, we encounter the first border patrol— four wolves who shift into human form when they recognize me, their faces transformed by disbelief and joy.

"Beta," their leader gasps, dropping to one knee. "Moon be praised."

"Up, Tomas," I say, uncomfortable with the deference. "I'm still just Lithia."

"News will spread fast now," Levi says as we continue our journey. "Ryker will know we're coming before we reach the den."

Sure enough, as we approach the final ridge overlooking the main den, I see a welcoming party assembled at the base of the stone steps carved into the mountainside. My heart leaps at the sight of familiar faces—pack members waiting with barely contained excitement.

Levi moves closer to my side, his hand coming to rest at the small of my back. "Your pack awaits," he says, his voice low and intimate.

I feel Kier's eyes on us, but when I glance back, his expression is carefully neutral. Only the slight tension in his jaw betrays his awareness of Levi's possessive gesture.

As we ascend toward the waiting pack, Levi never leaves my side, his hand a constant pressure at my back, guiding me forward as if I might disappear without his touch.

The contact feels wrong—too possessive, too claiming for something I've never offered him. My skin crawls under his palm, every nerve ending wanting to pull away from the unwelcome intimacy. It's not that Levi's touch is unpleasant exactly, but it's *not Kier's*, and that difference feels like a betrayal of something I can't even name.

I find myself hyperaware of the space between Kier and me, the deliberate gulf he's maintained since we encountered Levi. Gone is the easy closeness we'd found during our weeks together, the casual touches and shared warmth that had become as natural as breathing. Now he walks behind us, close enough to offer protection but far enough to make his message clear—whatever intimacy we'd shared belongs to the road, not to real life.

The loss of his nearness feels like a physical ache, even as a treacherous part of me whispers that this is exactly what I wanted. *Separation. Safety. Protection from feelings that could destroy me.* I should be grateful for the space, relieved that the temptation to fall further has been removed.

So why does it feel like I'm bleeding internally?

This is what you wanted, I remind myself firmly. *No attachments. No vulnerabilities. No one else to lose.*

But my wolf whines in protest, pressing against my consciousness with images of Kier's hands on my skin, his voice keeping me sane in the darkness. The rational part of me knows this separation is necessary—I'm Beta of Shadowmist, I have responsibilities, I can't afford the luxury of caring about someone who'll eventually leave.

The irrational part of me wants to turn around, shove Levi away, and pull Kier close enough to feel his heartbeat against mine.

Behind us, I can feel Kier's eyes on me, but when I risk a glance back, his expression is shuttered—the face of a man who's already begun the process of letting go. Just like I wanted him to.

My morose thoughts are interrupted by my pack. The reunion that follows is a blur of embraces, tears, and questions. We're bustled into the healing chambers where Elena, the head healer, starts to work on us. Elias, our head of security, arrives with his tools. It takes him a few minutes to work out the best way to remove the cursed cuffs, but soon they're falling away, freeing us from our silver prison.

Things move quickly after that. Dane, my twin brother, crushes me in his arms. Kitara and Ryker arrive, greeting me with joyous news of their impeding pup. Pack members press close, seeking reassurance that I've truly returned.

A wolf tries to comb the tangled mess that is my hair to check the cuts on my scalp, but I wave them off and reach for a razor. It takes barely any time to shave my hair.

Far easier to wait for hair to grow back than to deal with the multitude of people touching me.

Elena runs fingers over my ribs. "The cut is healing nicely, but the ribs will need to be rebroken and adjusted." She places a hand on my shoulder. "Without the silver cuffs, your healing should take less than a week."

I close my eyes. "Get it over with then. Might as well start the healing now."

Her touch is brutal and the pain rough, but I've lived through worse.

I catch the subtle shift in Kier's posture—shoulders pulling back, jaw tightening almost imperceptibly. His golden eyes flick to where Levi's fingers interlace with mine, and something dark flashes across his features before he masks it behind polite neutrality. The wolf in him recognizes the territorial display for what it is, even if he chooses not to respond to it.

I hesitate, wondering if I should remove my hand, but one glance at Levi's face and I decide to let him be. I don't have the energy to deal with him today.

Kier earns grudging respect for his restraint. A lesser wolf might have snarled, might have made a scene in front of my Alpha. Instead, he inclines his head respectfully to Ryker, his voice steady as he responds to questions about our escape.

But I can see the cost of that control in the rigid line of his spine, the way his hands curl into loose fists at his sides. He's letting Levi stake his claim without challenge, and something twisted and contrary inside me wishes he wouldn't.

Let the man piss where he thinks his territory may be. He'll soon realize I'm no one's to claim.

"Shadowmist welcomes you, Kier," Ryker says, his voice carrying the weight of Alpha authority. "Any who aids our Beta is friend to our pack."

Kier inclines his head respectfully. "Thank you, Alpha."

"Kier was in the cell beside mine," I explain, glancing at the copper-haired wolf. "Another of Thaddeus's prisoners. We kept each other sane. Talked through the walls when the guards weren't around. Then Thaddeus fell." I touch my chest. "I felt it—we all did. The power shift resonated through all territories. The guards were distracted, arguing about what it meant for them. Zella came for a bit, stirring up leadership trouble. It was then that Kier managed to break free. He could have run..." I swallow. "Instead, he came back for me."

My gaze meets Kier's, and we share a moment of understanding. I feel Levi tense beside me, but whatever he's feeling matters little to me.

"You escaped while wounded and in silver?" Kitara asks. She's small for a wolf, plump and curvy with a shock of long brunette hair. I suspect she's the most powerful seer alive— capable of eclipsing even Prudence.

"I made a promise to my Alpha and his mate. Death wouldn't release me from that oath." I shift, wincing. "But that's not what's important. What matters is what I learned while in captivity."

Ryker leans forward. "What did you learn?"

Unlike his small mate, Ryker is a towering and scarred wolf. His different colored eyes meet mine, one burning amber gold, the other a blood crimson. His black hair falls to his shoulders, threaded with gray at the temples.

"The betrayal goes deeper than Zella. There's a faction— wolves from multiple territories who believed in Thaddeus's vision of control and hierarchy. They're organizing, planning to disrupt the council system before it can fully establish."

Kitara's hand moves to her belly, and the protective gesture is not lost on me.

"The facility where they held us housed at least three seers," Kier adds. "All kept separate, all heavily guarded."

"Other seers?" Kitara asks.

Kier nods. "Not wolf though. One is a bear, another human. I'm not sure about the third."

Ryker's expression hardens. "Names? Locations?"

"Some," I confirm. "Enough to begin hunting them." I attempt to shift position and grimace. Both Levi and Kier move to help me, their hands overlapping before they exchange a look.

Down, boys.

"But that can wait until I've recovered enough to lead the hunt myself," I finish, waving the men off.

"Rest first," Kitara tells me. "Heal. We'll discuss the details when you're stronger."

I want to protest, but the pain in my side has me nodding.

Ryker rests a hand briefly on my shoulder—a rare gesture of affection. "Kitara is right. Rest now. That's an order."

A ghost of a smile touches my lips. "Yes, Alpha."

They leave and the medical team resume their checks and balances, poking and prodding until I feel like a porcupine.

"All right, that's enough," I snap, pushing away another needle. "Just let me sleep. All of you, out." I point my finger at Levi. "That includes you."

He glares at Kier, who's laying on the bed beside mine. "What about him?"

"Do you have silver poisoning?" I ask Kier, now done with Levi's theatrics.

He checks his wrists which are mattered scars from the cuffs. "Looks like it."

"Then you can stay." I raise my chin, glaring at Levi. "Out, Levi. Now."

He slinks off, shooting daggers at Kier as he goes.

"That gonna be a problem?" Kier asks when we're finally alone.

"Not if I can help it."

He nods. "So, about last night…"

It's my turn to glare at him.

"Right, got it." He pretends to zip his lips.

I don't for a minute believe him.

CHAPTER

NINETEEN

The healing chambers are quiet as the silver light of dawn filters through narrow windows carved into the stone. I've been here two days, mostly sleeping as my body purges the last of the silver from my system. Elena warned I'd have a fever, and the terrible chills then heat finally broke sometime in the night, leaving me weak but clearheaded for the first time since our arrival.

I trace the newly healed skin at my wrists, marveling at how quickly my wolf has repaired the damage now that the silver restraints are gone. The constant burn that had become my companion is just a memory, though sometimes I still wake reaching for the collar that's no longer at my throat.

A soft knock interrupts my thoughts. Before I can answer, the door swings open, revealing my brother's tall frame.

"Dane," I say, smiling a welcome. "Come in."

He steps inside, closing the door quietly behind him. We're twins, but not identical—where my hair was white-blonde before I shaved it, his is a shade darker, more gold than silver. His eyes are the same pale blue as mine, though set in a face that's all sharp masculine angles and stubborn determination.

"You're supposed to be resting," he says, dropping into the chair beside my bed. He picks up one of the maps I've been examining.

I snatch it back, smoothing it out on my lap. "I've been resting for two days."

"And Elena says you need at least five more." He leans forward, elbows on his knees. "How are you? Really?"

I consider lying, giving him the standard "I'm fine" that I've been offering everyone else. But this is Dane—my twin, my other half. He'd know the lie before it fully left my lips.

"I don't know," I admit. "Sometimes it doesn't feel like I escaped, and I start to question if all of this is real."

He reaches for my hand. "You did, though. You're home."

"I know." I squeeze his fingers.

We sit in comfortable silence. Even as children, we never needed many words to understand each other. After our parents' deaths, that connection had only deepened—grief making us inseparable.

"I thought you were dead," he says finally, his voice cracking slightly. "When we couldn't find you, when the days turned to weeks and then months…"

"I'm sorry."

"Don't." He shakes his head. "Don't apologize for surviving. I just—" He breaks off, looking away. "I just wish I'd been there when you needed me."

"And what? Been captured too?" I bump his shoulder with mine. "You're lucky you weren't. You'd have hated the gruel they fed us."

"But it should have been me in that prison. I'm just a hunter. You're the Beta."

I frown. "You're not 'just' anything, Dane. And if it had been you, I'd have torn the mountains apart stone by stone to find you."

"I tried," he whispers, and the raw guilt in his voice

makes my chest ache. "Every day, I tried. But there was nothing. No trail, no scent, no leads."

"Zella covered her tracks well."

His expression darkens at the traitor's name. "Ryker has hunting parties tracking her movements. When they find her—"

"When they find her, I want to be there," I cut in. "I want to be the one to end her."

"You've changed."

"Three months in a cage will do that to a wolf." I pause, my mind drifting to copper hair and golden eyes. *Three months changed me,* I think. *But what about three years? What was Kier like before they broke him down and rebuilt him into someone who talks to ghosts?*

The thought sends an unexpected pang through my chest. I've seen glimpses of who he might have been—in his easy humor, his protective instincts, the way he moves with lethal grace despite years of captivity. But how much of the man I'm falling for is real, and how much is just survival carved into human shape?

What dreams did they steal from him? What hopes did they bury under silver and stone?

The questions feel too intimate, too personal for someone I'm supposed to be keeping at arm's length. But I can't shake the image of a younger Kier, maybe less scarred, less guarded, with laughter that came easier and eyes that hadn't seen quite so much darkness.

Stop it, I order myself. *It doesn't matter who he was. It only matters who he is now.*

"It's more than that." Dane tilts his head, examining me with the same careful attention that's made him our pack's best tracker. "It's the way you carry yourself. You've always been ready for an attack, but this is something else."

I look away, uncomfortable under his scrutiny. "Let's change the subject. "

"Fine. We can talk about the nomad," he says simply. "Kier."

My pulse jumps at his name, an involuntary reaction I hate myself for. "What about him?"

"What's really between you?"

"He helped me escape," I say, keeping my voice neutral. "We survived together. That creates a bond."

Dane's expression tells me he's not buying my dismissal. "Lithia, this is me you're talking to. I saw how you looked at him when you arrived. How he watches you."

I sigh, running a hand over my freshly shaved head. The bristle of short hair against my palm is strange after years of long locks.

"It doesn't matter what it is," I say finally. "I'm Beta. My responsibility is to the pack."

"The pack doesn't need you to be alone. Look at Ryker and Kitara. Their bond makes them stronger, not weaker."

"That's different. They're true mates."

"And what if Kier is yours?"

The question catches me off guard. My wolf stirs, pressing forward with a low whine of longing that I ruthlessly suppress.

"He's not," I say, more sharply than intended. "And even if he was… you know why I can't."

Dane's expression softens. "Because of Mom and Dad?"

I swallow hard. "Everyone I've ever loved has been taken from me. I won't—I can't risk that again."

"Not everyone," Dane says quietly. "I'm still here."

"And every day I worry that will change too." The admission slips out before I can stop it.

Dane moves from the chair to sit beside me on the bed, wrapping an arm around my shoulders. "We lost them, Lithia. It broke us both. But hiding from love won't protect you from loss."

I lean against him, allowing myself a moment of vulnerability. "It's not that simple."

He sighs. "Just… don't push him away because you're scared. At least admit to yourself what you're feeling."

"And what about Levi?" I ask, changing the subject. "He hasn't exactly been subtle about his intentions."

Dane snorts. "Levi's been in love with you for years. Everyone knew it but you."

"I knew," I correct. "I just chose not to acknowledge it."

"Because of your no-attachment rule?"

"Because he deserves someone who can love him completely." I pull away slightly. "I'm not that person, Dane. I don't think I can ever be that person for anyone."

"Even Kier?"

I don't answer, which is answer enough.

Dane stands, recognizing when I've reached my limit for emotional revelations. "Get some rest. I'll bring you something to eat that isn't Elena's healing broth."

We both make a face. It might be healing, but it tastes about as good as the gruel I left behind.

"Bring me real meat and I'll love you forever," I joke weakly.

He pauses at the door, his expression serious again. "You already do. That's my point, Lithia. You never stopped loving people. You just stopped admitting to it."

After he leaves, I lie back against the pillows, his words echoing in my head. My gaze drifts to the empty bed beside mine where Kier had been for the first day. Elena moved him to a guest chamber in the main den yesterday, claiming he was recovered enough to no longer need her supervision.

I hadn't protested, though my chest had tightened when he'd left. Now the space beside me feels emptier than it should, the silence louder.

You're being ridiculous, I tell myself. *He's just down the hall.*

And this is what you wanted, isn't it? Distance. Space to think clearly without the distraction of his presence.

My wolf disagrees, pacing restlessly beneath my skin. She wants to seek him out, to check on him, to feel his solid warmth beside me as I've grown accustomed to over our weeks of travel.

Stop it, I order her. *We're home now. Things are different.*

But even as I think it, I find my senses straining to catch his scent, to hear his voice among the distant murmurs of pack activity. Without the silver suppressing her, my wolf is stronger, more insistent in her demands.

He's ours, she insists, images of our night together flashing through my mind—his mouth on mine, his hands on my skin.

I force the memories away, focusing instead on the pain in my healing ribs and the mission that awaits me once I'm recovered. I am Beta of Shadowmist. I have responsibilities and obligations that cannot be set aside for the sake of whatever this feeling is.

This will pass, I tell myself. *These feelings are just leftover adrenaline from our escape. Nothing more.*

But as sleep claims me again, it's his face I see behind my closed eyelids, his name that hovers unspoken on my lips.

And I hate myself for every second of weakness.

TWENTY

KIER

I wake before dawn, the remnants of a nightmare still clinging to my consciousness like cobwebs. In my dream, I was back in that cell—walls pressing in, silver burning against my skin, accusing eyes watching me from the shadows.

"You left us there to die," my sister whispers in my mind, her voice as clear as if she were standing beside me.

"You're not real," I mutter, pressing the heels of my hands against my eyes. "You're a memory. A hallucination."

"Then why can you hear me?"

Ants squirm under my skin as the walls close in. Desperate for fresh air, I throw off the blankets and shift. The den is quiet at this early hour—most wolves still sleeping, leaving the corridors empty and peaceful. Outside in the crisp mountain air, I inhale my first real breath since waking.

Three years of captivity taught me to value open spaces, to appreciate the stretch of horizons that seem to never end. The Shadowmist territory unfolds before me—towering pines silhouetted against the lightening sky, mountain peaks crowned with early snow, mist curling through valleys like smoke.

It's beautiful. Perfect, even. The kind of place I might have dreamed about during those endless days of isolation.

But I'm still an outsider here.

My wolf dances from side to side, restless after days of recovery. He doesn't like being surrounded by so many other wolves whose scents carry pack markers that aren't ours.

I know. I feel it too.

Every instinct I have screams that I don't belong—that I should move on before I get too comfortable, before I forget what it means to stand alone.

But there's Lithia.

Just thinking her name makes my chest tighten. We'd leave but for the white-blonde Beta who saved my sanity in that stone hell, who fought beside me to escape, who shared her body and her fears with me under the stars.

She's the woman I'm falling for with terrifying speed.

The woman who's been avoiding me.

I understand why, of course. She's Beta here—she has responsibilities, pack members who need her, a position to maintain. She can't afford the luxury of showing weakness or vulnerability, not when her pack is looking to her for leadership.

Doesn't make it any fucking easier.

My wolf whines in agreement.

With a huff, we pad back to our room and pull-on clothes. I need to stretch my muscles after days of enforced rest. But even I know running through an unfamiliar territory unescorted is a recipe for disaster.

I find my way to the training yard easily enough, grateful for the open space and the chance to work out some of the restlessness that's been building inside me. I begin with simple exercises—push-ups, pull-ups using a sturdy branch that overhangs one corner of the yard, sprints from one end to the other.

My body responds eagerly, muscles loosening as I push

harder. By the time the sun crests the mountain, I'm drenched in sweat but feeling more centered than I have in days.

"Impressive stamina for someone who spent three years in a cell."

I turn to find a tall wolf leaning against the fence, watching me with sharp eyes. The Alpha's presence is unmistakable, a quiet power that fills the space without effort.

Ryker.

"I worked out inside my cell," I reply, grabbing a towel someone left draped over the fence. "Push-ups, mostly. It was one of the only things to do unless you count antagonizing the guards."

"Most wolves wouldn't have survived what you did," he says, his tone matter-of-fact rather than sympathetic. "Three years in silver restraints? I'm not sure I'd be able to do it." His gaze drops to the scars around my wrists. "That kind of fortitude takes something special."

I shrug. "I was too pissed off to die."

Ryker's lips quirk into something approaching a smile. He studies me for a moment, then pushes off from the fence. "Want a real workout? I could use a sparring partner."

The invitation catches me off guard—sparring with the Alpha is no small thing. "You sure? I'm pretty rusty."

"I think you'll manage." There's a glint of challenge in his eyes. "Besides, I like to know the measure of wolves in my territory."

This is a test.

"I assume you've got rules about not maiming guests," I say dryly.

He laughs, the sound surprisingly warm from such an imposing figure. "First blood or yield. Nothing permanent."

"Fair enough."

We move to the center of the yard, circling each other warily. Ryker is built like the predator he is—powerful shoulders, efficient movement, eyes that miss nothing. His reputation as a warrior is legendary, and I can see why.

He strikes first—a quick jab that I barely deflect, followed by a sweep that nearly takes my legs out from under me. I counter with a straight right that he slips away from with insulting ease.

"Not bad," he comments, circling again. "But you're telegraphing your moves. And you're slow."

"I'm definitely out of practice," I admit. "Let's go again." His next attack comes faster, a combination that forces me to give ground. I block the worst of it but take a glancing blow to the ribs that makes me wince.

"Lithia's changed since she returned," Ryker says conversationally, as if we're not in the middle of a fight. I feint left, then drive in with a shoulder check that catches him by surprise. He stumbles back a step before regaining his balance.

"Is this where you tell me not to hurt your Beta?"

"Lithia can take care of herself," he replies, landing a solid hit to my solar plexus that leaves me gasping. "But she's more than my Beta. She's family."

I understand what he's trying to say. This isn't just the Alpha protecting a pack member, this is personal.

"I would never hurt her." I block his next strike and counter with one of my own. "Not intentionally."

"Intentions aren't always enough," Ryker replies, his tone thoughtful rather than accusatory. "Especially for someone who's spent so long alone."

The observation stings because there's truth in it. I've been a nomad for most of my adult life, never staying anywhere long enough to form real attachments. What do I know about commitment, about pack bonds, about the kind of loyalty that keeps a wolf in one place for years?

But I know Lithia. I know what she means to me.

Pissed off now, I unleash a flurry of attacks, driving Ryker back across the yard. He blocks most of them, but I manage to slip past his guard with a strike that opens a small cut above his eye.

First blood.

"Match," I say, stepping back.

Ryker touches the cut, looking at the blood on his fingertips. "Shit. Kitara's gonna give me hell if I come back with this." With his Alpha healing, the cut is already closing. He swipes his hand on his jeans. "You're not as rusty as you claimed."

I shrug. "Survival's a good teacher."

"So it is." He offers his hand, and I take it, surprised by the firm clasp of his fingers around mine. "You're welcome to train with us. The pack could use someone with your skills."

The invitation surprises me. It stretches beyond a simple sparring, to one that offers the opportunity to stay.

I can't help myself. "Playing matchmaker for your Beta, Alpha?"

Ryker's eyes sharpen, all traces of casual conversation gone. "Let me be clear, Kier. I don't invite wolves into my pack because they're fucking someone I care about."

I wince.

"I see a wolf who survived three years in a prison that would have broken most of my wolves in months," he continues, his voice low and serious. "I see you have combat skills sharp enough to draw blood from an alpha—despite your weakness. I see someone who risked his freedom to save one of mine." His mismatched eyes bore into me. "That's what I'm interested in. *Not* who you're sleeping with."

The rebuke is gentle but firm, and I feel properly chastised... and appreciated. It's a weird feeling. "Thanks. I'll consider your offer."

He nods, then turns to leave, but pauses after a few steps.

"For what it's worth," he says, his mismatched eyes holding mine, "I think you'd be good for the pack. And us for you."

He walks away, leaving me alone in the training yard with sweat cooling on my skin.

"They'll never accept you," Adelaide whispers from somewhere behind me. *"Not really. You don't belong here."*

"Shut up," I mutter. "You're not real."

"Neither is this fantasy you're building," she continues. *"A pack, a mate, a home? These aren't for wolves like you, Kier."*

I close my eyes, focusing on the grounding techniques Elena taught me. Blinking open, I start to name five things I can see. The training yard dirt, the wooden fence, a cloud passing overhead, a bird on a branch, the scuff marks on my boots. Then four things I can touch, the rough texture of the fence post, the soft cotton of my shirt, the cool morning air on my skin, the solid earth beneath my feet.

Adelaide fades, but the doubt she planted lingers. Is this all just another dream I've created to escape the reality of what I am—a wolf who doesn't belong anywhere?

"You'll only hurt her in the end," a different voice murmurs —not Adelaide this time, but an older wolf from my original pack. *"Better to leave now, before you cause real damage."*

I push away from the fence, needing to move, to escape the voices that follow me even here in this peaceful place. The den is coming alive now, wolves moving through corridors and courtyards as they begin their day.

I slip through them like a ghost, nodding when someone greets me but not slowing, not engaging. They're polite enough—Ryker has made it clear I'm to be treated as an honored guest—but I can feel their curiosity, their wariness.

I'm still the outsider, the nomad who helped their Beta escape but doesn't truly belong. And I've come after Zella— another stranger who they thought they could trust.

I round a corner and nearly collide with Levi.

"Watch it," he snaps, lips curled back with irritation.

"Sorry," I step back, giving him space. "Wasn't looking where I was going."

He eyes me with barely concealed hostility. "Looking for Lithia?"

His question pissed me off. "No. Just walking."

"Good. She's busy with *pack* business." The message is clear in his tone—she doesn't have time for me.

I could let it go. Should, probably. But his possessive attitude makes my wolf bristle. "I'm sure she can manage her own schedule."

His jaw tightens. "Look, Nomad. I don't know what happened between you two out there in the wilderness, and frankly, I don't care. But you're a guest here. A temporary situation. Don't forget that."

"Believe me," I say quietly, "I know."

Something flickers in his expression—surprise, maybe, at my candor. "Lithia is Beta of Shadowmist. Her duty is to this pack, not to some stray wolf she picked up along the way."

The words are designed to hurt, to put me in my place. But he's picked the wrong wolf to bother. I've faced worse than an insecure pup with a crush.

"You're right " I say, keeping my voice level. "Lithia is dedicated to this pack. It's one of the things I admire most about her." I step closer, not enough to be threatening but enough to make my point. "But you're wrong if you think I'm just passing through. I'm exactly where I want to be."

His eyes narrow. "For now."

"No." I meet his gaze steadily. "For as long as the pack will have me."

The simple truth of it resonates in my chest. I've spent twenty years running—from memories, from attachment, from the risk of losing something that matters. But Lithia matters more than the fear of staying.

And if Ryker's offer is legitimate, this pack might matter more too.

Levi studies me, then shakes his head. "You think you know her. You don't. I've watched her push away every wolf who's tried to get close to her for years. She doesn't let people in."

"She let me in."

"For now," he repeats, but there's a flicker of uncertainty in his eyes. "When we get back to normal, when the excitement of escape fades and reality sets in, she'll remember why she keeps her distance. And where will that leave you?"

It's a question I've asked myself a hundred times since we arrived. What happens when the extraordinary circumstances that brought us together give way to everyday life? When Lithia no longer needs me to survive, will she still want me around?

"I guess we'll find out," I say finally.

He snorts. "I guess we will."

With that, he brushes past me, deliberately bumping my shoulder as he goes. The childish display would be funny if I didn't understand the desperation behind it. He's loved her for years, probably, watching from a distance as she kept everyone at arm's length. And now some nomad has waltzed in and caught her attention.

I can almost sympathize.

Almost.

I continue my wandering, eventually finding myself in the den's main hall. It's a large, open space with high ceilings and massive stone fireplaces at either end. Tables are arranged throughout, some already occupied by wolves eating breakfast or discussing pack business.

My stomach reminds me that I haven't eaten yet today. I hesitate, then make my way to the serving area where platters of food are laid out buffet-style. I fill a plate—eggs, bacon, toast, fruit—and look for somewhere to sit.

Most tables are occupied, wolves clustered in familiar groups, conversation flowing easily between them. I scan the room, feeling increasingly out of place, when a voice calls my name.

"Kier! Over here."

Dane waves from a table near one of the fireplaces. Lithia's twin is sitting with several other wolves I recognize from the security team.

I make my way over, surprised by the invitation.

"Heard you went a round with Ryker this morning," Dane says as I sit down beside him. "And drew first blood."

News travels fast in a pack this tight-knit. "Lucky shot."

One of the other wolves—Felix, I think his name is— snorts. "Lucky shot, my ass. Ryker hasn't lost a sparring match in three years."

"Until today," another adds with a grin.

I shrug, uncomfortable with the attention. "He was probably going easy on me."

"The Alpha doesn't know how to go easy," Dane says, clapping me on the shoulder. "Trust me, if he lost, it's because you earned it."

The conversation shifts to upcoming patrol rotations and preparations for the rescue mission, and I'm content to eat my breakfast and listen. It's... nice. Sitting among wolves who don't seem to mind my presence, who include me in their jokes and stories without making a big deal of it.

I'm halfway through my meal when Lithia enters the hall.

She moves with the confidence of someone who knows exactly who she is and where she belongs. Her white-blonde hair is short fuzz, emphasizing the sharp lines of her face and the paleness of her eyes. She's dressed for business—fitted pants, boots, a top that allows for movement without sacrificing style.

Beautiful. Deadly. Perfect.

She scans the room as she walks, nodding to various pack

members who greet her. When her gaze lands on our table—on me—she pauses for the briefest moment before continuing on her way.

Mate, my wolf growls, frustrated.

But I caught the flicker in her eyes, the slight hitch in her breathing. She's not indifferent—she's deliberately keeping her distance.

She's pushing me away, I realize.

Dane notices my attention shift and follows my gaze to his sister. "She's been in meetings since dawn," he explains. "Planning the rescue mission."

"I figured," I reply, forcing my tone to remain neutral. "Lots to coordinate."

Dane studies me for a moment. I think he's about to say something but instead he turns away, laughing at something Felix has said.

A shiver runs down my back, and I glance over my shoulder to see Lithia approaching our table, her expression carefully neutral as she greets us.

"Morning," she says to the table at large, carefully avoiding direct eye contact with me. "I need volunteers for a reconnaissance run to the eastern facility. We need updated intelligence before we commit to a rescue operation."

Several of the wolves immediately offer their services, and Lithia nods in acknowledgment. "We'll meet in the war room at noon to go over details."

She turns to leave, but I can't let her go so easily.

"No 'good morning' for me, Beta?" I ask, injecting a teasing note into my voice. "I'm wounded."

She stiffens slightly, then turns to face me directly for the first time. "Good morning, Kier. Sleep well?"

"Like a baby," I lie smoothly. "Though my bed felt strangely empty without a certain white-blonde wolf hogging all the blankets."

I hear Dane choke on his drink beside me, and several of

the other wolves suddenly find their breakfasts fascinating. But I keep my eyes on Lithia, watching the subtle play of emotions across her face—surprise, embarrassment, and something that looks suspiciously like longing before she locks it all down behind her Beta mask.

"I'm sure you'll manage," she says dryly, but there's a hint of color in her cheeks that wasn't there before.

"Oh, I'm managing just fine," I reply with a deliberate wink. "But if you find yourself with a few minutes to spare, I'd love to show you what Ryker taught me this morning."

Her eyebrow arches. "You've been training with the Alpha?"

"Got to stay sharp somehow." I take a bite of toast, maintaining eye contact. "Though I'm open to other forms of exercise if you have suggestions."

The double entendre isn't lost on her. Her eyes narrow, but I catch the subtle quirk of her lips—not quite a smile, but close.

"I'll keep that in mind," she says finally. "Noon, war room. Don't be late."

With that, she turns and strides away, her posture perfect but her scent carrying notes of arousal and frustration that make my wolf preen with satisfaction.

Still want us, he rumbles.

Dane nudges me with his shoulder. "I think my sister might murder you later."

"Worth it," I reply, watching her disappear through the hall's main doors. "Besides, she can try."

The other wolves at the table are watching me with expressions ranging from amusement to grudging respect. Felix lets out a low whistle.

"Either you're the bravest wolf I've ever met," he says, "or the most suicidal."

"Little of both," I admit, returning to my breakfast with renewed appetite.

"You'll only hurt her in the end," Adelaide whispers from somewhere behind me. *"Better to let her go."*

Shut up, I tell the voice firmly. *You're not real. She is.*

"So Kier," Dane pokes his fork toward me. "Think you could keep up on a perimeter run?"

My wolf ripples eagerly under my skin.

"Just watch me."

CHAPTER
TWENTY-ONE

I'm done lying in bed like a lady of leisure.

The silver restraints are gone, my ribs are healed, and my wolf paces restlessly beneath my skin, desperate to move, to hunt, to *do* something useful.

I stand in the main council chamber, maps spread across the massive oak table that's served Shadowmist's leadership for three generations. The familiar weight of authority settles on my shoulders as pack members file in—security chiefs, trackers, senior wolves, all looking to me for direction.

This is where I belong.

"Beta," Dane greets me, taking his usual seat to my right. My twin's presence is a comfort, his steady energy helping to ground me after months of uncertainty.

Elias settles across from me, his weathered face grave. "Good to have you back in full capacity, Lithia."

I nod, checking the positioning of the maps one final time. "Let's get started."

The door opens, and my chest tightens as Levi enters. He's positioned himself as my shadow since my return, appearing wherever I am with convenient excuses. Need an escort to the armory? Levi volunteers. Someone to carry maps? Levi's already reaching for them. A guard for my morning run? Levi falls into step beside me without being asked.

Meanwhile, Kier has made himself scarce. I haven't seen him since Elena discharged him from the medical bay two days ago, though I find myself listening for his voice in the corridors, catching myself looking for copper hair in crowds. The guest quarters feel impossibly far away, even though I know exactly where he is—two doors down from my own room, close enough that I should be able to sense him but somehow feeling like he's on the other side of the world.

The contrast between Levi's overwhelming presence and Kier's conspicuous absence sits like a stone in my chest. One wolf won't leave me alone, and the other seems perfectly content to pretend our weeks together never happened.

Which is what you wanted, I remind myself, but the thought feels hollow.

I find my senses straining to catch his scent, to hear his voice among the distant murmurs of pack activity. Without the silver suppressing her, my wolf is stronger, more insistent in her demands.

Where is he? she whines.

We're not his responsibility anymore, I tell her firmly. *We're home now. Things are different.*

But even as I think it, I ache for the easy companionship we'd found on the road, the way he'd appeared whenever I needed him without being asked.

Levi takes the chair immediately to my left, close enough that his knee brushes mine when he settles. The contact is deliberate, possessive, and entirely unwelcome.

"Levi," I acknowledge coolly. "I didn't assign you to this briefing."

His jaw tightens, but he doesn't move. "As Gamma, I have a right to be here."

Technically true, though he's been using his rank to justify a lot of unwanted proximity lately. I let it slide for now—

picking this battle in front of the others would undermine pack unity.

Ryker and Kitara arrive together, his hand protective at the small of her back as he guides her to the head of the table. As if my thoughts have conjured him, behind them walks Kier. My pulse jumps at the sight of him.

He looks good. Better than good. His copper hair has been trimmed since our return, the unruly waves now tamed but still catching the light with hints of bronze and gold. He's traded his makeshift travel clothes for clean pants and a dark shirt that emphasizes the breadth of his shoulders and the lean strength of his frame. The shadows under his eyes have faded, and his golden gaze is clear and alert—no longer haunted by silver poisoning or the weight of captivity.

But it's more than his physical recovery that catches my attention. There's a confidence in his bearing now, a sense of belonging that hadn't been there during our first days back. He moves through the room like he has every right to be here

"I've asked Kier to join us," Ryker announces, settling into his chair with fluid grace. "His knowledge of their operations will be invaluable for planning our response."

Levi's spine stiffens. "Alpha, with respect, this is pack business. I think—"

"This conversation concerns facilities where he was held captive for three years," Ryker cuts him off, his tone carrying a warning edge. "Kier's experience makes him essential to this briefing."

"He's not Shadowmist," Levi presses, his yellow eyes flashing. "He has no oath to this pack, no—"

"He has my trust," I interrupt sharply, turning to face my Gamma. "Which should be enough."

Kier doesn't bristle at the challenge or try to defend his right to be here. Instead, he simply moves to an empty spot at the table, his attention focused on the maps spread before us.

"Report, Beta," Ryker says, his tone making it clear the discussion about Kier's presence is over.

I stand, pointing to the largest map, grateful for Kier's steady presence even as I feel Levi seething beside me. "Based on what Kier and I observed during our captivity, Thaddeus's network is far more extensive than we initially believed."

Murmurs of concern ripple through the assembled wolves.

"The facility where we were held is here," I continue, marking several locations with red pins. "But there's at least one other installation—"

"Two," Kier corrects quietly, stepping forward to point at the map. "There's another compound east of the main site."

"The scope of their operation extends beyond wolf-kind," I continue, placing different colored pins. "They held a bear seer named Adelaide—no older than sixteen. A human seer called Prudence with a sick infant daughter. At least one fae we couldn't identify." I meet each pair of eyes around the table. "I have no doubt there were many others."

"How many prisoners total?" Kitara asks.

"Unknown. The facility was compartmentalized—we couldn't see or scent others beyond our immediate section." The memory of those walls, the silver burns, the desperate voices in the darkness makes my wolf snarl. "Kier?"

"Conservative estimate across all facilities?" Kier looks to me, deferring to my leadership even as he provides expertise. "Sixty to eighty. But that's based on what I could observe. The actual number could be much higher."

"So we're looking at hundreds of missing persons," Elias finishes grimly.

Ryker leans forward. "What was their operation like?"

I flip to another map, this one hand-drawn from memory. "The facility where we were held had rotating shifts of twelve guards total. Three levels, heavily fortified, with silver-lined cells designed to prevent shifting."

"Fourteen guards," Kier corrects quietly, stepping forward to point at the map. "There were two additional rovers who moved between facilities."

"The cells were silver-lined to prevent shifting." I trace the escape route we took. "This was their weak point—"

"Was," Kier emphasizes, spreading another hand-drawn schematic on the table. "But they'll have reinforced it by now. They always adapted after escape attempts." His finger traces new defensive positions. "Here and here—they'll have added guard posts. And motion sensors along this corridor."

Elias leans forward, studying Kier's detailed drawings. "How can you be certain?"

"Because I tried to escape fourteen times," Kier says matter-of-factly. "Each time, they improved their security based on my attempt. By my last try, they had the place locked down tighter than a vault."

Murmurs ripple through the assembled wolves.

"The guard rotations follow a specific pattern," Kier continues, pulling out another sheet. "They change shifts every eight hours, but there's a fifteen-minute window during the transition where coverage is thinner. And every third week, they run equipment maintenance that requires them to be down to only two guards for a full shift."

"You memorized all of this?" Dane asks, impressed.

"When you have nothing but time and desperation, you notice patterns. The question is whether they maintain the same operational security at their other facilities."

"You want to plan a rescue?" Dane asks.

"Yes," I say firmly. "Every day we delay, more innocent people suffer." Images of Prudence's terrified face flashes through my mind. "I volunteer to lead the first team."

"Absolutely not," Levi says immediately, his hand moving to cover mine where it rests on the table. "You've barely recovered from your own captivity."

I jerk my hand away, anger flaring. "I'm perfectly capable of making my own decisions, Gamma."

"Your judgment may be compromised," he presses, his yellow eyes intense. "You've been through trauma. You need time to—"

"I need to do my job," I snap, standing abruptly. "Which is protecting this pack and the innocent people I failed to save."

The room falls silent, tension crackling between us. I can feel every pair of eyes on us, assessing, judging. Levi's presumption undermines my authority in front of wolves I lead.

Ryker's voice cuts through the silence, cold as winter steel. "Beta Lithia will determine her own fitness for duty. The Alpha makes deployment decisions, not the Gamma."

Levi's jaw works, but he inclines his head stiffly. "Of course, Alpha."

I resume my seat, fighting to project calm control. "As I was saying—rescue operations are a priority, but they require careful planning." I look directly at Ryker. "We can't afford another ambush like the one that took me."

"Agreed," Ryker says. "I want reconnaissance teams to scout each known location before we commit to action. Meanwhile, we'll reach out to other supernatural communities—bears, fae, covens. If this network spans multiple species, our response needs to as well."

"Timeline?" I ask.

"Two weeks for initial reconnaissance. If we find actionable intelligence, we'll move sooner." His mismatched eyes—one amber, one red—fix on me. "But I want experienced teams only. Volunteers who understand the risks."

I nod, already mentally assembling the roster. "I'll coordinate with our allies—"

"I'll assist," Levi interrupts, leaning closer. "Beta

responsibilities are significant. You shouldn't shoulder them alone."

The protective tone in his voice makes my teeth clench. "I've been Beta for five years, Levi. I think I can manage."

His hand finds my shoulder, fingers squeezing in what others might interpret as supportive contact. To me, it feels like a claim being staked.

"Of course," he says smoothly. "I just want to ensure you have all the support you need."

I force myself not to shrug off his touch, though my wolf paces in agitation. Making a scene would only give him more opportunities to play the concerned protector.

"We'll coordinate through normal channels," I say neutrally.

The meeting continues for another hour, covering patrol schedules, alliance communications, resource allocation. Through it all, Levi maintains his hovering presence— adjusting maps I can reach perfectly well myself, offering opinions on decisions that fall within my purview, generally treating me like a fragile thing that needs constant care.

I catch Kier watching this display with something unreadable in his golden eyes. When Levi leans over me to point at a location I can see perfectly well, Kier's jaw tightens almost imperceptibly. But he says nothing, doesn't challenge or interfere—just observes with the patience of a wolf who knows when to pick his battles.

By the time we adjourn, my patience is razor-thin.

"Lithia," Ryker says as the others begin to file out. "A word?"

Kier moves to Kitara's side as she rises carefully from her chair, offering his arm for support. "May I escort you back to your quarters?" he asks with quiet courtesy.

"Thank you," Kitara says, accepting his assistance with a grateful smile. As they reach the door, I catch her leaning closer to him, saying something too low for me to hear.

Whatever it is makes Kier's gaze flick back to me for just a moment before he nods to whatever she's said.

Then they're gone, leaving just Ryker and me in the chamber—and Levi, who lingers near the door like he's hoping to be invited to stay.

Ryker's expectant stare finally drives Levi from the room.

"How are you really?" Ryker asks once we're alone. "Fine. Healed. Ready to get back to work." I organize the maps with perhaps more force than necessary. "Though apparently my Gamma thinks I'm made of glass."

"Levi's... protective instincts have intensified since your return," Ryker says carefully.

"Protective?" I snort. "He's acting like he owns me."

"Do you need me to speak with him?"

The offer tempts me, but I shake my head. "I can handle Levi. He'll get the message eventually."

Ryker's expression suggests he doubts this, but he doesn't push. "And the nomad? Kier?"

My heart skips, though I keep my voice steady. "What about him?"

"He's been keeping to the guest quarters. Staying out of pack business." Ryker tilts his head. "But I sense there's more to his story."

"He saved my life." I meet my Alpha's gaze directly. "Whatever debt we owe him, it's significant."

"That's not what I'm asking about."

Heat creeps up my neck, and I curse my fair complexion for making every emotion visible. "I don't know what you mean."

"Lithia." Ryker's voice gentles. "You've served this pack faithfully for years. Your personal happiness matters to me— to all of us."

I stand abruptly, needing distance from his too- perceptive stare. "My duty is to this pack. Nothing else matters."

"Your parents' death was a tragedy," he says quietly. "But it doesn't mean you have to live your entire life in isolation."

"I'm not isolated. I have the pack."

"You have a responsibility as Beta, yes. But I don't expect you to martyr yourself. There's a difference."

I gather the maps, using the task to avoid his gaze. "Is there anything else, Alpha? I have patrol reports to review."

He sighs, recognizing dismissal when he hears it. "Just... consider that maybe it's time to let someone else carry some of your burdens."

After he leaves, I slump in my chair, rubbing my temples against the headache building behind my eyes. Every conversation lately seems designed to poke at wounds I've spent years learning to ignore.

The pack needs me focused, I remind myself. *Not be distracted by impossible wants.*

But as I work through patrol schedules and reconnaissance plans, my mind keeps drifting to copper hair and golden eyes, to gentle hands and a voice that kept me sane in the darkness.

Two doors down, my wolf whispers. *He's two doors down the hall.*

I know exactly where Kier is at any given moment—an awareness that's grown stronger since our escape. It's as if some invisible thread connects us across space. When he's in the training yards, I can feel the pull southward. When he's in the guest quarters, it's a warm pressure to the east.

Mate bond, my wolf insists, but I push the thought away.

There's been no claiming ceremony to judge if he's my mate. And there won't be—not for me.

The sun sets while I work, the council chamber growing dim around me. I switch on the lights, determined to finish the shift schedules before I rest. The work is familiar and comforting.

A soft knock interrupts my concentration.

"Come in," I call, expecting one of my security chiefs with an update.

Instead, Levi enters carrying a tray of food. "You missed dinner," he says, setting it on the table beside my papers. "I brought you something."

The gesture is thoughtful, but his presumption grates. "Thank you, but I can feed myself."

"When you remember to," he says, pulling up a chair close to mine. Too close. "You've been pushing yourself since you returned. It's not healthy."

I set down my pen deliberately. "Levi, we need to discuss something."

"Of course." He shifts closer, his knee pressing against mine. "I've been wanting to talk to you as well."

"Have you?" I lean back, putting distance between us. "Because I get the impression you've been doing more than talking. You've been hovering."

His brow furrows. "I've been supporting you. After what you've been through—"

"What I've been through was imprisonment and torture," I say flatly. "I know exactly what I've been through because I was there. I don't need a keeper."

"That's not what I'm trying to be." His hand reaches for mine, and I pull it away. "Lithia, I care about you. More than I think you realize."

"I realize perfectly well what you think you feel," I say carefully. "But it doesn't change anything."

"Doesn't it?" He leans forward, intensity radiating from every line of his body. "I searched for you every day. Every. Single. Day." His voice cracks slightly. "Do you have any idea what it did to me, thinking you were dead?"

The raw pain in his words makes my chest ache, but I can't let sympathy weaken my resolve. "I'm grateful for your efforts. Truly. But—"

"I love you," he interrupts, the words hanging between us

like a bridge I'm not willing to cross. "I've loved you for years. I thought maybe now that you've seen how precious life is, how quickly it can be taken... maybe you'd be willing to consider—"

"No." The word comes out harder than I intend, but I don't soften it. "Levi, you're pack. You're family. But that's all you'll ever be."

His face cycles through hurt, anger, disbelief. "Because of him, isn't it? The nomad."

"This has nothing to do with Kier."

"Doesn't it?" Levi stands abruptly, beginning to pace. "I've seen how you look at him. How you respond when his name comes up."

"That's enough," I say sharply, rising to face him. "My personal decisions are not your concern."

"Everything about you is my concern," he fires back. "You think I don't know you? I've watched you hold yourself apart from everyone for years. And then some random nomad shows up and suddenly—"

"Suddenly what?" I challenge. "Suddenly I'm tired of being alone?" The admission slips out before I can stop it.

Levi goes very still. "So there is something between you."

I close my eyes, cursing my loose tongue. "It doesn't matter what there is or isn't. This conversation is over."

"Like hell it is." He moves closer, his size and presence suddenly overwhelming in the confined space. "You think you can just dismiss me? Dismiss what we could have together?"

"There is no 'we,' Levi. There never has been."

"Because you won't let there be." His voice drops to something rougher, more dangerous. "Because you're too scared to take a chance on something real."

"Real?" I laugh bitterly. "You want to know what's real? Real is watching your parents die protecting you. Real is understanding that everyone you love becomes a target. Real is choosing duty over desire because it's the only choice that doesn't end in heartbreak."

"And what about what I want?" he demands. "What about my choice in this?"

"You'll find someone else," I say as gently as I can manage. "Someone who can give you what you deserve."

"I don't want someone else." His hand cups my cheek, thumb brushing over the scar that runs from temple to jaw. "I want you. Scars and walls and stubborn independence. All of it."

For a moment, I let myself feel the warmth of his touch, the genuine emotion behind his words. Levi is good, strong, and loyal. He's been my friend for years, someone I trust implicitly, someone I care about deeply.

But caring isn't the same as being in love.

The realization sits heavy in my chest—not just because I can't return his feelings, but because I finally understand the difference. What I feel for Levi is warm, familiar, rooted in years of friendship and shared experiences. It's comfortable affection, the kind that comes from knowing someone completely and appreciating their worth.

What I feel for Kier burns differently—hotter, deeper, with an intensity that terrifies me. It's not just attraction or gratitude or the bond forged through shared trauma. It's something that reaches into the darkest corners of my soul and demands I acknowledge it, something that makes my wolf pace with recognition and need.

That's the difference, I realize with painful clarity. With Levi, I could choose to love him if I tried hard enough. With Kier, I don't have a choice at all.

And that's exactly why I can't hurt Levi by pretending. He deserves someone who burns for him the way I burn for the copper-haired nomad. He deserves a mate who chooses him not out of duty or fondness, but out of the kind of desperate, consuming need that can't be reasoned away or controlled.

I can't give him that. I won't lie to either of us and pretend I can.

This isn't that life, and I'm not that woman.

I step back, removing his hand from my face. "I'm sorry, Levi. Truly. But my answer is no."

His expression hardens, hurt transforming into something colder. "Fine. But don't expect me to stand aside and watch you throw yourself away on some nomad who'll leave the moment things get difficult."

"Kier isn't—" I catch myself before I can reveal too much.

"Isn't what?" Levi's eyes sharpen. "Isn't temporary? Isn't going to break your heart when he moves on to the next territory?" He shakes his head. "You're smarter than this, Lithia. Don't let desperation make you do something you'll regret."

Anger flares in my chest. "Get out."

"Lithia—"

"I said get out." My voice carries the full weight of my authority as Beta. "Now."

He stares at me for a long moment, then turns and stalks from the chamber without another word. The door slams behind him hard enough to rattle the frame.

I slump back into my chair, emotionally drained. The food he brought sits untouched, my appetite destroyed by the confrontation.

That went well, my wolf observes dryly.

Shut up.

I try to return to my work, but concentration is impossible. My hands shake slightly as I organize papers, adrenaline from the argument still coursing through my system.

He's not wrong about one thing, my wolf says quietly. *You are scared.*

Of course I'm scared, I snap back. *I have good reason to be.*

Do you? Or are you using fear as an excuse to avoid something that might actually make you happy?

I don't answer, because I'm not sure I can handle the truth.

The night deepens around me as I work, the den settling into quiet. Most of the pack will be asleep by now, leaving only the night watch and insomniacs like myself.

By the time I finish the patrol schedules, exhaustion weighs heavy on my shoulders. I switch off the lights and gather my materials, finally ready to seek my own bed.

The corridors are dimly lit, emergency lighting casting long shadows on the stone walls. My room is at the end of the hall, past the guest quarters where Kier sleeps.

I pause outside his door, my wolf pressing against my consciousness with sudden intensity.

He's awake, she whispers. *Restless. Like us.*

I can feel it—a current of unease, of want, radiating from behind the wooden barrier. My hand rises toward the door without conscious thought, then falls back to my side.

Not tonight. Not when I feel so raw.

I continue to my room, closing the door firmly behind me. The space feels larger than I remember, emptier. The bed that had seemed perfectly adequate for years now feels vast and cold.

I strip out of my clothes mechanically, pulling on a soft sleep shirt that falls to mid-thigh. The routine motions should be comforting, but restlessness coils beneath my skin.

Sleep, I order myself, climbing into bed. *You need rest.*

But sleep doesn't come. I lie in the darkness, staring at the ceiling, hyperaware of every sound in the den. The distant murmur of guards changing shifts. The soft whisper of wind through stone passages. The barely audible creak of someone moving in the room two doors down.

Kier.

My body responds to just thinking his name—skin warming, pulse quickening, an ache building low in my belly. Memories surface unbidden, his thumb brushing across my knuckles before we'd even seen each other, his mouth on mine as fire raged around us, his hands on my body that night in the forest.

I squeeze my eyes shut, willing the images away, but they only grow more vivid. The way he'd looked at me that last night, golden eyes dark with desire. The feel of his fingers inside me, the perfect pressure of his mouth between my thighs, the way he'd whispered filth and praise until I came apart beneath his hands.

My thighs clench involuntarily, a soft whimper escaping my throat.

This is ridiculous. You're a grown woman, not some love-struck teenager.

But my body doesn't care about logic or propriety. Heat pools between my legs, demanding the attention I've been denying it.

Just get it over with, I tell myself. *Take the edge off so you can sleep.*

My hand slides beneath the hem of my sleep shirt, fingers tracing the sensitive skin of my inner thigh. I'm already wet, arousal slicking my fingers as I find the swollen bud of my clit.

Gods, I needed this.

I bite my lip to muffle the sound that wants to escape as I begin to stroke myself, slow circles that send pleasure spiraling through my core. But it's not enough—my body craves more, craves *him*.

I slide two fingers inside myself, arching slightly at the sensation. It's good, but nothing compared to the way Kier had filled me, the way his thick fingers had curved just right.

Kier. His name whispers through my mind as I work myself higher, thumb circling my clit while my fingers thrust in a rhythm that has my breath coming in soft pants.

I let myself remember the weight of his body over mine, the way he'd kissed me like he was drowning and I was air.

The rough velvet of his voice when he called me beautiful, the reverent way his hands mapped every inch of my skin.

The fantasy grows more vivid—I can almost feel his breath against my neck, his lips trailing fire down my throat. My free hand moves to my breast, pinching the sensitive peak through my shirt, imagining it's his mouth instead.

"So perfect," his voice whispers in my memory. *"Let me hear you, baby. Let me feel you come."*

My hips buck against my hand, the familiar tension building low in my belly. I'm close, so close, the pleasure coiling tighter with each stroke.

And then something shifts.

The fantasy becomes suddenly, shockingly real. I can feel him—not just imagine, but actually *feel* his presence, his arousal, his desperate need. The bond between us flares to life like a live wire, connecting us across the space that separates our rooms.

Through that connection, I feel everything. His hand wrapped around his hard length, stroking in time with my own movements. The way his breath catches when he imagines my mouth on him. The desperate way he whispers my name into the darkness.

"Lithia. Gods, Lithia."

The psychic connection intensifies, and suddenly I can see him. Not with my eyes, but with perfect clarity nonetheless—sprawled on his bed, head thrown back in pleasure, his hand working his cock with increasing urgency.

And he can see me too. His golden eyes snap open in the vision, meeting mine across the impossible distance, and I realize he's experiencing the same thing I am.

Mate bond, my wolf says with satisfaction.

The knowledge should terrify me, but I'm too far gone to care. Our eyes lock across the psychic connection as we touch ourselves, sharing every sensation, every spike of pleasure.

"Come for me," he whispers, and I feel the words like a physical caress. *"Let me feel you fall apart."*

The dual sensation—my own building climax and his echoing through the bond—is overwhelming. I feel his pleasure as if it were my own, feel how my image affects him, how desperately he wants to be the one touching me.

"Kier," I gasp, and watch his hand speed up at the sound of his name.

"That's it, baby. Come with me. Let me feel you."

The orgasm hits like lightning, pleasure crashing over me in waves so intense I arch off the bed with a cry I barely manage to muffle. Through the bond, I feel Kier's release echo mine, his pleasure amplifying my own until I can't tell where I end and he begins.

For several heartbeats, we're suspended in shared ecstasy, the bond pulsing between us like a heartbeat. Then slowly, gradually, reality reasserts itself.

I collapse back against my pillows, breathing hard, my body still trembling from the intensity of what just happened. The bond settles to a warm current beneath my skin, no longer the overwhelming flood but a constant, undeniable connection.

See? my wolf says smugly. *Mate.*

I stare at the ceiling, processing what just occurred. Shared orgasms through a psychic bond. The kind of connection that only exists between true mates.

Fuck.

There's no denying it now, no pretending this is just attraction or leftover adrenaline from our escape. The bond is real, powerful, and apparently permanent.

A soft knock at my door makes me freeze.

"Lithia?" Kier's voice, rough with recent pleasure and uncertainty.

I close my eyes, torn between the desperate need to see

him and the equally desperate need to maintain some semblance of control over my rapidly unraveling life.

Let him in, my wolf urges. *Stop fighting.*

My feet move before I make a conscious decision, carrying me to the door. I hesitate with my hand on the latch, knowing that opening it will change everything.

Everything's already changed, I realize. *The bond saw to that.*

I open the door.

Kier stands in the hallway, his hair mussed from sleep, wearing only loose pants that hang low on his hips.

"Well," he says, running a hand through his disheveled hair. "That was either the most intense spiritual experience of my life, or you're about to tell me I'm hallucinating again."

Despite everything, I snort. "We can't just put it down to a wet dream?"

"Hell of a dream." His golden eyes glint with familiar mischief. His gaze tracks over my face, then drifts to my shaved head—the short stubble all that remains of my once long hair. His expression softens with something that looks dangerously like tenderness. "Fuck, you're beautiful,"

My heart gives a little flip, and I hate how much I want him right now.

We stare at each other for a long moment, the bond humming between us like a tuning fork. I can feel his desire, his careful restraint, his desperate need to touch me.

"Can I come in?" he asks, then adds with a crooked smile, "Or should I just stand in this hallway all night making inappropriate comments about our psychic sex life?"

I step aside without a word, and he enters my room, closing the door behind him with a quiet click.

He leans against the door, watching me. "So, we're true mates."

"Apparently."

"How do you feel about that?" His voice is carefully neutral, but I can feel his nervousness through the bond.

I consider the question honestly. Terrified. Exhilarated. Confused. Desperate. "I don't know," I say finally. "This isn't... I never planned for this."

"Plans change," he says gently, taking a step closer. "The question is, what do we do now?"

I look at him—this beautiful, complicated man who saved my life and somehow managed to slip past every wall I've built around my heart. The bond pulses between us, warm and certain and absolutely terrifying.

"I don't know," I repeat, but this time it comes out as a whisper.

He closes the distance between us, his hands coming up to frame my face with infinite gentleness. "We don't have to figure it all out tonight," he murmurs. "But we can't pretend it doesn't exist anymore."

"No," I agree, leaning into his touch despite every instinct that screams danger. "We can't."

"Tomorrow, we'll deal with the pack, with your duties, and with whatever complications this creates." His thumb traces the scar on my cheek. "Tonight, can I just hold you?"

I study his face, seeing no pressure there, no demand for more than I'm ready to give.

"Yeah," I breathe. "But just for tonight."

He smiles then, soft and beautiful, and leans down to brush his lips against my forehead in the gentlest of kisses.

The bond sings between us, and for the first time, I let myself imagine what a future with someone—with Kier— might look like.

It's terrifying.

CHAPTER
TWENTY-TWO
KIER

I might be interested in joining Shadowmist, but twenty years as a lone wolf didn't prepare me for this.

The Shadowmist den pulses with constant activity—wolves moving through corridors, conversations echoing off stone walls, the perpetual hum of pack life that never seems to stop. After three years of silence broken only by screams and torture, followed by weeks of just Lithia's voice, the sheer *noise* sets my teeth on edge.

I lean against the balustrade overlooking the training yard. Below, pack members spar in organized chaos. They move with the easy familiarity of wolves who've known each other for years, finishing each other's movements, communicating with glances and subtle shifts in posture.

I don't belong here.

The thought sits heavy in my chest, a truth I've been avoiding for days. As much as I wish to stay, I can't become another Levi, watching the woman I love ignore me.

Shadowmist has been nothing but welcoming—but hospitality isn't the same as belonging.

A wolf steps beside me carrying two mugs that smell of something strong and bitter. He carries a trace of Lithia's

235

scent. I glance sharply at him, relaxing when I see it's Dane. Lithia's twin has her same sharp bone structure and pale blue eyes, but where she radiates controlled fury, he carries a gentler warmth.

"Thought you might want company," he says, offering me one of the mugs. "You've been keeping to yourself."

I accept the drink—some kind of herbal tea that burns pleasantly down my throat. "Not much of a joiner."

"So I gathered." Dane settles against the balustrade, mimicking my pose. "Though you did fine on those perimeter checks last week. I notice you didn't even complain about the rain like some of our softer pack members."

I smile, remembering the torrential downpour we'd trudged through together. "Your definition of 'light drizzle' needs serious recalibration."

"Hey, I warned you to bring a jacket," Dane grins.

"You said, and I quote, 'maybe grab something in case it gets chilly.' That's not the same as 'prepare for biblical flooding.'"

Dane laughs, the sound surprisingly similar to his sister's. "Semantics. At least you kept up." He takes a long drink before smacking his lips together.

The kid is as subtle as a punch to the face. I wait for whatever question he has to ask me.

"You know, twenty years as a nomad. That's a long time alone."

"No shit."

"Do you miss it?"

I shrug. "It suited me."

"Past tense?"

I take another sip, considering the question. "Your sister has a way of complicating things."

Dane snorts. "That's one way to put it. Lithia's never done anything the easy way." His expression turns serious. "What are your intentions regarding her?"

The directness catches me off guard, though I probably should have expected it. Pack bonds run deep, and twin bonds deeper still.

"Are you asking as her brother or as a member of this pack?"

"Both. And as someone who's just starting to enjoy having you around." Dane's tone shifts, becoming more earnest despite his casual posture. "It would be a shame to have to hate you just when I'm getting used to your terrible jokes."

"My jokes are excellent," I protest with mock offense.

"The pun you made about the elk tracks yesterday was unforgivable and you know it."

I can't help but smile at the memory. "Made you laugh, though."

"A momentary lapse in judgment," Dane counters, but his eyes are warm. He pauses, then adds more seriously, "Look, I care about my sister's happiness. And weirdly enough, I'm starting to care about yours too."

I meet his gaze. "I care about her. More than I've cared about anyone in a very long time."

"That's not what I asked."

Fair enough. I set down the mug, choosing my words carefully. "I want to stay. To be part of this pack, to be with her. But I won't force either situation if I'm not wanted."

"And if she pushes you away? Because she will—it's what she does when she starts catching feelings for something."

"Then I'll push back. Until she believes I'm not going anywhere."

Dane nods slowly. "Good answer." He pauses, then adds, "She's been alone too long. If it's possible to be a nomad in a pack, that's what she is. She's convinced herself that caring equals losing. Our parents died protecting us when we were children. She's never forgiven herself for surviving."

"Survivor's guilt." I know it well.

"Among other things." Dane looks down at the training

yard. "She'll test you, probably sooner than later. Make sure you're ready for it."

Before I can ask what he means, he changes the subject. "Want to spar? I could use the practice, and you look like you need to hit something."

"You really want to take me on?"

He flexes his muscles. "Might as well see if you can hold your own against a Shadowmist wolf."

"I beat your Alpha."

He hesitates then shrugs. "Maybe Ryker's getting old."

I snort. "I'd like to see you say that to his face."

The training yard is busy when we arrive, pairs of wolves working through drills while others watch and offer commentary. Conversations slow when Dane and I step onto the sand, curious gazes tracking our movements.

"Friendly match," Dane announces to the assembled wolves. "First to yield or first blood."

Great. An audience.

I strip off my shirt, noting how several of the watching wolves assess the scars that mark my torso—silver burns, knife wounds, evidence of a life lived hard. Dane does the same, revealing the lean muscle of someone who's spent years tracking through difficult terrain.

We circle each other, taking measure. He's fast, I can tell from the way he moves, but built for endurance rather than power. I have reach and weight advantages, but he's fast and has stamina.

It'll be a close match.

"Begin," someone calls, and Dane strikes.

He's even faster than I expected, darting in with a quick jab that I barely deflect. His follow-up comes immediately—a low sweep designed to take out my legs. I leap back, countering with a straight right that he slips away from.

The watching wolves murmur approval as we settle into a rhythm of attack and defense. Dane fights smart, using his speed to stay out of my reach while landing quick strikes whenever I over-commit. I fight like the nomad I am—aggressive, opportunistic, always looking for the decisive blow.

It's good. Better than good. For the first time since arriving at Shadowmist, I feel like myself.

Dane feints left, then spins right with a backhand that clips my jaw. I taste blood, grin, and surge forward. My shoulder catches him in the chest, driving him back several steps before he recovers his balance.

"Not bad for an old man," he pants, grinning.

"Old man?" I circle him slowly, looking for an opening. "I'm thirty-eight."

"Ancient," he confirms, then lunges.

We grapple, strength against speed, each trying to gain the decisive advantage. The watching wolves call out encouragement and advice, the atmosphere more like play than serious combat. For a moment, I can almost imagine belonging here.

Then Dane gets a grip on my arm and uses his momentum to throw me hard into the sand. I roll, come up spitting dirt, and nod to grant him the win.

"Yield," I say, earning approving nods from the spectators.

"Good match," Dane says, offering me a hand up. "You know your stuff."

"Occupational hazard."

We're cleaning ourselves off when another voice cuts through the ambient noise.

"What a touching display of male bonding."

I turn to find Levi approaching, his expression carrying the kind of predatory satisfaction that makes my wolf bristle. He's flanked by two other wolves I don't recognize, both watching me curiously.

"Levi," Dane acknowledges coolly. "Enjoying the show?"

Levi's yellow eyes fix on me. "I was wondering when our guest would demonstrate what he's capable of."

The emphasis on "guest" isn't subtle, and neither is the message.

"Something on your mind?" I ask, keeping my voice level.

"Just curious about your long-term plans." Levi moves closer, using his size to try to intimidate. "Will you be moving on soon? Or are you planning to make yourself at home indefinitely?"

Several wolves have gone quiet, sensing the tension building between us. Dane shifts position slightly, putting himself where he can intervene if necessary.

"I haven't decided," I say honestly.

"Ah." Levi nods as if this confirms something he suspected. "The life of a nomad. Never staying anywhere long enough to develop real attachments."

The jab hits closer to home than I'd like to admit. "Is there a point to this conversation?"

"Just making sure you understand the dynamics here." Levi's smile is all teeth and no warmth. "Shadowmist takes care of its own. We don't abandon pack members when things get difficult."

Unlike nomads, he doesn't say, but the implication hangs in the air.

Before I can respond, the crowd parts to reveal Lithia approaching. She moves with her characteristic predatory grace, but there's something different about her posture—tenser, more alert. Her silver eyes sweep the assembled wolves before settling on the standoff between Levi and me.

"Is there a problem here?" she asks, her voice carrying the authority of her Beta rank.

"No problem," Levi says smoothly. "Just getting to know our guest better."

Lithia's gaze flicks between us, and I can see her reading the tension in the air. "Kier, how are you settling in?"

"Fine," I say, though we both know it's not entirely true.

"Good." She turns to address the watching wolves. "Training time is over. Find something productive to do."

The crowd disperses with the efficiency of wolves who know better than to argue with their Beta. But Levi doesn't move, his yellow eyes still fixed on me with unmistakable hostility.

"Gamma," Lithia says, her voice carrying a warning edge.

"Beta," he acknowledges, but doesn't retreat. "I was just—"

"I know what you were doing." Her tone cuts off whatever excuse he was preparing. "Don't."

For a moment, the air crackles with competing dominance —Levi's barely contained aggression, Lithia's cold authority, and my own wolf's insistence that I shouldn't need her protection. Then Levi steps back, inclining his head in a gesture that's respectful but grudging.

"Of course, Beta. Excuse me."

He stalks away, his two companions falling into step behind him. But I catch the look he throws back over his shoulder—a promise that this conversation isn't finished.

"Charming fellow," I mutter.

"He has his moments," Lithia says dryly. She looks like she wants to say more, but Dane's presence stops her. "Brother."

"Sister." Dane glances between us, then grins. "I'm gonna go."

The impetuous pup doesn't even bother to make up an excuse. I like him.

After he leaves, silence stretches between Lithia and me. I can feel her studying me, cataloging details the way she would assess a potential threat.

"How are you really?" she asks finally.

"Adjusting." I retrieve my shirt from where I'd discarded it. "Your pack is intense."

"We're close-knit. It can be overwhelming for outsiders."

Outsiders. Even she sees me that way.

"Yeah," I say, pulling the shirt over my head. "I'm getting that impression."

She steps closer, close enough that I can smell her scent—still addictive, still enough to make my pulse quicken despite the frustration building in my chest.

"Kier—"

"Don't." I shake my head, stepping back. "Don't explain pack loyalty to me. I understand what I am here."

"What you are," she says quietly, "is the wolf who saved my life."

"Is that all I'll ever be?"

The question hangs between us, loaded with implications she's not ready to examine. My truth is, I stayed for her. Not for pack loyalty or honor or any noble reason. I stayed because the thought of leaving her behind was unbearable.

But admitting that feels like handing her a weapon she could use to destroy me.

She looks so lost and confused that I take pity on her.

"I should get back to my room," I say instead. "Thanks for the intervention with Levi."

Disappointment flickers across her features before she masks it behind her usual cool control. "Anytime."

I'm halfway to the den entrance when she calls my name.

"Kier."

I turn back, hoping for... what? Some sign that I matter to her beyond gratitude for services rendered?

"Stay safe," she says simply.

Not "stay." Just "stay safe."

"Yeah," I reply. "You too."

The rest of the day passes in a blur of restless energy. I try reading in the pack's library, but the words swim on the page. I attempt to nap, but sleep eludes me. Every time I close my eyes, I'm back in that training yard, feeling like an outsider trying to prove himself worthy of scraps of belonging.

By evening, I'm wound tight as a spring, my wolf pacing beneath my skin. The communal dinner is torture—surrounded by pack members who laugh and tease each other while I sit at the edges, included but not truly part of it.

Lithia sits at the head table with Ryker and Kitara, her posture perfect, her attention focused on pack business. She doesn't look at me once during the entire meal.

Message received.

I escape as soon as it's polite to do so, retreating to my guest quarters like the temporary resident I am. The room feels smaller than usual, the walls pressing in on all sides. I pace from wall to door and back again, my wolf's agitation bleeding into every muscle and nerve.

This is ridiculous. You're a grown man, not some lovesick pup.

But knowing that doesn't help. The truth is, I'm falling for Lithia in ways that terrify me. Not just physical attraction—though gods know that's intense enough—but something deeper. She challenges me, surprises me, makes me want to be better than I am.

And right now, she's doing exactly what Dane warned me she would—retreating behind her walls, pretending what we shared never happened.

I think about her sitting at that head table tonight, keeping her attention firmly on pack business, not once looking my way. Most men might take the hint, might accept the dismissal and walk away wounded. But I've survived three years of torture for a reason. Persistence isn't just my nature—it's how I stayed alive.

She can try to ignore me all she wants, I think with a grim smile. *I've outlasted professional torturers. I can outlast her stubborn denial.*

The next time I catch her glancing my way—and she will, I've seen how she can't help herself—I'll be ready. A wink, a smile, a subtle reminder that I see her game and I'm not going anywhere.

Let her build her walls. I've got nothing but time and determination to climb them.

A sharp knock at my door interrupts my planning.

"It's open."

But instead of Dane with another friendly overture, or one of the other pack members with some invitation I'll politely decline, it's Lithia who steps through the doorway.

She's changed out of her formal Beta attire into simple clothing—dark pants and a fitted shirt that emphasizes her lean strength. Her silver hair catches the lamplight, and her pale eyes are unreadable in the dim illumination.

"We need to talk," she says, closing the door behind her with a soft click.

My pulse spikes, though I try to keep my voice steady. "About?"

"This." She gestures between us.

I lean against the wall, crossing my arms over my chest. "I wasn't aware there was a 'this' to discuss."

Her eyes narrow. "Don't play games with me, Kier. I want to know what you expect from me."

The blunt question catches me off guard. I'd expected deflection, maybe another lecture. Not this direct confrontation.

"I don't expect anything," I say honestly. "You don't owe me anything."

"That's not what I asked."

No, it isn't. She's asking what I *want* from her.

"What do you want me to say, Lithia? That I think about you constantly? That I wake up hard every morning remembering the taste of you? That being near you without being able to touch you is torture?"

Her breath catches, pupils dilating slightly. "Yes. That's exactly what I want you to say."

"Why?"

She's quiet, and I can't resist twisting the knife a little. "Besides, based on tonight's dinner performance, I figured you'd mastered the art of pretending I don't exist. Barely looked in my direction once."

Her jaw tightens. "That's because I couldn't."

"Couldn't what?"

"Couldn't look at you." She takes a step closer, frustration bleeding into her voice. "Because every time I do, I remember everything. How you fed me when I was too weak to get out of bed. How you held me when my ribs were broken and I couldn't take another step. How you nursed me through fever dreams and never once complained."

She shakes her head. "I remember how you put yourself between me and that fire, willing to burn alive rather than let me get hurt. How you had freedom in your grasp—actual freedom after three years of hell—and you threw it away to come back for me."

Fuck.

"I didn't look at you tonight because every time I do, I see the man who puts my needs above his own. I see someone who makes me want to be brave enough to risk everything." Her breath hitches. "And that terrifies me more than any torture they could devise."

She takes another step, until she's standing directly in front of me. Close enough that I can feel the heat radiating from her skin, smell the scent that's been haunting my dreams.

"But tonight I also couldn't look at you," she continues, her voice dropping, "because all I could think about is your mouth between my legs. All I remembered is the way you touched me. The way you made me fall apart. I didn't look at you because I was too busy trying not to come just from smelling your scent across the room."

She reaches up to trace my jaw. "Because I feel the same way. About all of it."

Before I can process what she's said, she's pressing up onto her toes and crushing her mouth to mine.

The kiss is desperate, hungry, full of suppressed need finally cracking apart. I groan into her mouth, my hands gripping her waist to pull her closer.

She tastes like fire and home, like everything I've been denying myself since we arrived at Shadowmist. Her tongue slides against mine with the same fierce intensity she brings to everything, and I'm lost, drowning in sensation.

I back her against the door, pinning her there with my body while my hands map the curves I've been aching to touch. She gasps when I bite down on her lower lip, her nails digging into my shoulders hard enough to leave marks.

"Fuck," I breathe against her mouth, "I've missed you."

"Show me," she demands, her voice rough with need. "Show me how much."

I don't need to be told twice. My mouth trails down her throat, finding the spot that makes her arch against me with a soft cry. Her hands tangle in my hair, holding me against her as I work my way lower, tasting the salt of her skin.

She fumbles with the hem of my shirt, pulling it up and over my head with impatient efficiency. Her palms flatten against my chest, fingernails scraping lightly over old scars in a way that sends fire straight to my cock.

"Bed," I growl against her collarbone. "Now."

But she shakes her head, pressing me back against the opposite wall with surprising strength. "Here. Right here."

Before I can ask what she means, she's dropping to her knees in front of me, her hands already working at the fastenings of my pants.

"Lithia—"

"Shut up," she says, looking up at me with eyes gone dark with lust. "I need this."

Who am I to deny a lady her desires?

My brain shorts out as she frees my cock from my pants, wrapping her fingers around my length with a grip that's firm and sure. The first stroke nearly brings me to my knees, the pleasure so intense it borders on pain.

"Fuck," I gasp, my head falling back against the wall.

She smiles—actually smiles—and leans forward to run her tongue along the underside of my shaft from base to tip. The sensation is indescribable, wet heat and soft pressure that has my vision blurring at the edges.

When she takes me into her mouth, I nearly come on the spot.

My hands find her face immediately, palms cupping her cheeks as she works. One thumb traces the sharp line of her cheekbone while the other smooths over the bristled softness of her shaved scalp. The sensation is new, intimate—nothing between my touch and her skin, no hair to hide behind.

She's not tentative or careful—she takes me deep, her tongue working against me with devastating skill while her hand strokes what she can't fit. It's too much and not nearly enough, pleasure building at the base of my spine with alarming speed.

"Eyes on me," I growl, my voice rough with need. "I need to see you. Need you to see me."

Her pale blue gaze flicks up to meet mine, and the sight of her—lips stretched around my cock, eyes burning with determination and desire—nearly destroys what's left of my control.

"That's it," I breathe, my thumbs stroking over her cheeks. "Fuck, you're perfect. So fucking perfect."

My grip tightens slightly, not controlling but grounding, needing the connection as much as the pleasure.

"Lithia, I'm—fuck, if you don't stop I'm going to—"

She pulls back just long enough to look at me, her lips

swollen and slick. "Good," she says simply, then takes me deeper than before.

The orgasm hits like a freight train, pleasure exploding through every nerve ending as I come hard in her mouth. She doesn't pull away, doesn't flinch, just takes everything I give her with the same fierce determination she applies to everything else.

When the last tremors fade, she sits back on her heels, licking her lips with a satisfaction that nearly has me hard again already.

"Now," she says, rising gracefully to her feet, "we're even."

Before I can form a coherent response, she's straightening her clothes and moving toward the door.

"Wait," I manage, still struggling to think past the haze of post-orgasmic bliss. "Where are you going?"

"Back to my quarters." She pauses with her hand on the door handle. "I have early meetings tomorrow."

"That's it? You're just leaving?"

She turns back to face me, a devilish expression on her face. "Yep."

She slips out the door with a laugh.

This fucking woman. She'll be the death of me.

TWENTY-THREE

"I think we should have a feast," Kitara announces, her hand resting on her growing belly as she studies the scattered maps and reports covering the council table.

I look up from the reconnaissance photos, confused by the non sequitur. "A feast? Now? We're planning a rescue mission, not a celebration."

Ryker's mate smiles, that serene expression that always makes me wonder what future she's glimpsed with her seer abilities. "Precisely why we need one. The pack has been on edge since your return, everyone preparing for battle, worrying about what comes next. A night of good food and music will do wonders for morale."

"Plus," she adds with a knowing look, "it would give everyone a chance to properly welcome Kier to Shadowmist."

I suppress a wince but my wolf huffs in amusement, clearly more appreciative of the Alpha Female's matchmaking than I am.

"Kitara's right," Ryker says, setting down the facility blueprints he's been studying. "The pack needs this."

I want to argue that we don't have time for distractions, but I can see the wisdom in their suggestion. Wolves are pack animals—we draw strength from community and moments of connection that remind us of why we face danger together.

"Fine," I concede. "When?"

"Tonight," Kitara says decisively. "No point in waiting. We have enough food stored, and everyone could use the break from planning."

"That's… soon."

"It's exactly what's needed." She rises from her chair, her pregnancy making the movement slightly awkward. "I'll handle the arrangements. You just make sure you're there—and bring your nomad."

"He's not my nomad," I protest automatically.

Kitara's knowing smile makes me flush. "Of course not. My mistake."

After she leaves, Ryker turns to me with a more serious expression. "She worries about you, you know. We both do."

I straighten the stack of photos in front of me, avoiding his mismatched gaze. "I'm fine."

"Are you?" He leans forward. "Because from where I'm sitting, you've been running yourself ragged since you got back, barely taking time to heal, and doing everything possible to avoid being alone with Kier."

The direct hit makes me flinch. "I've been busy. There's a lot to organize."

"True. But that's not why you're avoiding him."

I look up then, meeting his gaze squarely. "With all due respect, Alpha, my personal life is my own business."

"Normally, I'd agree," he says calmly. "But when it affects pack dynamics, it becomes my concern."

"How is this affecting pack dynamics?"

"You're distracted. Off-balance. And the pack notices, whether you realize it or not." He pauses, his expression softening slightly. "Plus, I like him. He's good for you."

The simple assessment catches me off guard. "You barely know him."

"I know enough. I know he came back for you when he could have escaped alone. I know he looks at you like you're the moon itself." Ryker leans back in his chair. "And I know what it's like to find your mate when you least expect it."

"How many times do I have to tell you people that he's not—" I start, then stop, unwilling to voice the lie. My wolf stirs restlessly, aware of the truth I'm trying to deny. "It's complicated."

"Life usually is," Ryker agrees. "Question is, do you think he's worth the complication?"

I gather my papers, needing to escape this conversation before I say something I'll regret. "I should check on the reconnaissance preparations."

Ryker lets me go, but his parting words follow me out of the council chamber. "Tonight, at the feast. Give yourself permission to be happy, even if it's just for one night."

Give myself permission to be happy. As if it's that simple. As if happiness is something I could simply decide to allow myself, like an extra helping of dessert or a day off from training.

But as I make my way through the den's corridors, I can't shake his words. What would it be like to stop fighting this pull toward Kier? To simply let myself have what I want, consequences be damned?

Dangerous, my rational mind warns. *Giving your heart to someone means giving them the power to destroy you when they leave.*

If they leave, my wolf counters. *Kier is different.*

Just for tonight, I think, turning the idea over in my mind. *Maybe I can have this, just for tonight.*

The decision sends a thrill of anticipation through me, mixed with an edge of fear that I refuse to acknowledge. One night. What harm could there be in that?

THE MAIN HALL has been transformed by late afternoon. Tables have been arranged in a great circle, with space in the center for dancing. Garlands of pine and wildflowers hang from the rafters, their scent mingling with the mouth-watering aromas coming from the kitchen. Candles and lanterns cast a warm, golden glow over everything, creating an atmosphere of celebration and comfort.

I linger in the entrance, momentarily overwhelmed by the sight. Kitara has outdone herself in the few hours since she proposed this gathering. The pack moves around the space with easy familiarity, setting out plates and goblets, arranging seating, laughing and talking as they work.

This is what we're fighting for. Not just survival, but this— community, belonging, and joy that's shared among people who care for each other.

"Impressive, isn't it?"

I turn to find Kier standing behind me, and my breath catches in my throat. He's cleaned up for the occasion, his copper hair damp from a recent shower, curling slightly at the ends where it brushes his shoulders. He's wearing clothes borrowed from one of the larger pack members— dark pants and a forest-green shirt that brings out the gold in his eyes.

"You look..." I search for a word that won't reveal too much. "Different."

A smile plays at the corners of his mouth. "Different good or different bad?"

"Just different," I hedge, though we both know it's good. Very good.

He steps closer, his scent wrapping around me—pine and leather and something uniquely him that makes my wolf stir with interest. "You look beautiful," he says simply.

I glance down at my own attire—a deep blue dress that Kitara insisted I wear. "Thanks."

An awkward silence falls between us, and I scramble for something to say that doesn't involve how much I want to drag him out of this hall and back to my quarters.

"I saw you training with Elias this morning," I offer. "He was impressed."

"He said that?"

"Not in so many words. But he doesn't offer to spar with just anyone."

Kier's expression warms. "Your pack has been... welcoming. More than I expected."

"They're good people," I say, feeling an absurd surge of pride. "The best."

"I can see that." His gaze travels around the hall, taking in the preparations and the wolves working together. "This is something special you have here, Lithia. I haven't seen anything like it in a long time."

The wistfulness in his voice tugs at something in my chest. "You could be part of it, you know. If you wanted."

His eyes snap back to mine, suddenly intense. "Could I?"

The question carries more weight than the simple words suggest. He's asking about more than just acceptance into the pack, and we both know it.

Before I can answer, Kitara appears, looking radiant in a flowing dress that accommodates her pregnancy. "There you two are! Come in, come in. The feast is about to begin."

She takes both our hands, drawing us into the hall with a strength that belies her small stature. "I've saved seats for you at the head table."

Kier looks surprised by the honor but allows himself to be led to the table where Ryker and other senior pack members are already seated. As we settle into our places, I notice the speculative glances from the pack, the knowing smiles exchanged between some of the older wolves.

Great. Even more gossip fodder.

But as the food is served and wine begins to flow, I find myself relaxing despite the attention. The meal is a celebration of Shadowmist's bounty—venison and wild boar, fresh fish from the mountain streams, vegetables and fruits harvested from the pack's gardens, bread still warm from the ovens. It's a feast fit for a homecoming, which I suppose this is in many ways.

Conversation flows easily around the table, with Kier fielding questions about his travels as a nomad with good humor and interesting stories. He has a way of speaking that draws people in, making them laugh with his dry wit or lean forward to catch every word of a particularly harrowing adventure.

I watch him from the corner of my eye, fascinated by this side of him I've barely glimpsed before. He fits here, among my people, in a way I hadn't expected. There's none of the awkwardness or forced politeness that usually marks outsiders' interactions with the pack. He's just... himself. And they respond to that authenticity, including him in their jokes, their stories, their community.

"So, Kier," Felix asks from across the table, "is it true you once tracked a rogue alpha through three territories using nothing but a week-old scent marker?"

Kier chuckles, taking a sip of his wine. "It was ten days old, actually. And I had help—a particularly stubborn thunderstorm that refused to stop raining the entire time."

"How does rain help tracking?" one of the younger wolves asks, clearly fascinated.

"It doesn't, usually," Kier explains. "But this particular alpha had a habit of seeking shelter in abandoned human structures when it rained. All I had to do was check every dilapidated barn and shed along his likely path. Found him curled up in an old schoolhouse basement, still damp from the last downpour."

The story earns appreciative laughter, and I find myself smiling despite my attempt to maintain some emotional distance.

"What about you, Beta?" someone calls from farther down the table. "Any good stories from your time on the run?"

All eyes turn to me, including Kier's, and I feel a flush creeping up my neck. "Nothing as entertaining as Kier's adventures, I'm afraid."

"Oh, I don't know about that," Kier says, a mischievous glint in his eye. "The way you handled those pursuers when we reached the northern ridge was pretty impressive."

I narrow my eyes at him, sensing a trap. "That was just basic survival instinct."

"Basic survival instinct?" He turns to the others, his expression mock serious. "She led three armed guards on a chase through a burning forest, then climbed a sheer rock face with broken ribs while silver poisoning was still in her system."

Murmurs of approval ripple through the gathered wolves.

"And then," Kier continues, his voice dropping dramatically, "when we were cornered at the top with fire closing in from both sides, she found an underground stream that saved both our lives."

"That's not exactly how it happened," I protest, though the memory of those desperate moments brings heat to my face for entirely different reasons.

That kiss really was something else.

From Kier's knowing smile, I suspect he's thinking the same thing.

"Always modest, our Beta," Ryker says, raising his glass. "But worthy of celebration nonetheless. To Lithia—who survived against impossible odds and returned to us stronger than ever."

"To Lithia!" the pack echoes, raising their glasses.

I accept the toast with as much grace as I can muster,

uncomfortable being the center of attention. The meal continues and more stories are shared, and I find myself genuinely enjoying the evening. It's been too long since I allowed myself to simply be present, to enjoy the company of my pack without the weight of responsibility pressing down on me.

After the meal, musicians set up in one corner of the hall. The tables are pushed back to clear space for dancing, and soon the air is filled with lively music. Couples move onto the makeshift dance floor while the young pups run around, dancing in enthusiastic, if awkward, clusters.

"Dance with me," Kier says, holding out his hand. It's not a question, but not quite a demand either.

I look up at him, ready to refuse, but the words die in my throat at the expression in his eyes. There's want there, certainly, but also something softer, more vulnerable. He's offering his hand, but what he's really asking for is a chance.

Just for tonight, I remind myself. *I can have this, just for tonight.*

I place my hand in his, letting him lead me onto the dance floor. The music shifts to something slower, more intimate, as if the musicians somehow knew.

Kier's hand settles at my waist, warm and steady, while the other keeps hold of mine. He pulls me closer than strictly necessary, our bodies nearly touching as we begin to move with the music.

"You dance well," I observe, trying to keep my tone light despite the electricity crackling between us.

"My mother insisted all her pups learn. Said you never know when such skills might come in handy." His smile is tinged with grief. "She was right about a lot of things."

I squeeze his hand gently, offering silent comfort for the family he lost. "Tell me about her."

"She was fierce. Protective. Wouldn't take nonsense from anyone, especially her mate." His expression softens with memory. "But she was also the first to help when someone was in trouble, the one who made sure everyone had enough to eat, the voice of reason when tempers flared."

"She sounds wonderful."

"She was." He guides me through a turn, his movements graceful despite his size. "She would have liked you."

"Really?"

"Absolutely. She appreciated wolves who didn't back down from a challenge." His golden eyes meet mine, filled with warmth.

"I think I would have liked her too."

We dance in silence for a while, our bodies moving together with surprising harmony. It feels right, being in his arms like this. Safe in a way I haven't felt since childhood.

"Your pack loves you," Kier says after a while, his voice low enough that only I can hear. "I can see it in the way they look at you, the way they respond when you speak."

"They're my family," I reply simply. "The only real one I have, apart from Dane."

"Family is more than blood." His hand tightens slightly at my waist. "It's about choice. About who you decide to stand beside when things get difficult."

I look up at him. "Is that what you've been searching for? Family?"

"Maybe." He twirls me out, then pulls me back in, closer than before. "Or maybe I was waiting to find the right person."

My breath catches. "Kier—"

"I know," he interrupts gently. "You're not ready to talk about us. That's okay." His thumb traces small circles against my palm where our hands are joined. "But I want you to know something, Lithia. I'm not going anywhere."

The simple declaration sends warmth blooming through my chest. "You can't promise that. No one can."

"I can promise to try." His expression is serious now, all

teasing gone. "I can promise that whatever this is between us, it matters to me. You matter to me."

The music changes, shifting to something faster, but neither of us moves to break apart. We stand there on the dance floor, surrounded by laughing, spinning pack members, caught in our own private moment of truth.

"I'm scared," I admit finally, the words barely audible above the music.

His hand moves from my waist to my face, thumb brushing gently across my cheek. "I know. Me too."

"You don't seem scared."

"That's because you also make me brave." His smile returns, slow and warm. "Courage, Lithia."

Before I can respond, he steps back, his hand sliding from my face to catch mine. "Come with me. There's something I want to show you."

Curious despite myself, I let him lead me away from the dancing, through the hall and out of the den into the cool night air. The moon is high and bright, casting silver light over the den's courtyards and paths.

Kier guides me to a small garden tucked away from the main thoroughfares—a peaceful place where herbs and flowers grow in neat beds, with a stone bench set beneath an ancient oak. It's one of my favorite spots in the den, though I rarely have time to linger.

"How did you know I love it here?" I ask as we settle on the bench.

"Dane showed me. Said you used to come here as a pup when you needed quiet." He looks around, taking in the moonlit beauty of the garden. "I can see why. It's peaceful."

"I haven't been here in a while," I admit. "At least not to sit and just think."

"This seems like a place for reflection. And you've been working very hard not to be alone with your thoughts lately."

The observation is too accurate to deny. "Has anyone ever told you that you're annoyingly perceptive?"

"Once or twice." He stretches his arm along the back of the bench, not quite touching me but close enough that I can feel his warmth. "Usually right before they tell me to mind my own business."

"And do you? Mind your own business?"

"Almost never." His grin is unrepentant. "Curiosity is both my greatest strength and my worst flaw, according to most people who know me."

"I can believe that." I lean back slightly, allowing myself to relax into the space near his arm without quite admitting I'm seeking his touch. "It's probably what made you a good tracker."

"That, and stubbornness." His fingers brush against my shoulder, a touch so light it could be accidental. "Once I set my mind on something, I don't give up easily."

"I've noticed."

We sit in comfortable silence for a while, listening to the night sounds of the forest and the distant music from the hall. It's nice, this peaceful moment away from prying eyes and pack expectations. Just the two of us, the moon, and the quiet garden.

"Thank you," I say eventually.

"For what?"

"For knowing I needed this space to breathe." I turn to look at him, finding his golden eyes already watching me. "And for being patient with me, even when I've been... difficult."

"You, difficult?" He places a hand over his heart in mock shock. "I don't believe it."

I laugh, shoving his shoulder lightly. "You know what I mean."

"I do." His expression sobers, though warmth remains in

his eyes. "And you don't need to thank me, Lithia. I understand why this is hard for you."

I cock an eyebrow in question.

He shifts, turning to face me more fully. "You've lost people you love. Your parents died protecting you and Dane. That kind of trauma leaves scars that don't heal easily."

I swallow, the familiar ache of old grief tightening my throat. "I watched them die. Did I tell you that? I was hiding in a hollow tree with Dane, and I saw the hunters kill them. They died because of us, because they were trying to keep us safe."

"That's what parents do," Kier says gently. "They protect their children, no matter the cost."

"But the cost was too high." I look away, unable to meet his gaze as I voice the thought that's haunted me for years. "Sometimes I think it would have been better if they'd just run, saved themselves. Dane and I would have figured something out."

"Or you would have died too." His voice is firm but not unkind. "Your parents made a choice, Lithia. They chose your lives over their own. That's not something to feel guilty about—it's something to honor."

"By what? Hiding behind walls so thick no one can reach me? Pushing away anyone who tries to get close?" I laugh bitterly. "I don't think that's what they would have wanted for me."

"No," he agrees. "I think they would have wanted you to be happy. To live fully, not just survive."

"I don't know if I remember how."

His hand finds mine on the bench between us, his fingers intertwining with mine. "Maybe that's something we could figure out together."

The simple offer—not a demand, not a declaration, just a possibility—breaks something open inside me. A tear slides down my cheek before I can stop it, followed by another.

"Hey," Kier murmurs, his free hand coming up to brush away the tears. "It's okay."

"Is it?" I ask, my voice cracking. "Because it doesn't feel okay. It feels terrifying."

He pulls me closer, and I let myself be drawn into his embrace, my head resting against his chest where I can hear the steady beat of his heart. "You don't have to figure it all out tonight. There's time."

I close my eyes, absorbing the comfort of his arms around me, the security of his strength. "What if there isn't? What if something happens during the rescue mission? What if—"

"What if we focus on right now instead of all the what-ifs?" He presses a kiss to the top of my head. "Right now, you're here with me. The moon is full, the night is beautiful, and for once, neither of us is bleeding or being shot at."

Despite everything, I laugh. "When you put it that way, it does sound pretty good."

"It is good." His arms tighten around me slightly. "It's perfect."

We stay like that for a long time, wrapped in each other's arms beneath the ancient oak, the music from the hall a distant backdrop to our private moment of peace. I let myself savor it—the warmth of his body, the strength of his arms, the steady rhythm of his breathing.

Just for tonight, I'd told myself. But as I lift my face to his, seeking his lips in a kiss that feels like coming home, I know I'm lying to myself.

One night will never be enough.

CHAPTER
TWENTY-FOUR

The emergency summons comes at dawn—a sharp rap on my door that jolts me from restless sleep.

"Beta," the young scout pants, his eyes bright with excitement. "Elias needs you in the war room immediately. The reconnaissance teams have returned."

I'm dressed and moving within minutes, my heart hammering as I follow him through the winding corridors. Our scouts have finally returned from their surveillance of the three facilities we've identified—I can only hope it's good news.

The war room thrums with controlled urgency when I arrive. Maps cover every surface—hand-drawn schematics updated with fresh intelligence, guard rotations documented from days of careful observation, escape routes marked in red ink.

Elias looks up as I enter, his weathered face grim but determined. Around the table, I see the familiar faces of our senior staff—Dane studying reconnaissance photos, and Levi examining supply lists.

I'm surprised to see Kier leaning over facility blueprints.

His gaze meets mine, and I nod, understanding that Ryker's trying to include him in our pack.

"We have a window," Elias says without preamble. "Twenty-four hours, maybe less."

"What did the scouts find?" I ask, moving to the largest map where red pins mark the known facilities.

"They're moving prisoners," Dane reports from his position near the western maps. "Heath overheard a conversation that said they've got a large transport planned for tomorrow night. If we don't move now, we lose our chance."

My blood chills. "Is the large transport prisoners or something else?"

"Unknown," Elias admits. "But based on the preparations we observed, we think it is."

The implication hangs heavy in the air.

"How many total are at the facility?" I ask, studying the updated intelligence.

"Conservative estimate? Forty to fifty across all three facilities," another scout reports. "But here's the significant development—" He points to the map I know by heart, the facility where Kier and I were held. "This location has been completely evacuated. No prisoners, minimal guard presence."

I nod. "We thought they would."

"But it means they've either got another facility we haven't been able to track, or they've consolidated operations at their last two heavily fortified sites." He indicates the eastern and western facilities. "Best intelligence suggests the high-value targets—the seers—are being held here." His finger taps the eastern location.

Prudence.

"Guard strength at the active sites?"

Elias shrugs. "Eastern facility—the one likely holding the seers—twenty-plus guards, definitely enhanced based on what we could scent in the breeze. The western site has standard security, maybe fifteen guards total."

I study the fresh intelligence, my mind racing through tactical possibilities. Two facilities, limited time, innocent lives hanging in the balance.

"We hit them simultaneously," I decide. "Divide their attention, prevent coordination between sites."

"Agreed," comes Ryker's voice from the doorway. Our Alpha enters with Kitara at his side, both looking like they've been awakened as urgently as I was. "What's our timeline?"

"Teams need to be in position by sunset," Elias replies. "Simultaneous strikes at midnight when the guards are due to change will create maximum confusion."

Ryker nods, his mismatched eyes scanning the maps with tactical precision. "Team assignments?"

The war room fills as more pack members arrive for the emergency briefing—senior wolves, specialists, fighters. Soon we have enough personnel for two full assault teams.

"What about our allies?" Kitara asks. "The bear clans, the witch covens? They have people missing too."

"Already reached out," Ryker confirms. "Ghost River and Greyback packs are sending support teams, the other packs are considering who they can provide. The Northern Bear Clan is contributing a strike force. Three covens from the eastern territories are providing magical support and healing expertise."

"The fae courts?" someone asks.

A heavy silence falls over the room. Ryker's expression darkens. "No. There's too much bad blood from the war years. They might use this as an excuse to settle old scores rather than focus on rescue operations. I'll not risk our people like that."

I nod, understanding his decision. The fae courts' involvement in the Blood Wars left wounds that still haven't healed.

"So we're looking at coordinated strikes across multiple species," Elias summarizes. "Wolves, bears, witches and warlocks. Should we have a unified command structure?"

"Lithia coordinates the eastern facility assault, Elias will take the west." Ryker decides. "I'll handle overall strategic command from here, maintaining communication between all teams."

"I don't know. The eastern facility is where we'll face the strongest resistance," Levi interjects from his position at my left shoulder. "I think it makes sense for Elias to lead."

"Why?" I ask. "The mission parameters are similar to what Kier and I faced during our escape—underground facility, enhanced guards, silver-lined security measures."

"Last time you got taken. The risk is too great. You're too valuable to—"

"I'm Beta," I snap, whirling to face him. "I make tactical decisions for this pack, not you."

"And I'm Gamma," he fires back, his yellow eyes blazing. "Which means when the Beta makes reckless decisions that endanger the pack's command structure, I have a duty to intervene."

The room goes deadly quiet. Every wolf present can feel the dominance struggle crackling between us, can scent the tension that's been building for weeks finally boiling over.

"Step back," I tell him, my voice a growl. "Now."

He turns to Kier. "Aren't you gonna say something?"

Kier looks at me, and I brace, waiting for him to cut me down as well. "Nah. She seems to have it in hand."

After years of people either dismissing my authority or feeling the need to defend me when I'm perfectly capable of defending myself, Kier's endorsement of my abilities catches me off guard. He's not trying to fight my battles for me or undermine my position—he's simply acknowledging what should be obvious, I'm Beta of this pack for a reason.

My wolf preens at his quiet confidence in us, and I have to

fight back a smile despite the tension crackling through the room.

Levi throws up his arms, opening his mouth to protest when Ryker cuts him off. "Enough."

We both turn to face our Alpha, Levi's jaw tight with barely contained frustration, my hands clenched into fists at my sides.

"Beta Lithia will lead the assault on the primary facility," Ryker states with cold finality. "Levi, you'll coordinate the overall operation from here."

"Alpha, I respectfully protest—"

"Your protest is noted and overruled." Ryker's tone is filled with an unmistakable warning. "The decision stands."

Levi's face cycles through anger, hurt, and resignation before settling into cold acceptance. "Of course, Alpha."

But I catch the look he throws my way as he steps back—a mixture of desperation and possession that makes my wolf snarl in response. This isn't over.

"If you'll let me, I'd like to be on the eastern facility team," Kier says, straightening from where he'd been studying the facility schematics. His golden eyes meet mine across the table. "I have the most experience with their operational security, and Lithia will need someone who understands how these bastards think."

"You're not pack," one of the senior wolves mutters, but Ryker silences him with a gesture.

"He's proven himself," Ryker says firmly, his tone carrying the weight of alpha authority. "Kier's experience makes him invaluable for this operation."

The casual way Ryker defends Kier's place in our circle warms me. Whether he realizes it or not, Kier has become part of Shadowmist in truth, not just in name.

The bond between us thrums—I can feel his determination to protect me, my gratitude for his support, the electric awareness that never fades no matter how professional we try to keep things in public.

"All right, questions?" Ryker looks around the room.

Silence greets his inquiry, though the tension is thick enough to cut.

Kitara raises her hand.

Ryker grins, nodding at her. "You don't need to raise a hand, mate."

"I just thought you should know that I saw something." She rubs her temples. "Zella is there. But that's all I saw. They've got too much silver around the facility for me to get anything else."

I stiffen, my resolve hardening.

It's time to make that bitch pay.

My wolf is in agreement.

"Good. Lithia?"

I nod at my Alpha. "I'll handle it."

"Fine. Teams deploy at dawn. Dismissed."

As the room empties, wolves moving to their various preparations, I find myself alone with the maps and my thoughts. The rescue mission should be my only focus—innocent lives depend on our success. But I can't shake the feeling that the real danger won't come from enemy guards or silver weapons.

It'll come from the explosive dynamic between the three of us, trapped together in close quarters with months of unresolved tension ready to ignite at the worst possible moment.

"Beta."

I turn to find Dane approaching, his expression carefully neutral. "Brother."

"Walk with me," he suggests, gesturing toward the door. "I want to show you something."

I follow him through the winding corridors of the den, past the common areas where pack members go about their evening routines. We end up in the weapons room—a cavernous space lined with racks of blades, staffs, and projectile weapons of every description.

"Thought you might want to test some new gear before tomorrow," Dane says, moving to a rack of particularly wicked-looking knives. "Elias had these specially made."

I accept the blade he offers, testing its weight and balance. The metal has an unusual sheen to it, darker than normal steel but not quite silver. The handle is wood, inlaid with a beautiful pattern.

"He made it from your cuffs," Dane explains, watching my reaction.

I make a few practice swings, appreciating the weapon's balance. "How many do we have?"

"Enough to equip your team." He pauses, then adds quietly, "And to make sure you come home."

"I'll be fine," I assure him, though we both know the risks involved.

"I know physically." He moves closer, his pale blue eyes serious. "Lithia, what's going on between you and Levi?"

The question I've been dreading. "Nothing that affects pack business."

"Bullshit." His tone is gentle but unyielding. "I've watched him hover around you for weeks. Watched you get more and more tense every time he's near. And don't think I haven't noticed how Kier watches it all happen."

I set down the shadow silver blade, suddenly needing something to do with my hands. "It's complicated."

"Uncomplicate it for me."

I lean against the weapons rack, choosing my words carefully. "Levi has feelings. That I don't return. He's having difficulty accepting that."

"And Kier?"

Heat creeps up my neck despite my best efforts to remain

composed. "Kier is a friend who helped me survive captivity."

Dane snorts. "Right. And I'm secretly a unicorn." He crosses his arms, studying me with the patience that makes him such an effective tracker. "Sister, I've seen how you look at each other."

My cheeks flame. "I have no idea what you're talking about."

"Don't you?" He steps closer, his voice dropping to the tone he used when we were children and he was trying to talk me out of some reckless plan. "Lithia, you're my twin. I know you better than anyone. And right now, you're scared."

The accuracy of his assessment makes my wolf whine. "I'm not scared."

"You're terrified," he corrects gently. "Do you really think you should go out into the field knowing that if something were to happen, you'd have regrets?"

"Everyone leaves, Dane." The words slip out before I can stop them, raw with pain I've been carrying for years. "Everyone dies or betrays or just... goes away. It's better to keep a distance."

"Mom and Dad didn't choose to leave," he says quietly. "They died protecting us. That's not the same as abandonment."

"Isn't it? The result is the same—we're alone."

"We're not alone." His hand finds my shoulder, squeezing gently. "You have me. You have this pack. And if you'd stop being stubborn for five minutes, you might have something even better."

Before I can respond, the sound of approaching footsteps interrupts us. I turn to see Kier entering the weapons room, his expression carefully neutral.

"Sorry," he says, noticing our serious conversation. "Didn't mean to interrupt. Elias said I should come select gear for tomorrow."

"No interruption," Dane says smoothly, though his pointed glance at me makes me want to smack him. "I was just leaving." He heads for the door, pausing to add, "Think about what I said, sister."

Then he's gone, leaving Kier and me alone among the weapons with tension thick enough to cut.

"Everything all right?" Kier asks, moving to examine the selection of blades.

"Fine," I say too quickly. "Just sibling stuff."

He nods, but I can feel his attention on me as I busy myself organizing weapons that don't need organizing. The silence stretches between us, comfortable and uncomfortable at the same time.

"You know," he says finally, his tone deliberately casual, "if you're having second thoughts about me joining the team—"

"I'm not." The response comes out sharper than intended, making him raise an eyebrow. "Your knowledge of the facility is valuable. It makes tactical sense."

"Tactical sense," he repeats, something unreadable in his voice. "Right."

I risk a glance at him and find him studying a particularly vicious-looking dagger with more attention than it warrants. His dark copper hair falls across his forehead, and there's tension in the line of his shoulders that suggests he's as affected by our proximity as I am.

Just be professional, I tell myself. *Focus on the mission.*

But when he moves to test the weapon's balance, his shirt pulls tight across his chest and shoulders, and I'm suddenly remembering the feel of those muscles under my hands, the taste of his skin, the way he'd gasped my name when I'd taken him in my mouth.

Heat pools low in my belly, and I have to look away before I do something stupid.

"These blades," he says, thankfully oblivious to my

internal struggle, "they're specifically designed for enhanced enemies?"

"According to Elias, yes." I force my voice to remain steady. "He's tried to include anything in them that he knows is a weakness for supernaturals. Silver, salt, iron. We don't know what those guards are spliced with. Their DNA could be anything."

"Clever." He sheaths the dagger, moving to examine a set of throwing knives. "What about armor? If we're facing enhanced guards—"

"There's limited protection available in human form," I interrupt. "And nothing in were. If you want, there's some leather which is better than nothing, but won't stop a determined assault."

"So the key for dealing with them is speed and stealth over direct confrontation."

"Exactly." I move to the armor rack, pulling out a set in his size. "Try this."

He strips off his shirt, and I immediately regret my suggestion.

My mouth goes dry as he pulls on the armored vest, adjusting the straps across his chest. When he reaches for the side buckles, I step forward instinctively.

"Here, let me—"

My fingers brush his skin as I work the fastenings, and electricity shoots up my arm. He goes very still, his breathing shallow as I adjust the fit across his shoulders and torso.

"How's that?" I ask quietly.

"Good."

Our eyes meet, and the air between us crackles with the tension. I'm close enough to smell his scent—pine and leather and something uniquely him that makes my wolf whine with need.

"Lithia," he starts, his voice low.

"We should test mobility," I say quickly, stepping back

before I do something I'll regret. "Make sure the armor doesn't restrict your movements."

He nods.

I move to the center of the room, drawing one of the practice blades. "Come at me. Let's see how the armor affects your speed."

He draws his own practice weapon, settling into a fighting stance that speaks of years of training. We circle each other slowly, testing distance and reaction time.

"The leather's heavier than I expected," he says, making a quick thrust that I easily deflect. "But the balance is good."

I counter with a low sweep that he blocks, our blades ringing together in the empty room. The sound is sharp and clean, echoing off stone walls.

"Not bad," I praise.

"I've been practicing with a den full of warriors," he replies, deflecting my attack. "Your people don't believe in going easy on the outsider."

The word "outsider" carries more weight than it should, and I find myself faltering. He takes immediate advantage, stepping inside my guard to place his blade at my throat.

"Point," he says, but he doesn't step back.

We're close now, close enough that I can feel the heat radiating from his body, can see the flecks of darker gold in his amber eyes. His free hand comes up to rest on my waist, the touch burning through my clothes.

"You're not an outsider," I hear myself say. "Not anymore."

"Lithia—"

"Again," I say, stepping back before I lose what's left of my control. "But faster this time."

We resume sparring, but there's a different energy to it now—less practice and more dance, each movement flowing into the next with increasing intensity. He presses forward with renewed aggression, forcing me to work harder to match his speed and strength.

I duck under a high slash, coming up inside his guard to drive my elbow toward his ribs. He twists away, grabbing my arm to spin me around until my back is pressed against his chest, his blade at my throat while mine is trapped uselessly at my side.

"Point," he breathes against my ear, but neither of us moves.

His arm bands across my stomach, holding me against him, and I can feel every line of his body pressed to mine. The armor does nothing to hide his strength, the solid warmth of his chest against my back, the way his breathing has gone ragged.

"Kier," I whisper, not sure if it's a warning or a plea.

His grip tightens fractionally, and I feel something else pressed against the small of my back—hard and insistent and absolutely inappropriate for a training session.

"Fuck," he mutters, starting to pull away. "Sorry, I—"

I lean back into him instead, grinding my ass against his erection in a movement that's pure instinct and terrible judgment. His sharp intake of breath tells me exactly how much he appreciates the contact.

"Lithia, we shouldn't—"

"I know," I agree, but I don't stop moving against him. His free hand slides down to grip my hip, holding me still even as his body betrays how much he wants me to continue.

"Don't start what you won't finish."

"Right," I breathe, but I turn in his arms instead of stepping away. Now we're face to face, his hands on my waist, his erection pressing against my belly through our clothes.

For a heartbeat, we just stare at each other, balanced on the knife's edge between distance and desire. Then his control snaps.

"Fuck it."

He kisses me with desperate hunger, backing me toward the weapons rack until I'm pinned between cold metal and his burning body. I respond with equal ferocity, cracking apart under the weight of need.

His hands slide into my hair, angling my head to deepen the kiss while I claw at the buckles of his armor. I need to feel his skin, need to touch him without barriers between us.

"Fuck, you taste good," he growls against my mouth, his teeth scraping my lower lip. "I fucking hate when my mouth isn't on you."

I manage to get his vest undone, pushing it off his shoulders where it hits the floor with a heavy thud. My hands map the planes of his chest, relearning every scar and line of muscle while he tugs at my shirt, pulling it up and tossing it away.

His mouth follows the path of his hands, trailing fire down my throat to the curve of my breast.

"Kier," I gasp, my head falling back against the weapons rack as he takes my nipple into his mouth through the thin fabric of my bra.

The sensation shoots straight to my core, making me arch against him with a soft cry. His responding growl vibrates against my breast as he sucks harder, his hands sliding down to grip my ass and lift me against him.

I wrap my legs around his waist instinctively, bringing our centers into perfect alignment. Even through our remaining clothes, the friction is incredible—hot and desperate and exactly what I've been craving.

"We need to stop," I pant even as I rock against him, chasing the pleasure building between us.

"Yeah," he agrees, his mouth moving to my other breast. "We definitely need to stop."

But his hands are sliding under my sports bra, palming

my bare breasts while I grind against the hard length of his cock. Nothing about this feels like stopping.

"We'll stop," he says, grinding against me. "Just watch me stop."

I bite his shoulder, growling as he sucks my breast into his mouth.

I'm reaching for the ties of his pants when the sound of approaching footsteps freezes us both.

"Shit," I breathe, scrambling to untangle myself from him and grab my discarded shirt.

Kier steps back, running a hand through his disheveled hair as he tries to control his breathing. His erection is still prominently visible through his pants, and his eyes are dark with frustrated desire.

"Lithia?" Levi's voice calls from the corridor. "Are you in here?"

Of course it's him.

"Just finishing up," I call back, pulling my shirt over my head with hands that shake slightly. "Be right out."

Kier has managed to retrieve his armor, though he's making no attempt to put it back on.

Levi appears in the doorway, his yellow eyes immediately taking in the scene—my mussed hair, Kier's shirtless state, the tension crackling between us.

"I was looking for you," he says, his voice carefully controlled. "There are some last-minute details about tomorrow that need your attention."

"Of course there are," I mutter, checking to make sure my clothes are properly arranged. "What details?"

But his attention has shifted to Kier, and I can practically see the calculations running behind his eyes. The possessive anger that flares in his expression makes my wolf bristle in response.

"Perhaps we should discuss them privately," Levi suggests, his gaze never leaving Kier.

The emphasis on the last word is a clear insult, and I see Kier's jaw tighten in response. The testosterone in the room ratchets up another notch, and I suddenly feel like prey caught between two predators.

"Any pack business can be discussed in front of a team member," I say firmly, moving to position myself between them. "What details, Levi?"

He reluctantly drags his attention back to me, though I catch the warning look he shoots Kier. "The coven have called. They'd like to know more about the enhanced guards."

Something Levi could have easily told them about. This is pure territorial posturing, and we all know it.

"Fine," I say, picking up my gear. "Let's go handle it."

As I move toward the door, Levi falls into step beside me, his hand coming to rest at the small of my back in a gesture that's clearly meant to mark territory. I resist the urge to shrug him off—barely—and keep walking.

Behind us, I hear Kier gathering his equipment, and I don't need to look back to know he's watching us leave with an expression that could melt steel.

Tomorrow, I tell myself. *After the mission, we'll figure this out.*

But even as I think it, I know tomorrow might be too late. The tension between the three of us is reaching a breaking point, and when it finally snaps, someone's going to get hurt.

I just hope it's not in the middle of a life-or-death rescue operation.

THE EVENING PASSES in a blur of final preparations and briefings that feel more like exercises in avoidance than actual planning. Levi finds reasons to keep me busy until well past midnight, reviewing issues we've already discussed a dozen times.

By the time I finally escape to my quarters, exhaustion weighs heavy on my shoulders. But sleep remains elusive as I lie in my empty bed, staring at the ceiling and replaying every moment of what happened in the weapons room. Particularly Levi's interruption.

This can't continue. My wolf paces restlessly, torn between desire for our mate and frustration at the complications his presence creates.

A soft knock at my door interrupts my brooding. For a wild moment, I hope it's Kier, coming to finish what we started. But when I open the door, it's Levi standing in the hallway, his expression serious.

"We need to talk," he says.

"It's after midnight, Levi. Whatever it is can wait until—"

"No," he cuts me off, stepping closer. "It can't wait. Not when I see you making poor choices."

The presumption in his tone makes my temper flare. "What choices would those be?"

"You know exactly what I'm talking about." His yellow eyes burn with intensity. "The nomad. You're letting him cloud your judgment."

"My judgment is fine," I snap. "And my personal relationships are none of your business."

"Everything about you is my business," he says, echoing the words from our earlier confrontation. He steps closer, his voice dropping to something rougher. "I would die for you, Lithia."

"And I would for you. But I call that loyalty," I say gently. "And friendship. It's not romantic love, Levi. It never has been."

His jaw works for a moment, emotions cycling across his face too quickly to track. "You're only saying this because of him."

"This isn't about Kier—"

"Everything is about him!" The words explode from him with enough force to make me flinch. "I've watched you these past weeks, Lithia. Watched you come alive around him in ways you never did before. And I know what that means."

"You don't know anything."

"I know you're in love with him," he says quietly, and the certainty in his voice makes my heart stutter. "I know you've never looked at anyone the way you look at him. Including me."

The admission hangs between us like a blade. Because he's right, and we both know it.

"Levi—"

"I also know he'll break your heart," he continues, his voice hardening. "Because that's what nomads do. They take what they want and move on when it becomes inconvenient. And when he does, I won't be here. I'm not going to pick up the pieces."

Anger flares in my chest, hot and protective. "You don't know him. And I've never needed anyone to hold me together, Levi. I've never asked you or anyone else to pick up the pieces. I'm not broken, and I don't need rescuing."

His jaw tightens, but I'm not finished.

"Real friendship isn't something you withhold and use as a weapon when you don't get what you want. What you're doing right now—this resentment, this bitterness because I can't return your feelings—this isn't the Levi I know. This isn't my friend."

I step closer, my voice growing harder. "My friend would want me to be happy, even if it wasn't with him. My friend wouldn't try to manipulate me with guilt and ultimatums when his feelings weren't reciprocated. And my friend sure as hell wouldn't stand in my quarters insulting someone who saved my life just because he's jealous."

The words hit their mark—I can see it in the way he flinches.

"I know his type. I've seen a dozen wolves like him over the years—charming, dangerous, completely unreliable when it matters. They're addictive until they're not, and then they're gone."

"I don't recognize this version of you," I continue, my voice softening with genuine hurt. "The Levi I know is better than this. He's honorable and kind and puts the pack's needs above his own desires. But this wolf standing in front of me? This wolf is letting his wounded pride turn him into someone I don't want to be around." I point at the door. "Get out."

"Lithia—"

"I said get out." My voice carries the full weight of my Beta authority, and he steps back as if struck. "This conversation is over."

For a moment, I think he'll argue. Then his shoulders slump slightly, defeat flickering across his features.

"I love you," he says simply. "That's not going to change, no matter how many nomads you take to your bed. But I can't wait around for you to work that out. Once this mission is over, I'm leaving."

"Levi—"

He shakes his head. "I've told you what I want, Lithia. Now the choice is yours."

But there is no choice.

I close the door and lean against it, my hands shaking with residual anger and just a touch of fear. Because part of me—the part that remembers every loss, every betrayal, every moment of abandonment—whispers that he might be right. That Kier will leave eventually, and I'll be left with nothing but regret and the memory of what it felt like to want someone completely.

A whisper touches my mind. *Our bond.*

He's our mate, my wolf whispers. *He'll stay.*

I know, with bone-deep certainty, that whatever Kier is, he's not the kind of wolf who disappears when things get difficult.

I swallow, my decision made. *I'll tell him after the mission.*

TWENTY-FIVE

Restlessness coils through my limbs making it impossible to stay still. I've tried lying down, tried reading, tried organizing tomorrow's mission gear for the third time. Nothing works. The walls of my quarters feel like they're closing in, suffocating me.

Tomorrow we hunt monsters. Tomorrow I lead my pack into danger, knowing some of us might not return. And tonight, I'm hiding in my room like a coward, too afraid to cross two doors and claim what my heart demands.

Pathetic.

My wolf stirs beneath my skin, impatient with me. She knows what she wants—has known since the moment we heard his voice through the prison wall. She's tired of my excuses, my fears, my stubborn refusal to listen to what every instinct is screaming.

Go to him, she demands. *End this.*

I push to my feet, decision crystallizing. Enough.

The corridor is quiet at this hour, most of the pack settled for the night. My bare feet make no sound on the stone as I pad toward his guest room, my heart hammering against my ribs with each step.

When I reach his door, I hear him speaking. I'm about to retreat when his door swings open, revealing Kier dressed in dark clothing and sturdy boots.

He freezes when he sees me, golden eyes widening in surprise. "Lithia."

"Sorry," I say quickly, suddenly self-conscious about appearing at his door in sleep clothes. "I didn't realize you were busy—"

"I'm not." He steps aside, gesturing for me to enter. "I'm speaking to myself again. Turns out the hallucinations aren't so easy to let go."

I step into his room, closing the door behind me. "Are they getting worse?"

He runs a hand through his hair. "Not worse, exactly. Just... persistent. Elena says it's normal after prolonged isolation and trauma. The mind creates voices to fill the silence, and even when the silence is gone, the pathways remain."

I lean against the window ledge, watching him. "Are they the same from when you were inside?"

"Mostly. Sometimes it's Adelaide, sometimes my old pack members. Other times it's prisoners asking why I left them to die." He meets my eyes, pain flickering in the golden depths. "And lately, you."

"Me?"

"A version of you that tells me I'm not good enough for this pack. That I'll mess this up somehow, hurt you, disappoint everyone." He shakes his head. "Elena says they're manifestations of my own fears and guilt, not real external voices. She's been working with me on grounding techniques, ways to distinguish between what's real and what's my damaged psyche trying to protect itself."

I reach for his hand, threading our fingers together. "How long does she think it will take?"

"Months, maybe longer. Maybe I'll never get rid of them.

Three years of that kind of isolation..." He shrugs. "The brain doesn't heal quickly. Elena's been having me practice reality checks—touching something real, naming five things I can see, focusing on physical sensations. I can differentiate what's real by trying to touch them. If they move, I know they're false. It helps, but the voices still come."

"Is that what you were doing when I knocked? Reality checking?"

A rueful smile tugs at his lips. "Adelaide was lecturing me about going out alone tonight. She likes to tell me I make silly decisions when I'm emotional. I was explaining to her that she's not real and I'm perfectly capable of making my own choices." He squeezes my hand. "Though she might be right."

"You survived three years of hell," I say firmly. "That's incredible strength."

"Elena says the same thing."

"She's right. Can I help? Is there anything I can do?"

He shakes his head. "You're already doing it." He brings our joined hands to his lips, pressing a soft kiss to my knuckles. "Elena's explained that healing isn't linear and setbacks are normal. She offered medication, but I want to see if I can manage it with the other strategies we're building. She also says having real connections and relationships will help, as this was brought on by the trauma of isolation."

Before I can respond, he clears his throat and changes the subject. "Did you need me for something?"

"Where were you headed?" I ask, noting his outdoor gear.

"Running trail. The kind that requires four legs." He studies my face in the lamplight. "Couldn't sleep either?"

"Too wired. Too much energy for tomorrow."

Understanding passes between us—that electric tension that comes before battle, when your body knows violence is coming and prepares accordingly. We're both predators, both warriors. We both feel the storm approaching.

"Want company?" The offer slips out before I can second-guess it.

His entire expression shifts, something hungry and hopeful flickering behind his controlled facade. "You sure? I was planning to hit the northern trails. Rough terrain."

"I know those trails better than anyone," I counter, lifting my chin. "Question is, can you keep up?"

His grin is sharp as a blade. "Try me."

Within minutes we're outside, the crisp night air filling our lungs as we strip down and shift. My wolf emerges with a satisfied growl, stretching muscles too long confined. Beside me, Kier's wolf is breathtaking—powerful shoulders, intelligent eyes, coat like burnished copper in the moonlight.

Perfect, my wolf purrs, and I can't disagree.

I take off at a sprint, leading us into the forest depths. Behind me, Kier's paws thunder against the earth as he gives chase. The familiar trails blur past—streams we leap, logs we vault, rocky inclines that test our agility. With each mile, the tension in my body transforms from anxiety into exhilaration.

This is what I needed. Wild movement. Primal freedom.

When we reach the meadow clearing where the mountain trail begins in earnest, we shift back to human form. Both of us are breathing hard, energized rather than tired.

"Where to now?" Kier asks, his eyes bright with adrenaline.

I point toward the steep path that winds up the rocky face. "The summit. Best view in the territory."

"Lead the way."

The climb is challenging even for seasoned wolves, requiring careful placement of paws on the narrow, rocky trail. We ascend in companionable silence, both focused on the technical aspects of the route.

By the time we reach the top, the moon has moved across the sky, bathing everything in silver light. The view from the summit takes Kier's breath away—I can see it in the way he goes completely still, drinking in the panorama of forest and mountain that stretches endlessly in every direction.

We shift back to human, standing shoulder to shoulder as we take in the view.

"Now I understand," he says quietly, his voice full of reverence.

"Understand what?"

"Why you'd fight so hard to protect all this." He turns to face me, moonlight catching the planes of his face. "This isn't just about Shadowmist territory, or the pack. It's about legacy."

His words pierce straight through my defenses, hitting something deep and vulnerable I rarely let anyone see. He doesn't just appreciate the view—he comprehends what it represents. I'm a continuum of the generations of wolves who've called this home, the blood that's been spilled to keep it safe. There's a responsibility that comes with guardianship, one that's been bred into me and carved into my bones.

When our lips meet, it's different from the desperate moments we've shared before—deeper, more deliberate, full of promise rather than desperation.

My hands slide into his hair, pulling him closer, trying to pour everything I can't say into this kiss.

I want you. I need you. I'm falling so hard I can't see the bottom.

The words burn in my throat, but I can't force them out. Instead, I let my body speak for me, arching against him, my hands mapping the solid strength of his shoulders with desperate reverence.

"Lithia," he breathes against my mouth, his voice rough with desire. "I need you."

"Then take me."

He lowers me gently to the soft grass, his hands reverent as they explore my skin. Every touch sends fire racing through me, and I want to tell him how he makes me feel— safe, wanted, alive in ways I'd forgotten were possible. But the words stick in my throat, caught behind walls I've spent years building.

So I show him instead. My hands trace the scars that map his chest, my lips following the path, trying to convey through touch what I can't say aloud.

You're extraordinary. You make me want to be brave.

"You're trembling," he whispers, his golden eyes searching my face with concern.

I am trembling, but not from cold or fear. I'm shaking with the weight of feelings too big for words, with the desperate need to claim this moment, this man, this terrifying hope that maybe I don't have to face everything alone.

"You're beautiful," he whispers, pressing kisses along my skin. When he reaches the sensitive spot where my neck meets my shoulder, I arch beneath him with a soft gasp.

His mouth trails heat along my collarbone, over the swell of my breasts, teasing one nipple into a tight, aching peak before he sucks it deep into his mouth.

I cry out, clutching at his shoulders, gasping his name as his tongue circles, flicks, licks—his hands slipping down to part my thighs.

"Cold?" he asks as I shiver under him.

"No." I'm shaking from need. From want.

From you.

He touches me, and I pour everything into the sounds I make—every gasp, every moan, every whispered plea. My body becomes my voice, telling him things my mind isn't ready to acknowledge.

Don't leave.

"Kier—"

"Gods, I need—" He cuts himself off with a shaky breath, sliding lower, pressing my thighs apart with a low, feral growl.

When his tongue drags through the slick heat between my

legs, I shudder violently, thighs clenching around his shoulders.

"Fuck, you're soaked for me," he rasps, voice muffled as he dives back in, licking me open, sucking hard on my clit until I'm sobbing his name. His fingers slip inside, thick and sure, curling just right, and I nearly come undone right then, bucking against his mouth.

But I'm not passive—gods, I can't be. My hands are searching blindly, needing him, all of him. I reach down, wrapping my fingers around the hard, heavy length of him, stroking as he groans against me, hips jerking helplessly into my grip.

"Fuck, Lithia—" he gasps, voice breaking, fingers tightening on my thighs as I work him, feeling him pulse in my hand, thick and hot and desperate.

When I'm trembling on the edge, dizzy with need, I push up onto my elbows, tugging him up, flipping him onto his back with a strength that surprises us both. His eyes flare wide, breath shuddering out in a laugh—proud, turned on, undone.

I slide down his body, kissing, licking, tasting every inch, until I wrap my mouth around him, taking him deep, hollowing my cheeks, sucking hard.

"Fuck, baby, gods—" He fists his hands in my hair, not pulling, just holding on, groaning raggedly as I swallow him down, working him with mouth and hand until his hips stutter and his head tips back with a choked-off cry.

He comes hard, hips jerking, warm and salty against my tongue, and I moan softly around him, licking him clean, not pulling away until he's trembling under me, laughing breathlessly as he pulls me up into his arms.

I wish I could laugh so easily, but the words I wish I could say are choking my throat, cutting off all thoughts.

Stay. hold me. Be with me.

I close my eyes, listening to his heartbeat under my ear as

I remember pressing my face to my mother's chest and hearing nothing but silence.

I wish...

In the aftermath, as we lie tangled together under the star-filled sky, I wish everything were different. I wish my parents were alive. I wish we'd met in a claiming ceremony rather than a prison. I wish I could tell him how he makes me feel, what this means, how grateful I am that he stayed, that he chose me. But the words are still trapped, caught behind years of grief and self-preservation.

"Fuck, Lithia," he murmurs, voice wrecked, still catching his breath. "What are you doing to me?"

I bury my face in his chest, heart pounding so hard it hurts. *Don't leave. Stay. Please stay.*

So I press closer to him instead, letting my body say what my voice can't. *You matter. This matters. I'm terrified of losing you.*

"We should head back," I whisper eventually, though I don't want to move.

"We should," he agrees, but neither of us makes any effort to leave.

Finally, the cool night air and the approaching dawn force us to dress. We shift, our run back through the forest to our clothes is filled with less urgency. It's a slow lope, and though Kier tries to nuzzle me into play, I flick my ears back, letting him know I'm tired and not in the mood.

Tonight is ending.

As I pull my clothes back on, I feel the familiar walls start to rebuild themselves, brick by brick. The vulnerability of moments ago feels overwhelming and dangerous.

What did I do?

The walk back is quiet, but I can feel myself retreating with each step. By the time we reach the sleeping quarters, the space between us feels huge.

"Kier?" I pause at my door, not quite meeting his eyes.

"Mm?"

"Tonight... this doesn't change anything. I still don't see—"

"I know." He steps closer, and I have to fight the urge to step back. "Lithia." His voice is gentle but firm, cutting through my spiraling retreat. "What's wrong?"

I look down, recognizing the pattern even as I'm trapped in it. "I don't know how to do this."

"Do what?"

"This. Whatever *this* is. I don't know how to... stay close to someone without panicking."

He touches the scar at my temple, studying my face. "What if I told you I don't know how to do it either?"

"You seem to be managing fine."

"Do I?" He lets out a quiet laugh. "I spent three years talking to people who weren't there. I'm not exactly the poster child for healthy relationships."

Despite everything, I almost smile. "We're quite a pair, aren't we?"

"Disasters attract, apparently." His thumb traces along my cheekbone. He grins—that crooked, self-deprecating smile that always catches me off guard. "Can I admit something?"

I nod.

"I'm terrified. Tomorrow I'm walking back into hell. I could really use the Shadowmist Beta to wrap herself around me tonight and keep me safe." The vulnerability in his admission, disguised as a joke, breaks through my defenses more effectively than any argument could have. He's asking for comfort, making it about his need instead of mine, giving me permission to care for him instead of having to admit I need care myself.

"You need me to be the big spoon?" I ask, forcing a lightness into my tone.

He nods. "I definitely do."

I reach for the doorknob behind me. "Then I guess I better stay."

TWENTY-SIX

Dawn arrives gray and cold, with mist clinging to the mountains like smoke. I dress in tactical gear—dark clothing that won't catch light, weapons secured but accessible. Everything I'll need for what's coming.

The team assembles in the main courtyard as the sun breaks over the peaks. Twelve wolves total, each one chosen for specific skills that complement our mission objectives. Kier stands near the equipment packs, checking and rechecking gear with the methodical precision of someone who's survived by being prepared.

Levi arrives last, his expression carefully neutral as he approaches our group. If anyone notices the tension between us, they're smart enough not to mention it.

"Final intelligence update," I announce, unrolling the facility map one last time. "Guard rotations confirmed as of last night. Entry point here." I tap the service tunnel Kier and I had used for our escape. "Primary objective is prisoner extraction. Secondary objective is intelligence gathering. We're not there to fight a war—we're there to save lives and get out."

Nods around the circle confirm understanding.

"Questions?"

"Rules of engagement?" asks one of the senior wolves.

"As minimal force as necessary to complete the mission. We're not executioners, but we're not martyrs either. Protect yourselves and your teammates." I look each of them in the eye. "Everyone comes home."

I roll up the map, tucking it into my pack. "We leave in ten minutes."

As the team disperses to make final preparations, I find myself alone with Kier and Levi—the three of us forming an uncomfortable triangle of unresolved tension.

"Lithia," Levi starts, but I cut him off.

"Professional conduct only," I say firmly. "Whatever personal issues we have get resolved after. Understood?"

Both men nod, though the look that passes between them could power the den's heating system for a week.

"Good." I shoulder my pack, checking the weight distribution one final time. "Let's go save some lives."

As we move toward the den's exit, I catch Kier's eye and see something there that makes my chest tight.

Hold that thought, I tell myself. *Just hold that thought until we get home.*

KIER

The eastern facility crouches in the valley like a cancer, its industrial bulk scarring the mountainside. From our position on the overlooking ridge, I can see the steam vents that mark the underground levels, the guard towers that pierce the darkness like silver needles, and the razor wire that crowns the perimeter walls.

"Twenty-three guards visible," Lithia murmurs beside me, her voice barely audible as she tracks movement through her scope. "Plus however many are inside."

"Shift change in ten minutes," I add. "That's our window."

Behind us, our team of twelve makes final preparations. The Ghost River wolves move silently, their gray-furred leader nodding his readiness. The bear clan fighters are mountain-solid and patient, waiting for blood. The three witches from the eastern covens whisper final protections over our gear, their magic shimmering like heat waves in the cold air.

"Teams Charlie and Delta in position," comes the crackling voice through our earpiece. It's Elias reporting in from the other facility.

"Team Charlie in position," Dane confirms from the other side of the eastern facility. If all goes to plan, he'll meet us somewhere in the middle.

Levi checks his watch from his position near our equipment packs. "Synchronized strike in three minutes."

The tension between him and me remains sharp as a blade, but we're dealing so far. Whatever personal conflicts we have, innocent lives hang in the balance.

Lithia's hand finds mine in the darkness, her fingers intertwining with mine for just a moment. No words needed —just the connection, the promise that we're in this together.

"One minute," she whispers.

I close my eyes, letting my wolf stretch beneath my skin. Three years of silver poisoning have left their mark, but anger and determination burn hotter than any toxin. Somewhere in that concrete tomb below us, prisoners suffer as we once did.

Not anymore.

"Go."

We move like death itself descending the mountainside— twelve predators flowing through shadows toward prey that has no idea what's coming. The perimeter guards die silently, their throats opened before they can raise alarm. I take the first one myself, a young wolf whose eyes widen in recognition before I end him.

I remember you, I think as I lower his body behind a supply crate. *You liked to watch them break us.*

The main entrance is heavily fortified, but we easily find the service tunnel Dane's team used to scout two days ago. We slip inside like smoke, the concrete walls closing around us with familiar, terrifying weight.

Nope, don't like this.

"Split formation," Lithia commands in the barest whisper. "Kier and I take point. Levi secures intelligence. Teams sweep and clear."

The tunnel system is a maze of maintenance corridors and storage areas—perfect for an ambush.

We encounter the first real resistance at a security checkpoint where the service tunnels meet the main complex. Four guards, armed with silver-laced weapons and body armor that gleams with protective runes.

They see us coming.

"Intruders in sector seven!" one shouts into his radio as he brings up a silver-lined rifle. "Code black! Code—"

Lithia puts three shadow silver throwing knives into his chest before he can finish the transmission. I surge forward, shifting just my face as I tackle the second guard, ripping out his throat with my wolf-jaw. His weapon discharges into the ceiling, concrete dust raining down as we grapple.

The third guard manages to fire once—a silver-core bullet that burns past my shoulder, close enough to sear. Then the Ghost River Alpha is on him, massive jaws clamping down on his weapon arm with a wet crunch.

The fourth turns to run, but one of the bear clan fighters moves with surprising speed for his bulk, crushing the guard's spine with a single powerful blow.

"Clear," Lithia reports, but alarms are already sounding deeper in the facility. "So much for stealth."

I shift back, examining my shoulder. "We knew this would happen," I remind her. The wound stings but won't slow me down.

"That was impressive," she murmurs as we head deeper into the complex. "Not many wolves can hold a half-shift."

"What can I say, I'm full of surprises."

Someone pulls an alarm, the siren deafening in the narrow corridors, as red emergency lights cast everything in bloody shadows.

"Movement ahead," one of the witches calls out, her magic allowing her to sense life forces through the walls. "Twelve hostiles, armed and moving to intercept."

"Let them come," Lithia draws her primary weapon—a shadow silver blade. "We go through them."

The ambush comes at a corridor junction where three passages meet. Silver-jacketed rounds spark off concrete as enhanced guards pour fire into the intersection.

"Suppression!" I shout, diving behind a structural pillar as bullets chew chunks from the concrete. "Witches, can you blind them?"

"Working on it!" The lead coven member begins a rapid incantation, her voice rising above the gunfire as magic builds around her hands.

The spell releases in a burst of searing white light that floods the corridor. Enhanced wolf eyes, adapted for night vision, are momentarily useless. The gunfire stops as our enemies cry out in pain and confusion.

"Now!" Lithia commands.

We surge forward catching the guards while they're still blinded and disoriented. My blade finds the gap between one guard's armor plates, punching through to pierce his heart. Lithia moves like deadly poetry beside me, her weapon singing through the air to open throats and find vital organs with surgical precision.

The fight is brutal but brief. Enhanced guards are tough, but they're not expecting Elias' weapons or our coordinated assault. Within minutes, bodies litter the junction, their blood pooling in the harsh emergency lighting.

"Casualties?" Lithia calls out, checking each of our team members.

"Minor wounds only," the bear clan leader reports. "Nothing that won't heal."

We continue deeper, following our noses toward the primary cell block. The facility's layout becomes increasingly familiar—concrete and steel designed for suffering, silver threading through every surface to weaken prisoners.

"Contact," I warn, hearing voices ahead. But these aren't guards.

We round a corner to find a cluster of cells, their doors standing open, confused prisoners emerging into the corridor. Various weres, witches, and a few humans who might be seers—maybe twenty people total, all bearing the telltale marks of prolonged captivity.

"Who's in charge here?" demands a tall woman with the scent-markers of lynx shifting. Her clothes hang loose on a frame that speaks of months of inadequate feeding, but her eyes burn with undiminished fury.

"Shadowmist Pack," Lithia identifies herself, stepping forward. "We're here to get you out."

"Shadowmist?" A younger man pushes forward—he's in his mid-twenties with the distinctive aura that marks him as a warlock. His dark hair is matted, his face gaunt, but there's something compelling about his features even though they're marked by torture. "Thank the gods. We heard the alarms and thought they were moving us again."

Dane appears at my shoulder.

"Lithia, we've secured—" His pale blue eyes lock on the young warlock.

"Are you injured?" he asks, his voice gentler than I've ever heard it. The warlock looks up at him with wide, exhausted eyes that hold flecks of green and gold.

"I'll live," the warlock says, but he sways slightly on his feet. "Been worse."

Dane's hand reaches out to steady him, and I catch the way both men freeze at the contact—electric awareness crackling between them despite the chaos around us.

Interesting.

"What's your name?" Dane asks quietly.

"Rohan," the young man replies, not pulling away from Dane's supporting touch.

"Well, Rohan," Dane says with a small smile, "let's get you somewhere safe."

"Where are the seers?" I ask the lynx woman. "I'm looking for a fear-seer named Prudence?"

The lynx shakes her head grimly. "They moved her three days ago. Took all the high-value targets—they took them to another facility."

My heart sinks. "Where?"

"North," Rohan says, his voice growing stronger as Dane helps him stand. "I heard the guards talking. Some kind of compound in the mountains, heavily warded. They called it the Sanctum."

"I know that place," one of the other rescued prisoners adds—an older witch with silver-streaked hair and calculating eyes. "It's where they take the ones they don't want found. Ever."

Lithia and I exchange grim looks. Prudence is still out there, still suffering, but at least now we know where.

"Lithia," Levi's voice crackles through our earpieces from deeper in the facility. "I've found their command center.

Maps, communications, the works. And you're not going to believe what they're planning."

"Collect what you can," Lithia orders. "We need to get out of here."

"Extraction time," I announce, though we've barely begun to search the facility. "Let's go everyone."

"There's a warded storage room," Rohan says urgently, still leaning against Dane for support. "Two levels down, past the guard station. That's where they keep the important documents."

"Dane, get these people out of here," Lithia orders. "Kier and I will deal with the intelligence."

We move quickly through the facility, following Rohan's directions while our rescue teams shepherd the freed prisoners toward the exit routes. The sound of approaching vehicles grows louder—reinforcements that will arrive too late to stop our escape but in time to make it significantly more dangerous.

"Got it!" Levi's voice carries triumph as we reach the command center. He's stuffing folders and hard drives into a waterproof pack. "Facility locations, guard rotations, prisoner manifests."

There's a map on the wall and I study it, memorizing the key details. The scope of this is staggering. If the map's to be believed, there are facilities like this all over the world. Hundreds, if not thousands of prisoners, a trafficking network that spans the entire supernatural community.

Explosions echo from the direction we came, followed by the staccato chatter of automatic weapons. Our exit routes are under attack.

"Time to go!" Lithia shouts over the noise. "Levi, pack it up. Everyone else, move to the alternate exit."

We reach the service tunnels just as pursuit catches up with us. Silver bullets spark off tunnel walls as enhanced guards pour fire into our escape route, forcing us to move in short rushes between cover points.

"Kier!" Lithia's warning comes just as I spot the muzzle flash—a guard with a clear shot, rifle trained on center mass, finger already contracting on the trigger.

I throw myself sideways, tackling Lithia to the tunnel floor as the silver bullet burns through the space where she'd been standing. The round catches me instead—not center mass, but high on my left shoulder, the silver core punching through muscle and bone with agonizing precision.

"Fuck!" The pain is immediate and overwhelming, silver poisoning flooding my system as the bullet lodges against my shoulder blade. My vision grays at the edges, wolf strength draining away like water.

"Kier!" Lithia's voice, sharp with panic and fury. She rises from beneath me, shadow silver blade already in motion, throwing with deadly accuracy. The guard who shot me drops with her knife buried in his throat.

"I'm fine," I manage through gritted teeth, though we both know it's a lie. Silver bullet wounds don't heal quickly, and the poison is already making my limbs heavy. "Keep moving."

"Like hell," she snarls, hauling me to my feet with surprising strength. "Levi! We need cover"

He lays it down as Lithia half supports, half drags me to the exit.

We emerge from the tunnels into the pre-dawn darkness, our extraction vehicles waiting with engines running. The witches have warded our escape route with concealment spells, but those won't last long against determined pursuit.

"Home," Lithia orders as she helps me into the back of an armored truck. "Hurry."

As our convoy pulls away from the burning facility, I catch a glimpse of Rohan and Dane sharing the back of another truck. The warlock has finally collapsed from exhaustion, his head resting against Dane's shoulder while the twin keeps protective watch.

Lithia's hand finds mine in the darkness, her fingers interlacing with mine despite the blood and silver poisoning.

"Stay with me," she whispers. I can hear her fear.

"Always," I manage to whisper back.

Always.

THE JOURNEY back to Shadowmist territory passes in a haze of pain and silver-induced delirium. I drift in and out of consciousness, vaguely aware of Lithia's voice keeping me anchored, her hand never leaving mine.

When we finally arrive at the den, Elena and her medical team are waiting with a fully equipped surgical bay. The silver bullet comes out in pieces, each fragment burning like liquid fire as it's extracted from my shoulder.

"He'll be fine," Elena assures Lithia as she stitches the wound closed. "No major damage to bone or arteries. The silver poisoning will take a few days to clear his system, but he's young and strong."

"Thank you," Lithia says quietly, and I can hear the relief in her voice.

I drift back to consciousness sometime later to find myself in a medical bed, my shoulder immobilized but the agonizing burn of silver finally gone. Lithia sits beside me, her pale blue eyes showing exhaustion and worry.

"How do you feel?" she asks when she sees I'm awake.

"Like I've been shot," I reply, managing a weak smile. "But alive. How did the other teams do?"

"Successful extractions at both facilities. Thirty-seven prisoners rescued in total. No casualties on our side beyond your wound." Her expression darkens. "But Adelaide and Prudence weren't at any of the sites."

"That lynx said they're at something called the Sanctum?"

"We'll find them," she promises fiercely. "This was just the beginning."

I shift position slightly, testing the limits of my mobility. The shoulder is stiff and sore, but functional. "What about the intelligence Levi gathered?"

"Still being analyzed, but it's extensive. Facility locations, operational plans, financial records. It's enough to start dismantling their network."

She catches my hand, her fingers trembling slightly as her thumb grazes across my palm. The simple touch sends electricity up my arm, but it's the vulnerability in her eyes that nearly undoes me.

"Kier, when that guard took aim at me..." Her voice wavers, barely above a whisper.

I turn my hand over, catching her fingers with mine. "I wasn't going to let him hurt you," I say simply, though the memory of that moment—seeing the rifle trained on her, knowing I had seconds to act—still makes my chest tight with panic.

"You could have died." The words come out strangled, like they're being torn from somewhere deep inside her. "The bullet hit bone, Kier. A few inches lower and it would have severed an artery."

"Better me than you."

She stares at me, and I watch emotions war across her face —disbelief, gratitude, something that looks dangerously like love before fear chases it away. Her pale blue eyes search mine like she's trying to solve a puzzle.

"Why?" The question is barely audible, but it hits me like a physical blow.

The question hangs between us, loaded with implications neither of us has been ready to acknowledge. But lying here, her hand in mine, silver bullet wound still aching in my shoulder, having nearly lost everything that matters—pretense seems not just pointless but cruel.

My throat works as I struggle to find words equal to what's burning in my chest. Three years of isolation taught me to survive on scraps of hope, but this woman gave me something to live for. The thought of losing her, of a world where she doesn't exist, makes something fundamental inside me rebel.

"Because I love you," I say quietly, each word deliberate, weighted with everything I've been too afraid to voice. "Because a world without you in it isn't one I want to live in."

Her breath catches audibly, pupils dilating until they nearly swallow the silver of her irises. I watch the words hit her, see the way they make her entire body go still except for the rapid flutter of her pulse at the base of her throat.

"Kier—" My name comes out as barely a breath, full of wonder and terror in equal measure.

"I know you're scared," I continue, needing to say this while I have the courage, while the nearness of losing her still burns fresh in my memory. My free hand comes up to cup her cheek, thumb tracing the scar that runs from temple to jaw. "I know you think caring about people means losing them. I know you've built walls so high even you can't see over them anymore."

Tears gather in her eyes—the first time I've seen her cry since our escape. "Everyone I've ever loved has been taken from me," she whispers, her voice breaking. "My parents, and now almost—" She can't finish the sentence.

"But I'm here," I say firmly, pressing my forehead to hers. "I'm here, and I'm not going anywhere. You couldn't get rid of me if you tried."

A sound escapes her—half laugh, half sob. "You don't know that. You can't promise that."

"I can promise that I'll fight like hell to stay. That I'll

choose you, every day, for as long as I have breath in my body." My voice grows rougher with emotion. "I can promise that loving you is the easiest thing I've ever done, even when you make it difficult. Especially when you make it difficult."

The tears spill over now, cutting silver tracks down her cheeks. "I love you too," she whispers, the admission torn from somewhere deep. "Gods help me, I love you so much it terrifies me."

The words hit me like lightning, like coming home, like every prayer I never knew I was making. My chest swells with something too big to contain, and I have to close my eyes against the intensity of it.

"Say it again," I whisper, desperate to hear it, to believe it's real.

"I love you." Her voice is stronger now, more certain. "I love your stubborn refusal to give up. I love how you see the best in everyone, even when they don't deserve it. I love your terrible jokes and your protective instincts and the way you make me feel like I'm worth saving."

I open my eyes to find her watching me with an expression so tender it takes my breath away. "You are worth saving," I tell her fiercely. "You're worth everything."

When I kiss her, it tastes of salt and promises and the kind of desperate hope that comes from finding something you didn't know you were looking for. She kisses me back with equal fervor, her hands fisting in my shirt like she's afraid I might disappear.

"I'm terrified," she admits against my lips.

"So am I," I confess. "But I'd rather be terrified with you than safe without you."

She nods, tears finally spilling over as she leans down to kiss me.

"Beta?"

We break apart, Lithia scrubbing at the tears on her face before she turns around. Levi stands in the doorway, his expression carefully neutral though something raw flickers in his yellow eyes as he takes in our intimate position.

"Seriously?" I growl.

"What is it, Levi?" Lithia asks, straightening but not moving away from my bedside.

"Ryker's holding a debriefing in an hour." His gaze flicks to me. "He doesn't expect you to be there."

"Appreciate the concession."

Levi's attention returns to Lithia, and for a moment his professional mask slips. "I'm glad you're both safe."

My eyebrows rise. He actually seems genuine.

"Thanks, Levi," Lithia says gently.

Levi nods, something settling in his expression—acceptance, maybe, or resignation. "I'll see you both later."

After he leaves, Lithia helps me get dressed. The medical bay is quiet except for the soft sounds of other patients recovering—several of the rescued prisoners are being treated for malnutrition, poisoning, and injuries.

"He's taking this better than I expected," I observe as we prepare to leave.

"He's a good wolf," Lithia says quietly. "He'll find his own path."

"And us? What's our path?"

She stops, turning to face me fully. The woman who stands before me isn't the guarded Beta who's kept everyone at arm's length for years. This is someone who's chosen to be vulnerable, to risk everything for the possibility of something real.

"Forward," she says simply. "Together."

It's not a claiming ceremony or a grand declaration. But it's enough.

It's everything.

TWENTY-SEVEN

KIER

I wake to find Lithia gone from her bed, her scent still warm on the sheets but her presence absent. For a moment, panic claws at my chest—old instincts from three years of captivity screaming that she's been taken, that this peace was just another dream.

Then I hear the shower running.

I lie still, listening to the sound of water and letting relief wash through me. She's here. She's safe. She chose me.

She chose me.

I stretch, pleased to find that my shoulder has only the slightest twinge of protest.

My wolf stirs beneath my skin, restless with need. *Claim her*, he demands. *Make her ours completely.*

I've been patient. Gods know I've been patient. But patience has its limits, and mine shattered the moment she whispered I love you.

The shower cuts off, and a few minutes later she emerges from the bathroom wrapped in a towel, her short hair damp.

"You're awake," she says, noticing me watching her.

"Hard to sleep when my mate is wandering around

naked," I reply, sitting up against the headboard. The sheet pools around my waist, and I don't miss the way her eyes track the movement.

"How's your shoulder?"

I lift it, rotating my arm. "Nearly good as new. Got to love our fast healing."

She drops the towel.

Just like that. No hesitation, no self-consciousness, no careful negotiation of boundaries. She stands before me gloriously bare, her pale skin marked with fading bruises from our mission, and scars that tell stories of survival and strength.

She moves toward the bed with predatory grace. "I believe, mate, we have unfinished business."

This is the Beta of Shadowmist Pack—confident, commanding, done with half-measures and hesitation. My wolf surges forward, recognizing the change in her. *Yes. Finally.*

I'm out of bed and crossing to her before conscious thought kicks in. When I reach her, I don't gentle my touch or ask permission. My hands frame her face, thumb tracing her scar.

"You choose me," I say, voice rough with barely contained hunger.

"I do." Her silver eyes hold mine steadily. "Now what are you going to do about it?"

The challenge in her tone is deliberate. She's not asking for tenderness or sweet words. She's demanding I claim what's mine.

Be careful what you wish for, mate.

I growl and slam my mouth to hers.

The kiss is fierce, consuming. She meets my hunger with her own, her nails digging into my shoulders as she presses against me. No hesitation, no fear—just pure filthy want.

I walk her backward until her spine hits the stone wall, pinning her there with my body. The contrast of cool stone and burning skin makes her gasp, and I swallow the sound, deepening the kiss until we're both breathless.

"I've wanted this," I bite out against her mouth, "wanted you, since the first moment I heard your voice in that cell."

"Then take me," she demands, wrapping her legs around my waist.

Fuck. The feel of her—wet and hot and ready—pressed against my cock nearly undoes me.

"You sure about that?" I ask, grinding against her. "Because once I start, I'm not stopping until you're screaming my name."

Her smile is wicked. "Promise?"

I don't answer with words. Instead, I lift her higher against the wall, position myself at her entrance, and thrust home in one brutal stroke.

The sound she makes—part gasp, part moan, completely mine—sends fire racing through my veins. She's tight, so fucking tight, her body gripping me like a velvet fist. For a moment, neither of us moves, adjusting to the overwhelming sensation of finally being joined.

"Say you're mine," I demand, pulling back only to drive into her again.

"Yours," she gasps, her head falling back against the stone. "Only yours."

The words unlock something primal in me. I set a punishing pace, each thrust driving her higher up the wall, the sound of our bodies meeting echoing through the room. She meets me stroke for stroke, her nails raking down my back hard enough to draw blood.

"More," she commands breathlessly. "Harder. Please, Kier."

I give her what she wants, what we both need. This isn't

gentle or romantic—it's claiming, pure and simple. The desperate hunger of two people who've found their perfect match and refuse to let anything stand between them.

Her first orgasm hits without warning, her body clenching around me as she cries out. But I don't slow, don't give her time to recover. I carry her to the bed, never breaking our connection, and lay her down beneath me.

"Turn over," I order, my voice rough with command.

She obeys without question, rising to her hands and knees, presenting herself to me with a trust that makes my chest tight. From this angle, I can see everything—the elegant curve of her spine, the perfection of her ass, the evidence of her arousal glistening between her thighs.

"Beautiful," I murmur, running my hands over her skin. "So fucking perfect."

I enter her again, this position letting me go even deeper. The angle has her gasping, pressing back against me for more. I give it to her, setting a rhythm that has the bed frame creaking with each thrust.

"Is this what you wanted?" I ask, my hands gripping her hips hard enough to leave marks. "To be taken? Claimed? Owned?"

"Yes," she pants. "Yes, gods, yes."

I can feel her building toward another peak, her body tensing beneath me. This time, when she comes, I let myself follow, buried deep inside her as we both shatter.

But we're not done. Not even close.

Before she can catch her breath, I'm moving again, rolling us so she's straddling my hips. Her eyes are glazed with pleasure, her lips swollen from my kisses, and she's never looked more beautiful.

"Your turn," I tell her, hands spanning her waist, my cock already rock hard once more. "Show me how much you want this."

She doesn't need to be told twice. Rising up on her knees, she sinks down on my cock with agonizing slowness, taking me inch by inch until I'm fully seated inside her. The view is incredible—her head thrown back, breasts bouncing as she begins to move, the place where we're joined slick and swollen.

"That's my good girl," I encourage, watching her find her rhythm. "Take what you need."

She rides me with increasing confidence, her movements becoming more desperate as another orgasm builds. When she's close—so close I can feel it in the tremor of her thighs—I flip us again, driving into her with renewed intensity.

"Now," I growl against her throat. "Come for me now."

This time, when she breaks apart beneath me, I sink my teeth into her shoulder at the exact moment of her climax. The mating bite—claiming her as mine in the most primal way possible.

She gasps, then leans forward, sinking her own teeth into my neck.

The shadow of the bond that was already there snaps into place with the force of a lightning strike.

Suddenly, I can feel everything she feels—the echoes of her orgasm still pulsing through her, the overwhelming love and satisfaction and rightness of being claimed. Her emotions flood through me. Relief, joy, a bone-deep contentment the likes of which I've never experienced.

And underneath it all, her wolf finally settles, recognizing her mate.

"I can feel you," she gasps, her eyes wide with wonder. "Inside my head, in my heart. I can feel everything."

"Good," I murmur, licking the mating bite closed. "You'll never be without me now."

The truth of it rolls through our connection—this isn't just physical joining anymore. We're mated, bonded, two halves of the same whole. I can feel her wonder at the connection, the way it settles something restless that's lived inside her for years.

Mine, my wolf says with deep satisfaction. *Finally.*

Ours, her wolf responds, and the rightness of it makes us both shudder.

But even mated, the hunger isn't satisfied. If anything, the bond makes our need for each other more intense, the drive to claim and be claimed burning hotter than before.

"Again," she whispers, and I can feel her desire through our connection, amplifying my own until it's almost overwhelming.

"Insatiable," I accuse, but I'm already hardening inside her, my body responding instantly to the hunger I can feel pouring through our bond.

"You made me this way," she points out, rolling her hips in a slow, deliberate circle that has us both groaning. The sensation, enhanced by our newfound connection, is almost too intense to bear.

I watch her closely, needing to memorize every expression as I claim her completely this time. Her silver eyes are dark with desire, pupils blown wide as she stares up at me.

"I can feel everything you're feeling," she whispers, wonder coloring her voice. "Your need, your hunger for me. It's like—like I'm drowning in it."

"Good," I growl, settling between her thighs. "Because you're about to feel a lot more."

I slide into her slowly, savoring the way her body welcomes me, the perfect heat of her surrounding my cock. But this time, I can feel it from her perspective too—the stretch, the fullness, the way I hit that spot inside her that makes stars explode behind her eyes.

"Fuck," I breathe, overwhelmed by the dual sensation. "Is this what you felt before? This incredible—"

"Yes," she gasps, her nails digging into my shoulders. "But it's stronger now. So much stronger."

I begin to move, each thrust deliberate and deep, building a rhythm that has both of us climbing toward something bigger than before. Through our bond, I can sense exactly what she needs—a little more pressure here, a change of angle there. It's like having a direct line to her pleasure, and I use that knowledge ruthlessly.

"Right there," she moans when I hit the perfect spot, but I already knew from the spike of sensation that echoed through our connection. "Gods, Kier, don't stop."

"Never," I promise, grinding against that spot until she's writhing beneath me. "I'm going to make you come so hard you forget your own name."

As our pleasure builds, I feel a tightening at the base of my cock—but this time it's different. Stronger. More insistent. My knot is forming, preparing to lock us together in the most primal claiming possible.

True mates.

"Lithia," I warn, my voice strained. "My knot—it's going to—"

"I know," she pants, her legs wrapping around my waist to pull me deeper. "I can feel it starting. Claim me, Kier."

The knot begins to swell, growing thicker with each thrust. I can feel her awareness of it through our bond—her anticipation, her slight nervousness, her overwhelming desire to be claimed completely.

"Tell me you want it," I demand, my thrusts becoming shorter as the knot grows. "Tell me you want to be locked to me, filled with my seed until it takes."

"Yes," she gasps, her back arching. "I want it. Want you. Want to be yours completely."

The knot catches at her entrance on my next thrust, and we both cry out at the sensation. It's thick now, demanding entry, stretching her in ways that border on too much but somehow still feel perfect.

"Breathe," I command, holding still to let her adjust. "Relax for me, baby. Let me in."

She does, her body gradually accepting the invasion, and when the knot finally pops inside her, the sensation is indescribable. Through our bond, I feel her shock at the fullness, the way it stretches her inner walls, the incredible pressure as it continues to swell.

"Oh gods," she keens, her head thrown back in ecstasy. "It's so—so big. I can feel it growing."

"That's it," I encourage, barely able to speak through the intensity. "Take my knot. Take all of me."

I try to thrust, but the knot has already locked us together, trapping my cock deep inside her. Instead, I grind against her, the movement sending shockwaves through both of us as the knot presses against every sensitive spot inside her.

"Kier," she sobs, overwhelmed by sensation. "I can't—it's too much—"

"You can," I assure her, one hand sliding between us to find her clit. "Come for me, Lithia. Come on my knot while I fill you up."

The moment my thumb circles her clit, she explodes. Her orgasm tears through her with devastating force, her inner walls clamping down on my knot so hard I see stars. Through our bond, I experience every second of her climax—the way it builds from her core and radiates outward, the way her whole body locks up in ecstasy, the way my name tears from her throat like a prayer.

Her pleasure triggers mine, and I roar as my release hits. My knot pulses inside her, expanding even further as I spill into her in hot, thick spurts. The sensation is overwhelming—not just the physical pleasure, but the emotional satisfaction of finally, completely claiming my mate.

Through our bond, I feel her awe at the sensation of being filled, the way my seed floods her womb, held in place by my knot. She can feel my satisfaction, my possessive pleasure at marking her from the inside out.

"Mine," I growl against her throat, my knot still pulsing. "Completely mine now."

"Yours," she agrees breathlessly, her hands threading through my hair. "Always yours."

We lie locked together, both of us trembling from the intensity of what just happened. My knot shows no signs of subsiding—it could be anywhere from twenty minutes to an hour before we can separate. The thought of being joined to her for that long, of feeling our connection strengthen with every passing moment, makes my cock twitch inside her.

"How long?" she asks softly, echoing my thoughts.

"Could be a while," I admit, shifting slightly to relieve some of the pressure on her hips. "First knotting between mates usually lasts longest."

She hums contentedly, her fingers tracing patterns on my back. "Good. I don't want to let you go yet."

My wolf preens with masculine satisfaction, finally having marked and claimed his mate properly.

"Tell me what you're feeling," I request, wanting to hear it in her own words.

"Full," she says immediately. "So incredibly full. I can feel you pulsing inside me, feel your seed filling me up." Her cheeks flush at the explicit words. "And the bond—gods, Kier, I can feel everything. Your satisfaction, your possessiveness, your love. It's like you're part of me now."

"I am," I confirm, pressing a kiss to her temple. "We're mated now. Truly mated. There's no undoing this."

"I don't want to undo it," she whispers.

I feel her truth through our bond, the way our connection has settled something restless inside her. My knot gives another pulse, drawing a soft moan from her lips.

"Still sensitive?" I ask with a grin.

"Everything feels more intense," she admits. "Like every nerve ending is connected to you now."

To test her theory, I contract the muscles at the base of my cock, making my knot swell slightly. She gasps, her back arching.

"Kier," she warns, but there's no real protest in it.

"Sorry," I say, not sorry at all. "I like watching you react."

"You're going to drive me mad," she mutters, but I can feel her arousal building again through our bond.

"Good," I reply, settling more comfortably over her. "We have time."

And we do. All the time in the world to explore this new connection, to learn each other's bodies and minds through the bond that now ties us together. My knot may trap us physically, but emotionally, we're both exactly where we want to be.

When my knot finally begins to soften forty minutes later, neither of us is eager to separate. But when I finally slip free, the sight of my seed leaking from her body fills me with primitive satisfaction.

"Mine," I murmur, gathering the evidence of our claiming on my fingers.

"Yours," she agrees.

"Any regrets?" I ask, though I can feel the answer through our bond—contentment so deep it makes my throat tight.

"Only that we waited so long," she admits, pressing a kiss to my collarbone. "I wasted so much time being afraid."

"Not wasted," I correct, tightening my arms around her. "You needed to heal. To learn to trust. I would have waited forever if that's what it took."

She lifts her head to look at me, something vulnerable in her expression despite everything we've just shared. "What happens now?"

"Now?" I brush my knuckles across her cheek. "Now I officially join Shadowmist. Permanently. No more guest quarters, no more being an outsider looking in." I pause, letting her feel my certainty through our bond. "I belong here. With you. With this pack."

Relief floods through our connection—relief that she doesn't have to choose between duty and desire, that I'm not asking her to abandon everything she's built here.

"The pack will accept you," she says confidently. "Ryker already sees you as one of us. The others will follow his lead."

"And Levi?"

She's quiet for a moment, and I feel her working through complicated emotions. "Levi will be fine. He's a good man— he deserves to find someone who can love him the way he deserves."

Through our bond, I sense there's more to the story, but I don't push. Whatever complicated history exists between them, it's in the past now. We're mated, bonded, committed to each other in the most fundamental way possible.

"I should go," she says eventually, though she makes no move to leave my arms. "Pack business, mission debriefings, all the tedious details of being Beta."

"You should," I agree, running my hand down her spine. "But you won't. Not yet."

"No," she admits, snuggling closer. "Not yet."

We stay like that as the sun climbs higher, learning the feel of our new bond, memorizing this moment of perfect peace before the world intrudes again. Because it will intrude— there are still prisoners to rescue, Zella to hunt down, the complex business of integrating our mated bond into pack life.

But for now, none of that matters. For now, there's just us —mated, bonded, complete.

"I love you," she whispers against my throat.

"I love you too," I reply, and mean it with every fiber of my being. "My mate. My partner. Mine."

"Yours," she agrees, and in that single word is a promise that will last forever.

Outside, I can hear the den coming alive—voices in the corridors, the sound of pack life continuing. But in here, in this room, there's just the two of us.

Finally, my wolf sighs, settling into contentment.

Finally, I agree.

And for the first time in twenty years, I truly know what it means to belong.

CHAPTER
TWENTY-EIGHT

The ancient traditions of wolves have always run deep, carved into our bones like the runes that mark our territory stones. Tonight, under the full moon's silver light, Kier and I will complete the claiming ceremony that binds us not just as mates, but as part of the pack's eternal legacy.

"You ready for this?" Dane asks, adjusting the ceremonial wreath of mountain flowers in my hair. The blooms are white and silver, their petals catching the full moon's light.

"As ready as anyone can be for running naked through the forest while their mate hunts them," I reply, checking the ties on my simple white dress.

Mate. The word sends a thrill through me every time I think it. After years of believing I'd never have this—never allow myself to have this—the reality feels almost too good to be true.

Inside, my wolf practically purrs with contentment. She's been restless for weeks, pacing beneath my skin, demanding I acknowledge what she's known all along. Now, finally, she settles with deep satisfaction.

Ours, she growls.

I smooth the white fabric with hands that want to tremble —not from nerves, but from pure, overwhelming joy. When was the last time I felt this kind of happiness? This bone-deep contentment that comes from being exactly where I belong, with exactly who I belong to.

He chose me. This incredible man who could have anyone. He looked at all my walls and fears and sharp edges, and he said yes.

I've never felt so essential to another person, so fundamentally needed. Not as Beta, not as a protector or leader or weapon, but simply as Lithia. The woman behind all the roles, the one I'd almost forgotten existed until a finger touched mine in the dark.

The flowers in my hair catch the moonlight, and I can't stop the smile that tugs at my lips.

Finally, I think. *Finally, I'll truly be Kier's.*

"This is *so* romantic," Kitara observes dryly from her position near the sacred circle. Despite her advanced pregnancy, she insisted on overseeing the ceremony. "Nothing says 'eternal love' like a primal chase."

I laugh, some of my nervousness easing. "Says the woman who was claimed by an alpha who literally fought three wolves to keep her."

"Point taken." She smiles. "I guess I can't complain."

The pack has gathered in the ceremonial clearing, the ancient stones forming a perfect circle. Wolves of all ages line the perimeter, their eyes bright with anticipation. This will be the first claiming ceremony that isn't overseen by Thaddeus. That in itself is a celebration not just of our bond, but of the pack's continued strength and growth.

Ryker steps forward, his commanding presence silencing the gentle murmur of conversation. In the firelight, he looks every inch the Alpha.

"Tonight we witness the claiming," he begins, his voice

carrying easily across the clearing. "Any who wish to try for a mate may step forward."

There's three females who do so, along with me.

"The ancient ways demand the hunt," Ryker continues. "The female runs, testing her mate's worthiness. The male pursues, proving his dedication. When caught, the claiming is complete, and both become part of the eternal pack."

This isn't just about Kier and me—it's about him becoming part of something larger, finding the home he's searched for his entire life.

"Would-be mates, step forward."

I spot Kier across the circle, and my breath catches. He's stripped to the waist, ceremonial paint marking his chest and arms in swirling patterns. His copper hair gleams in the firelight, and his golden eyes are fixed on me with an intensity that makes my pulse race.

Mine, my wolf whispers, pressing against my consciousness. *Hunt. Claim. Complete the bond.*

Heat licks over my skin, a restless shimmer under the surface. My breath shortens, thighs pressing together as something low and primal begins to stir. Not yet, I tell myself, but my body has other ideas—scent thickening, pulse hammering, skin prickling with need. The first threads of heat, unwelcome and unstoppable, unfurl through me.

Kier's giving me the kind of look that strips away clothes, distance, and reason. My wolf claws at my insides, snarling for him, and, from the tension rolling off Kier, I know he's barely holding back from tearing through the crowd just to get to me.

Come claim me.

"Lithia of Shadowmist," Ryker's voice pulls my attention back to the ceremony. "Do you accept this hunt? Do you offer yourself to be claimed by the wolf who proves worthy?"

"I do," I reply, my voice carrying clearly in the night air.

Ryker goes round the circle, asking the three other females

and four other males the same questions before he gets to Kier.

"Kier of the wandering path," Ryker turns to my mate. "Do you accept the challenge? Will you pursue what is yours by right of love and dedication knowing that to do so will bind you to the Shadowmist pack?"

"I will," Kier responds, his voice rough with barely contained hunger.

"Levi of Shadowmist," Ryker says, and my head lifts. I turn, seeing Levi standing in the circle.

He ignores me, his gaze locked on Ryker.

"Do you accept the challenge? Will you pursue what is yours by right of love and dedication?"

"I do."

I relax when he turns to look over the three females, not even sparing a glance my way.

"Then let the hunt begin."

The pack erupts in howls and cheers as I step forward, my hands moving to the ties of my dress. The white fabric falls away, pooling at my feet, leaving me bare to the moonlight and my mate's burning gaze.

I shift, my wolf emerging with a joy bark. I feel free, powerful, and ready to run. I throw back my head releasing a howl, the sound echoing off the surrounding mountains, then bolt for the tree line.

Behind me, I hear Kier's answering call as he shifts and gives chase.

The forest welcomes me like an old friend, pine needles soft under my paws, the scent of earth and growing things filling my nostrils.

I run, but this isn't about escape. We both know how this hunt ends. It's about the chase itself, the primal dance of pursuit and surrender that awakens something ancient in our wolves.

I leap over fallen logs, weave between towering pines,

splash through a shallow creek that runs silver under the moon. My heart pounds with exhilaration, every sense heightened. I can hear him behind me—paws hitting earth, branches rustling as he follows my trail.

Getting closer, I realize with a thrill of anticipation.

I dart left, hoping to throw him off, but he anticipates the move. His howl splits the night, closer than before, and I feel the first stirrings of something deeper than excitement.

Heat.

My wolf's season, triggered by the chase, by the certainty of being caught by our mate. It starts as a warm glow in my belly, spreading outward until my skin feels electric.

I risk a glance back and see him—a magnificent wolf with dark copper fur and eyes like molten gold. He's gained significant ground, maybe fifty yards behind me now. Close enough that I can see the determined set of his ears, the power of his movement.

Beautiful, my wolf sighs. *Strong. Worthy.*

I put on a burst of speed, but the heat is building now, making my legs weak and my thoughts fuzzy. The scent of my arousal mingles with the pine-sharp air, and his answering growl tells me he's noticed.

The moonlit clearing appears ahead—a perfect circle of silver grass surrounded by ancient oaks. I know without looking that this is where I'll be caught. Where the hunt will end and the claiming will begin.

I reach the center of the clearing and turn to face him, my sides heaving from the run. He emerges from the tree line like something out of legend—powerful, predatory, absolutely magnificent. For a moment, we simply stare at each other across the clearing, predator and prey locked in an eternal dance.

Then he moves.

He doesn't rush—there's no need now. His approach is deliberate, confident, the walk of a male who knows his prize is won. I could run again, extend the chase, but the heat building in my core demands satisfaction.

When he's close enough to touch, we both shift.

The transformation back to human form leaves me gasping, need flooding through me with overwhelming intensity. The heat—gods, the heat is like nothing I've ever experienced. It burns through my veins, sets every nerve ending on fire, demands immediate satisfaction.

"Kier," I whimper, swaying on my feet. "I need—"

"I know," he growls, his hands framing my face. "I can smell it." His pupils are blown wide, nostrils flaring as he breathes in my scent. "You're burning for me."

Before I can respond, he's tackling me to the soft grass, his mouth crashing to mine in a kiss that's pure claiming. I meet his hunger with my own, desperate and wanting, my nails raking down his back hard enough to draw blood.

"Mine," he snarls against my throat, his teeth scraping the sensitive skin. "My mate. My female."

"Yours," I gasp, arching beneath him. "Always yours. Please, Kier, I need—"

He doesn't make me finish the plea. His hand slides between my thighs, finding me already wet and ready, swollen with need. The first touch of his fingers against my clit sends electricity racing through me.

"Fuck, you're soaked," he breathes, circling the sensitive bundle of nerves until I'm writhing beneath him. "All this for me?"

"Only you," I pant, my hips bucking against his hand. "Only ever you."

He slides two fingers inside me, and I cry out at the sensation. It's good, but not enough—the heat demands more, needs to be filled completely.

"Please," I beg, not caring how desperate I sound. "I need your cock. Need you inside me. Now."

He positions himself at my entrance, the head of his cock

sliding through my wetness. "Look at me," he commands. "I want to see your face when I claim you."

Our eyes lock as he pushes inside, stretching me, filling me completely. The sensation is incredible—not just the physical pleasure, but the emotional satisfaction of being joined to my mate under the eyes of the moon and pack.

"Perfect," he groans, bottoming out inside me. "So fucking perfect. Made for me."

He starts to move, and the heat explodes through me like wildfire. Every thrust drives me higher, each withdrawal leaves me aching for more. This isn't gentle lovemaking—this is primal, desperate claiming.

"Harder," I demand, my legs wrapping around his waist. "Please, I need—"

He gives me what I need, driving into me with enough force to drive us both across the grass. I can feel his knot beginning to form, the thick swell at the base of his cock that will lock us together.

"Going to knot you," he pants against my ear. "Fill you so full you'll feel me for days. Mark you inside and out."

"Yes," I sob, teetering on the edge of climax. "Please, I need it. Need your knot."

When my orgasm hits, it's with the force of a tsunami. I scream his name as pleasure tears through me, my body clamping down on his cock with devastating intensity. The sensation triggers his release, and he roars as his knot swells, locking us together as he spills into me.

But the heat isn't satisfied. If anything, being filled makes it burn hotter.

"More," I gasp when we can both breathe again. "I need more."

He chuckles, dark and promising. "Heat's not done with you yet, is it?"

I shake my head, already moving against him despite his

knot still locking us together. The movement sends sparks of pleasure through us both.

"Tree," I manage to say between gasps. "When your knot goes down. Against the tree."

His eyes flash with renewed hunger. "Whatever my mate wants."

Twenty minutes later, when his knot finally releases, he's hauling me to my feet and pressing me against the nearest oak. My legs wrap around his waist as he drives into me again, this angle hitting spots that make me see stars.

"So good," I moan, my head falling back against the rough bark.

He sets a punishing pace, his hands gripping my ass to support my weight as he fucks me against the tree. I can feel another knot forming, my body already anticipating the claiming.

"Come for me," he demands, one hand sliding between us to circle my clit. "Come on my cock so I can knot you again."

I shatter around him, and this time when his knot locks us in place, I feel something deeper click into position. The bond between us strengthens, deepens, becomes something more profound than physical joining.

You're inside me completely, I whisper through our mental connection.

As you are me, he responds, and I feel the truth of it—his thoughts, his emotions, his very soul intertwined with mine.

The heat drives us through three more rounds—me riding him frantically while he lies on his back, gasping out praise and encouragement; him taking me from behind while I brace against a fallen log; finally, a slow, deep claiming on the soft grass as dawn begins to touch the sky.

By the time my heat finally eases enough for us to return to the den, we're both exhausted, sated, and more deeply bonded than I thought possible. I can feel his contentment, his satisfaction, his overwhelming love flowing through our connection.

"How do you feel?" he asks softly, gathering me against his chest.

"Sore." I pull his hand between my legs, letting him feel the slick mess he's made. "You've ruined me."

He growls, catching his cum and spreading it across my chest. "Good."

We return to the claiming circle and dress slowly, reluctantly, knowing the pack will be waiting for our return. When we emerge from the forest, hand in hand, we're greeted by cheers and howls of celebration.

Tables have been set up in the main courtyard, laden with food and drink. Pack members surround us with congratulations and well-wishes, but it's Ryker who steps forward first.

"Welcome home, brother," he says simply, clasping Kier's shoulder.

The word "brother" brings tears to my eyes. Kier has found what he's searched for his entire life—not just love, but family. Belonging.

"Welcome to Shadowmist," Kitara adds, pulling him into a gentle hug. "You're pack now. Truly."

The celebration continues until dawn, traditional songs and ancient rituals welcoming our newly completed bond. Through it all, Kier and I remain connected—mentally, emotionally, spiritually.

Mine, my wolf purrs with deep satisfaction.

Ours, his responds, and the rightness of it fills every empty space I didn't even know existed.

He pulls me onto his lap, holding me close as we watch our friends celebrate.

"Any regrets?" I ask, though I can feel the answer through our bond.

"Only that we waited so long," he murmurs against my hair. "I love you, Lithia of Shadowmist."

"I love you too, Kier of Shadowmist," I correct, and feel his smile against my skin.

TWENTY-NINE

KIER

The courtyard is alive with celebration. Three other couples managed to complete their claims during the hunt, and the pack is still reveling in the success. I watch Heath spin his newly claimed mate around while she laughs, her red hair flying. Near the fountain, another pair sits close together, sharing quiet words and gentle touches. The third couple has disappeared entirely—probably still working off the heat that drove their claiming.

But there's one wolf sitting alone by the fire, staring into the flames with the hollow expression of someone who ran but didn't catch a bride. My chest tightens in sympathy. With five males and only four females to claim, it was inevitable that someone would miss out. The claiming hunt is ancient tradition, but it doesn't guarantee success for everyone. Some wolves run alone, and some return alone.

"Where's Levi?" I ask, scanning the courtyard. He ran, but it doesn't look as if Levi has returned.

"Is he still out there looking for a bride?" Lithia frowns, her gaze searching as well. "Surely he would have heard Ryker's howl announcing all the brides had been claimed."

I shrug. "I guess not." My gaze strays back to the lone wolf slumped at the table.

"He'll find his mate," Lithia murmurs, following my gaze. Through our bond, I feel her compassion for the unsuccessful hunter. "Maybe not tonight, but he will."

I squeeze her hand, marveling again at how perfectly she fits against my side, how right this all feels. After twenty years of wandering, of never belonging anywhere, I'm home. Not just with Shadowmist, but with her. My mate, my anchor, my everything.

"Ready to get some sleep?" I ask, pressing a kiss to her temple. "We've had a long night."

She hums in agreement, leaning into my touch.

We walk through the crowd toward the den, and I catch sight of Rohan and Dane dancing together, locked in a tight embrace.

I glance at Lithia who is smiling as she watches them.

"You're not worried?" I ask.

"He's a big wolf. He'll work it out."

We're just walking up the small slope to the den's entrance when I notice something that makes me pause. There's movement at the bottom of the courtyard. A figure emerges from the shadow of the stone archway, moving slowly, carefully.

Levi.

But he's not alone.

He's supporting a woman—small, pale, and clearly exhausted. Her clothes are torn and dirty, her hair matted, and even from this distance I can see the bruises marking her exposed skin. In her arms, she clutches a bundle of rags.

No, not rags. A baby.

Recognition hits me like a physical blow.

"Prudence."

The fear-seer from our captivity. The human woman who was forced to torture us, all to protect the child she's now holding. She looks even smaller than I remember, and as fragile as spun glass, swaying on her feet despite Levi's support.

"How did they get here?" Lithia breathes beside me, her shock resonating through our bond.

Elena rushes forward from across the courtyard, her healer's instincts kicking in at the sight of obvious injuries.

"Let me see her," she calls. "She needs medical attention—"

"No."

Levi's voice cuts across the courtyard like a blade. He shifts position, placing himself between Elena and Prudence.

Prudence cowers behind him, one hand gripping his shirt.

"Don't touch her," he growls, baring his teeth at Elena.

Elena stops short, confusion flickering across her features. "Levi, she's injured. I can help—"

"No one touches her!"

The words roar across the courtyard, silencing the festivities. Levi's yellow eyes are blazing, his stance protective.

"Mine," he says, his voice rough. "My mate. No one touches her."

"Levi," Ryker's voice carries authority as our Alpha steps forward, but there's understanding in his tone too. "She needs healing."

"I'll heal her," Levi snarls, baring his teeth at his own Alpha—a display of dominance that would normally earn swift retribution. "I'll take care of her. Both of them."

Ryker, Kitara and Elena approach, arguing with Levi as Prudence looks on, cringing behind the giant wolf.

"Come on," I murmur to Lithia, pressing a kiss to her temple. "Let's give them some space. Looks like they have a lot to figure out." I squeeze her ass. "And I can smell your heat coming on."

She squirms against me, the scent of her arousal blooming. "I thought you were tired and wanted to sleep."

"Who needs sleep when I've got the only dream I've ever wanted right here?"

She groans, laughing. "You're terrible."

I grip the back of her neck, pressing our foreheads together. "And you're mine," I whisper against her lips. "Always."

Thank you so much for reading
Lithia and Kier's story!
I hope you fell in love with the
Shadowmist Pack.

Next up will be Levi's story, and let me tell you,
YOU DO NOT WANT TO MISS IT!

Want more sexy shifters and bonus content?
Be sure to check out my website
EvieMitchell.com

ABOUT E.V. MITCHELL

E.V. Mitchell is the darker, wilder side of bestselling romance author **Evie Mitchell**, venturing into the realms of romantasy, paranormal romance, and monster romance.

Known for writing body-positive romance with heart-pounding spice, E.V. Mitchell blends monsters, myths, and magic with scorching hot heroes and heroines who embrace their darkness.

Find the rest of her books at EvieMitchell.com.

You can catch up with Evie on all socials at @EvieMitchellAuthor or @EVMitchellAuthor

Visit Evie's website for her current booklist www.EvieMitchell.com